Children
by Katherine Gilbert

Dedication:

For Armida. who angelically keeps me sane, whatever sort of prisons we're caught in

Katherine Gilbert's More in Heaven and Earth Universe

Chapter 1
Michael

There was something about being dead which made actors even more unruly than they usually were.

While Michael was watching, he was already bored.

"Now, in this scene, Juliet . . ."

"Uh, wrong play. This is *Julius Caesar*."

That had gotten the first ghost going, but the minor arguments which covered the stage were many.

Being the only ones who had known each other while alive, the Bickering Twosome were the worst.

"You never could find the spotlight."

"Why do you think I'm dead?"

A detailed description of her last role followed, but her old rival had apparently heard it many times already, interrupting to argue about costumes.

Michael, who had never paid quite enough attention to learn their names, focused elsewhere in the mishmash of actors at the Terminally-Confused Ghost.

"I thought it was, 'Ecru, Bruté.'"

The ghost near him rolled his eyes. "You are a freaking moron, my friend."

Knowing better than to interrupt, Michael sort of agreed. For an actor, the Terminally-Confused Ghost knew next to nothing about acting or any of the actual lines.

3

As always, Michael watched silently. It wasn't as though there was much else to do. He kept his black clothes well-tended, his face neutral, showing nothing he felt. While the ghosts were some sort of distraction, the next summons wouldn't take long, one mission or another always making their captor send someone to get him. If the man had made one thing clear, it was that their time was no longer their own.

In the meanwhile, there was the daily ritual of Ghost Rehearsal, which was always more like one giant undead argument.

Repressing a sigh so as not to give his captor any outer sign of his feelings, should he be watching from somewhere, Michael pondered the group. This old theater now housed the spiritual remains of many actors who had followed them from place to place, apparently many from suicide. Having no idea why they followed and didn't just pass on, he'd never had much to do with them, besides witnessing the spiritual chaos, but he supposed if their creepy reputation kept visitors away from each of their current homes, it was enough. He had no idea what their captor would do if an ordinary mortal came snooping but was happy with his ignorance.

Still, having just one director kill himself to herd the unruly bunch seemed to be too much to ask.

The Lady in Red was now having her say. A new addition, she was apparently this theater's most famous post-life resident, mostly for her habit of hanging out in the men's dressing room, flashing the living actors.

It wasn't really her fault, the area having been the women's dressing room during her time. Apparently, she considered noticing the living bad form. To her mind, the theater was still hers. Why acknowledge the ridiculous creatures with pulses who happened to inhabit it now?

Having managed to make her way to center stage with ease, the other ghosts giving her a pathway wherever she wished without even realizing it, her voice was deep and mellifluous, reaching to the very last seat without any seeming effort. "You're all being very silly."

She had struck a pose quite naturally, really did have a nice profile. "Shakespeare is so old-fashioned. Ibsen is so much more *real.*"

The arguments around her had stopped momentarily, but Michael wasn't certain that the ex-people who had been having them really noticed.

"In my last role, I was playing..."

That broke the spell, as every single ghost around her finished the thought.

"Hedda Gabler, we know."

There was a series of disgruntled noises from them, and Michael suspected—not for the first time—that they were mostly upset at having been so fascinated by her, if only for a moment.

Simply raising her eyebrow at the crowd, the Lady in Red turned, and their complaints trailed off, as every one watched her slow retreat.

Say what you would about her. She did have a *fabulous* presence. Even Michael was caught in her spell for a moment, till he was interrupted by a smiling voice beside him.

"Watching the chaos?"

Looking up, he saw Isis settle in a chair next to him. Despite the fact that he was certain she had been sent by their captor, he couldn't really be angry at her. She was just as trapped as he was. And the long legs she stretched out onto the seat in front of her were rather distracting, as well.

Partly because he realized she was noticing, he tried to pull his attention back. Generally, he attempted not to think about the fact that he kept the slight curls of the auburn hair of this incarnate form long and not shorn because he knew she liked them. Hairstyles were such a strangely *human* obsession, and it amazed him sometimes that she shared it.

Of course, her own hair fell to her waist in long black waves—and he also did his best not to admit that enjoyed that too.

Still, for all her beauty, he didn't want to encourage her attempts to entice. Their captor had been using her for seduction missions whenever he found an excuse for them. She was very good at them, and he didn't want to encourage her in that direction. It wasn't her traditional role, and he wasn't certain that any of them were doing any good by helping their captor more than they actually had to.

In many ways, this was a sore spot. While he knew there must be some reason why The Lady had allowed all of their captures, he was still highly unclear about what it might be, and playing along with the whims of their tormentor had never sat well with him.

Somehow, Isis took it all in stride. The only thing which seemed to annoy her about being brought into being in this current time was that, as she would put it, "some group of murderous lunatics are taking my name in vain."

As he would have been at least as annoyed at such an insult, Michael understood.

Thankfully, they weren't being tormented particularly at the moment, unless he counted the ongoing, repetitive arguments on stage.

Isis smiled at the ghosts with a sort of maternal affection, and he wondered again at her patience. Many times, he'd noticed that she'd made friends with several of them.

His gaze traced along her lovely face. If he had to put up with their captor's nonsense, at least he had some interesting companions in his pain. He might wish her better, but she never complained, and he wondered whether she too knew there must be some reason for all of this.

If only either of them could discover what it was.

"If you keep staring at me like that, I won't be able to concentrate for rehearsals," she smiled.

Laughing a little, he looked back to the stage, and she flipped the long, dark waves of her hair behind the chair, wafting some scent of a desert flower toward him. A few of the strands caught on his jacket, and he wondered at the luck of the fabric.

Still, he was determined not to give in to touching them while they were in public—and that said nothing about the guilt he felt over her. He was well aware that he was simply her distraction, and, as much as he enjoyed her company, she was not the piece of him which was missing, either. Of course, where that one piece was, he had no idea, as The Lady had sent that part of him on a mission years before—and he had no idea when they might ever be reunited.

This was an impossible idea to explain to Isis, though, as no relationship in his home was a sexual one, only spiritual—and even calling that missing piece "he," as he often did, tended to cause confusion in a much-too-physical world. In many ways, he wasn't entirely certain what to feel about having given into this human shape so much as to become anyone's lover, and he knew Isis was . . . what was an appropriate human term for it? Ah, yes—she was slumming. Anything to distract her, until she could return to her own beloved partner.

As inevitable as it was, Michael was a little jealous over this truth. He himself had no particular love to return to, even if he did manage to complete whatever this mission was. To return to the Lady was to return to peace. There was a comfort to be found there, surely, but the one he was closest to wouldn't be there to greet him, anyway.

Well aware that none of these questions could be answered now, he went back to business.

"How soon do you think he'll come with another mission?"

It was Michael's constant worry. So far, he had managed not to do anything too irreparable on their captor's orders, but he knew the man wasn't happy over this fact. Michael was no stranger to war, but just because he was good at fighting—and even killing, as necessary—didn't mean he enjoyed it. That had been true even with The Lady.

For their current master, he had no guarantee over the guilt of their targets—rather the opposite, in fact. So long as he continued getting results, he hoped to avoid taking such a path again.

Of course, this was not the reason their captor had called him into being, but he cared little for that. No slaves in their right minds would ever care much for the happiness of their masters, except as it shielded them from harm. All any of them could do was try to get by until they understood what the man wanted enough to discover how to end this and break free.

Still, this didn't seem to be happening any time soon. There had already been several years of captivity on this painful plane of existence with no end in sight.

He had always had a sympathy for those in the physical world, for all of The Lady's creations. While there were compensations to all the torments and annoyances of material existence—his hazel eyes slid over to his companion's long legs again, and he caught her smile from the corner of his glance—he knew that, for many of those here, there was little more than suffering.

All those lost souls on the stage were only one example of this truth.

Now, they were bickering even more heatedly, seemed to have teamed up to be rehearsing at least four different plays simultaneously. He counted a Jacobean revenge drama, two Shakespearian tragedies—The Lady in Red hadn't talked them out of that one, apparently—and what appeared to be the opening of Edward Albee's *The Sandbox*. His years with them had made him somewhat of a theater connoisseur. The cacophony they presented would have made the most avant-garde producer proud.

Watching them tenderly, Isis sighed. "Y'know, someday soon, someone's going to catch on that all we do is 'rehearse' and expect an actual opening from us."

Although he doubted it, Michael smiled. Every time there was too much suspicion on them, their "tour" simply moved on. There was always something else their captor wanted and some better place to use as a base to get it—although why they took up their homes anywhere in the mortal world was a little uncertain, as all of them had the ability to go wherever they needed.

Just one more mystery I can't solve.

Pulling himself back to his companion, he answered. "Maybe we can put the ghosts on, instead."

One eyebrow raised, she looked at him.

"If nothing else, it will confuse them."

The eyebrow went higher. "An empty stage?"

Shrugging, he half-acknowledged her point. Only a psychic or those in their position would actually be able to see the performance.

"What's the old saying: 'If you can't dazzle them with your brilliance, baffle them with your . . .'?"

He had trailed off, and Isis shook her head. He knew she found his unwillingness to curse amusing.

Still, he had been The Lady's servant too long. Not that she would care—she could manage a good blue streak when annoyed—but, as her representative, sometimes a terminal one, he felt the need to be a bit more formal.

But it wasn't something he wanted to explain. It made him feel the ache of how far he had fallen too much.

He was just about to try to distract Isis again when their captor finally appeared. He always did, eventually.

Unmoving, Michael watched, as the man came up to them, his gray hair pomaded and perfect, his suit probably designer. He didn't look like the sort of man to be hanging around disused theaters, but Michael supposed everyone had their cover.

Out of the corner of his eye, he noticed Isis tuck her feet back down. She might give into the man's orders for the seduction of some outsider, but she never courted their captor's eyes.

As always, the man was brusque. "You'll need to go out tonight. I'll leave the address with Hermes when I have it."

Seeing no point in arguing, Michael sighed—but that didn't mean he had to be polite.

"What is it you want this time?"

Their captor raised a silver eyebrow above very sardonic blue eyes but didn't comment on his tone. "You'll know it when you see it."

He grinned—not a pretty sight, even for all his perfect white teeth.

"It's a spear, a rather old one." The evil in his eyes deepened. "You may even recognize it."

Damn him.

Knowing all too well whose spear it would be, Michael hated this.

The man's awful grin continued.

"I don't think your 'lady' will miss it much."

Michael said nothing.

"And don't give me that glare."

The man started to stalk away.

"You're not a goddamned archangel anymore."

His look burning, Michael knew this *much* too well. But, as soon as he could, he would end this—and get back to The Lady with as much of his soul as he could salvage.

Chapter 2
Gabriela

The huge old warehouse looked deserted, but they always did. After six months of these assignments, she knew better than to trust anything she could see.

Gabriela rested her head back against a girder of the deserted underpass as she listened, waiting for her targets' arrival. Eventually, unfortunately, they would be here. Her trainers were never wrong. They always knew when there was something "unnatural" which had to be dealt with.

Now, if only she weren't starting to question their every ideal . . .

Waiting in the cold for her final orders, she was uncomfortably aware of the ridiculousness of her situation. Should anyone but her enemies see her, she would appear completely out of place—her armored chest-plate and short leather skirt, the laced sandals, her long, fire-red hair braided, now to her side, not exactly fashion-forward. And that said nothing of the spear.

Still, if anyone happened to be in this forgotten part of town to witness her, they would hopefully imagine her to be either a rather dedicated cosplayer or simply crazy enough to give a very wide berth. Either one would work for her purposes now.

It hadn't always been like this. When she had believed, it had been so much simpler. Believing made her strong.

She could go in, deal with the target—as she had been raised to do, in one way and another, for 18 years—and leave, knowing that she was doing God's work. True, something about it had felt . . . off, even that first time, but it had been easier when she had simply been able to ignore her concerns.

After the last two targets, though, she couldn't.

There had only been six targets in her short career, much of her work aimed at tracking down her prey, and the first four hadn't made her question particularly.

The first time, that vampire had been feasting on some young woman in an alley. That she had seemed to be enjoying it was clearly only because of the mind control such creatures possessed. Even Hollywood had gotten that right, once upon a time. Now, it was all dewy-eyed, eternal high schoolers watching boring girls sleep.

She *really* didn't get it—but she supposed her training didn't exactly make her the ideal target demographic.

Anyway, that vampire had clearly been doing something wrong, despite how upset his victim had been at his death. That had just been the mind control talking—some supernatural version of Stockholm syndrome.

Or so she had told herself at the time.

In kills two to four, there had been little to make her question—two ghouls and a zombie. True, none of them had been actively feasting when they had met their demise, but the simple fact of what they were was an abomination.

For a while, the doubts had quieted. But then there had been that damned werewolf—and every sense of right and wrong she had so carefully cultivated had started to shake loose. Two weeks since that day wasn't long enough to let them go.

It had been a very easy kill, the creature seeming to sense her, walking into the blind alley all on its own. At the time, she had thought that it had just anticipated an easy victim, but it hadn't acted that way, once confronted.

Instead, it had just sat there in its wolf form, waiting. She had at least expected it to pounce or bite at the end, but . . . nothing. It had just watched calmly as the spear rose above it, had even shifted slightly to give her a better target.

Until her trainers had sent a powerful bolt of compulsion at her, blurring out her senses, she had almost stopped. By the time they were clear again, the spear had pierced the creature's heart—although it was no longer a beast, was instead a beautiful young woman, about her own age. Two words had escaped with her dying breath: "Thank you." And then the last glow of yellow had faded from her eyes along with the rest of her life.

Despite all her trainers' continuing lectures, it was this which had shaken Gabriela. If all the creatures she had been born and raised to hunt, all these infectious evils upon the earth, were truly as demonic as she had been taught, then why would one of them be waiting for death—even thank her for it?

Her trainer had said that it was just a demon's last trick to shake her, or perhaps it had been happy to return to Hell, but Gabriela couldn't quite force herself to believe anymore.

There had been something far too human in the wolf's eyes, some sense of a holy creature which had been violated, who was happy to be given peace again. There had been nothing there to suggest that the creature's fate after death was anything but joyous—and it was this which she couldn't quite rectify with all that she had been taught.

Of course, she had been too well-trained not to continue to follow orders, but even she recognized that her efforts recently were half-hearted. The steel of the girder behind her cold, she sighed. And even that had been before the siren, before seeing the family which had mourned her loss so thoroughly. That had been the absolute last straw.

Of course, as directed, she was still here. There had never been any doubt about that. Even if she had been crazy enough to try to leave, where would she go? Her family was all in the compound, her trainers the closest she had to friends. Her parents had ensured that she was raised for only one purpose: to kill the unnatural. She had nothing to start over with, no idea of how to live a "normal" life. That was what she was supposed to be protecting in the outside world, to keep all those people who had no idea that such creatures existed happy in their ignorance. No matter how tormented she was over the life she led, she had no idea how to go anywhere else but here.

There was almost a part of her which wished she knew an answer, especially since it was becoming obvious that her trainers sensed her questions. A warrior who doubted became an enemy—and there were more than enough who didn't to easily take her out.

Quite thoroughly caught, she waited for confirmation to begin her mission, trying to believe. True, the ones she would be confronting tonight *were* evil: demons, two or three of them. The leaders weren't entirely sure, and she couldn't afford to get sloppy. After all, it would take every bit of her training, determination, and skill just to survive.

Unfortunately, it had occurred to Gabriela, as she was driven from the sparse familiarity of the compound to this abandoned, darkened underpass in the parts of D.C. the tourists never saw, that this might be their way of getting rid of her. Despite her lifelong training, she could easily be overpowered by such formidable threats. The fact that no one in the compound would miss her was too obvious a truth to even feel sad about. After all, she had never had any illusion that she was loved. She was simply a useful tool—and, as her trainers had told her all too often, broken tools were extremely disposable.

Her wait ended with the sign she needed, as little as she actually wanted it, the words glowing in the air in front of her: "There are two. Back corridor exit. Spare no one. Give up nothing."

Lovely.

The extra reminders made it obvious that her reluctance hadn't gone unnoticed. Still, if they *were* really demons . . .

Even as part of her mind wondered whether this were just some final test, she moved in quietly toward the abandoned warehouse she'd been watching. If tonight's enemies were as bad as she feared and she hesitated, they would kill her. If they weren't, she would kill them and give her trainers yet another proof of their control—and herself more nightmares.

She didn't like either outcome particularly, especially since, if she were killed by demons, her soul might be in danger—and that was far more precious to her than her life.

It didn't take long to find them, either, as they didn't seem to be hiding. Moving as stealthily as she could, she rather feared that the pair she was approaching were well aware she was coming. Their cautious stance made that clear—although, unlike herself, they didn't creep.

Sadly, she didn't doubt that they were demonic, as they were too beautiful to be anything else. Staring around a corner at them through the dark—only her trainers' spell allowing her to see clearly—it was obvious that the woman was dark and lovely, with flowing black hair which only supernatural powers could have kept that perfect. She had an ankh hanging off of her bracelet which glowed a very electric blue in the gloom, undoubtedly a sign that she had tucked a few extra spells up her sleeve. That she looked deadly as well as beautiful in her black leather catsuit and full voluptuous form just made her powers all the more evident.

However, the man with her was even more magnetically attractive, although possibly that was just the way he appeared to Gabriela, who tended more toward his gender. In a dark modern suit which was thoroughly out of place with the glowing sword he held, his body seemed powerful, yet not in a showy, bulging way. Still, something about it suggested that everything there was to him was perfect sleek muscle and tone, honed for use. His eyes were dark, his skin lighter than his companion's, his curls brown and down to his shoulders, his face also a sculpted perfection, as she caught another glimpse of it, as he looked around.

In short, the two of them were distractingly perfect, which was only to be expected from demons.

Creeping closer, not giving herself time to think, she held up her spear and prepared to leap. She would only get one chance—and she had to remember that all that beauty was a lure which would steal her soul if she gave it half a chance.

Unfortunately for these plans, the demons were not taken unaware.

Gasping, all of Gabriela's fears were brought into focus as the beautiful male creature before her turned suddenly, raised one hand, and, with compelling eyes which shone a kind of golden light which her spear now seemed to reflect all down its length, stopped her attack in mid-air. A moment later, she thudded to the ground away from him, and the metal burned too brightly for her to hold. Then, it flew to the man's hand, resting there as if it had been his all along.

Clearly, there was no way to fight.

Nonetheless, she wanted to, certain that—whatever untruths her trainers had told her before—they had been very reliable in their assessment here.

These two were undoubtedly demonic, the man's eyes trying to speak to her, his power impossible to overcome. She couldn't even bring about the will to attack him again, shook there on the floor like some barely-trained novice—a beauty too great to be born of anywhere but the utter temptations of Hell spellbinding her.

Despite her need not to have her soul ripped from her just as the spear had been, she scrambled up from the floor and backed up to the wall, knowing there was no way out. Even if she could escape, where would she go? Her trainers' motto was, "Win or Die." If she came back to them without these creatures' lives and possessions, without even the spear they had trained her with from such an early age, it would clearly be the latter. As she had been taught repeatedly, mercy was not a quality God could afford.

The beautiful man before her gasped, his hair whipping behind him in the wind the spear put out after having been stolen by him, and she could see the more auburn tinges to the strands in its glow. Hating that she was so easily taken in by his demonic tricks, she tried not to notice that his look seemed amazed, even hurt.

"Gabriel?" he whispered, taking a step toward her—and she wondered how he knew and yet didn't know her name. "Gabriel is that . . ."

Widening, his eyes trailed along her.

". . . you?"

Gabriela's back was pressed so hard to the wall she could feel a leftover nail gouging into her, more worried over her fate by the moment. The demon was talking to her as though she were a man, although, in this outfit, and with her extremely ample body—she had never been a lightweight—she would have thought that it was clear she wasn't.

The female demon raised her hand to the male, stopping his approach. "Wait, Michael. Don't you see it?"

Gabriela shuddered, the woman coming closer, that ankh on her wrist now glowing the same color as the spear.

"Don't you see what they've done to her?"

Knowing she should fight, Gabriela only felt weak and sad. The female demon was projecting some sort of maternal image, the light which flowed from her supposedly warm and loving, asking her to beg for an embrace. While Gabriela knew it was a lie, these demons much too powerful, a part of her ached for it, wanted to walk steadily toward her doom.

Her eyes widened. In just another second . . .

The woman's hand reached for Gabriela's neck, and she closed her eyes, saying a quick prayer for her immortal soul.

Although the woman didn't squeeze the life out of her as she had feared, her touch branded Gabriela's skin, making her scream. A thousand images flashed, the terror drowning most of them out, and she wished she had the will left to fight.

But she didn't.

As the light burned through her, her mind dimmed further. And, when she lost grip on consciousness, it was with only one, final thought: *They're going to possess me, too.*

But, slumped on the floor in a heap before her enemies, she didn't have the opportunity to fear any further than that.

Chapter 3
Michael

Fighting on orders from your captor was never easy. As Michael was about to find out, finding your oldest and dearest friend at the end of your sword was much, much harder.

The warehouse was astoundingly silent, although he sensed someone was there. When he heard the slightest sound, more a movement of the air than actual footsteps, he thought it far too stealthy for a mere human, although he wasn't certain it was truly supernatural, either.

Sword drawn, he waited. At least he knew the sound was too quiet to be some bemused night watchman. The last one they had run into had been convinced they were playing some sort of sex game, had wanted to join in. It had taken all of Isis' charm—and Michael's patience—to tempt him to walk away.

Closing his eyes, Michael knew he could detect the visitor better without the distraction of sight. Sometimes, he found human form quite annoying. Despite its obvious appeal when given a companion like Isis, it was so easy to fool. All the senses played tricks, seemed to have minds of their own. He would be better off if he just . . . felt.

This he did, then, but what he sensed was rather odd.

It came first in a wave of surprise from Isis, her whispered, "She's coming," really more of a surprised, "*She's* coming?"

He could feel her stare on him for just a moment, before she too refocused—but that was before he sensed the power of the spear.

Impossible to ignore its pull, the weapon had been a longtime, powerful ally. That he was supposed to bring it back to his captor disgusted him. But surely the Lady must have a plan . . .?

It was in worrying over this ever-present question that his distraction was born. Turning, he opened his eyes to see the spear aiming for his heart. All he could focus on, it was a shining gold—powerful as always.

His reaction was more instinct than thought. Raising his hand, he greeted it like a much-missed friend. Unsurprisingly, it abandoned its current user and came to him instantly.

In calling the spear, he had also pushed away his attacker, which meant that a beautiful, desperately young, sturdily-built woman with very long red hair was looking up at him from the floor with terror in her lovely gray eyes. This form was a total stranger to Michael—but the spirit which moved that body was Gabriel's, and he had known and wrapped his soul through his fellow angel's since the beginning of time.

That this girl was dressed in the most ridiculously out-of-place costume didn't make understanding any easier. But he didn't need to know the details. All he wanted to do was go to him . . . well, her . . . and greet this part of himself he had so desperately missed.

It was only Isis' command which kept Michael from running to this female form of his old friend—that, and what he had seen on her neck.

It was a three-pronged trident, could have been a holy symbol in some times and places, but not here—not as it was. The power, the ugliness which flowed from it nearly altered space, was a cancer on the world.

Besides, as always, Isis didn't need him, holding the woman back from attacking again, as her hand shielded reality from that terrible symbol. When Gabriel had stopped screaming from the pain and collapsed, Isis moved her hand away, and there was only a deep, pink patch left on the skin there—but the ugly stain had left the room.

Worried, Michael moved to her in a heartbeat, truly wanting to question his senses.

"Gabriel," he whispered, hand stroking back over the unconscious woman's hair. The moment didn't seem real, as his eyes took her in again. Especially not like this . . .

Isis was still holding the woman up, looking at him curiously. "She is clearly a woman. Why do you make her sound like a man?"

Embarrassed, Michael glanced at her. It wasn't something they had discussed, as he knew Isis wouldn't understand. "We don't really have sexes . . . over there."

Her eyebrow raised, her look ran over him momentarily. When it returned, memories of their previous activities shone there clearly. "You could have fooled me."

Floundering, Michael didn't like it. He was not a man, or an angel, who floundered.

"No. I mean . . . We don't . . ."

Refusing to sound as ruffled as he felt, he huffed out a slightly annoyed breath.

"We're spirits there, you see."

Isis shook her head, her eyebrow still raised. "Your worldview is so . . . odd."

Still, she didn't question further, simply lifted the unconscious woman, carrying her like a sleeping child.

Michael was a little appalled, and only partly because he felt this was his job. "What are you doing?"

Shrugging, his companion led the way. "Our captor never said we couldn't bring back friends."

That settled the question. Apparently, they were taking her back.

Michael glanced over the sleeping woman's face, as they returned, his heart aching at a million new factors: the reunion, Gabriel's lack of recognition of him, this . . . very different body. And that said nothing of what their captor would do with her.

Now, he needed not only to get himself and Isis out of this somewhat intact—along with leaving an opening for escape for the others
their captor held—but Gabriel, too.

Right now, he really hoped the Lady had a plan, because he was
stumped.

Marveling at the "weirdness factor" of this entire situation, Michael
followed Isis and her warm burden back through the night and the portal to the disused theater in silence. Listening to the ghosts had taught
Michael the phrase, and he was grateful for it. It described their whole
situation much too well.

All of it was weird: the conglomeration of angels, goddesses,
demigods, and others which their captor had put together; the ghosts
of actor suicides who came along with them, their number increasing
with every new theater they passed through; his half-relationship with
Isis, who liked him well enough but was simply amusing herself with
him until she could be reunited with her beloved Osiris. Now, too,
there was Gabriel . . . a.

Isis had summoned her current name when she brought her down
to a room in the tunnels which were currently below this particular theater, not that they really existed anywhere. His eyes ran over his, highly
altered, old friend once more. How he was supposed to get used to this
last change, especially, he had no idea.

It wasn't that he had a prejudice for either of the sexes, really, all the
Lady's creations precious to him. But the one before him had an effect
he could not easily put into words.

With Isis, he was soothed, aroused, and comforted. With his heavenly brothers and sisters, he was embraced. But, with this form before
him, there was an ache—and part of him was unwillingly certain that
there would be no soothing it, until she welcomed him happily into her
arms.

*And that's about as likely to happen as me giving the ghosts daily
marimba lessons.*

While they were keeping her in this disused room, he honestly wasn't certain whether she were their captive or not. The sparkling magic which surrounded her, confining her in a bubble of isolated protection, certainly argued that she was, but he understood Isis' motives too well. It wasn't so much that their captor had told them to watch her as the fact that she might end up hurting herself, or trying to hurt one of them, when she woke.

Feeling distinctly like a creep—and grateful for the added vocabulary he had picked up from the ghosts—he still wasn't willing to try to undo the magic just yet. He had to discover exactly what had happened to Gabriel . . . Gabriela first—and his old friend hadn't seemed anything like willing to talk before.

Sitting sideways in a chair, watching her, he couldn't help but wonder how she had gotten here. Just her clothes were so odd, nothing like anything in this century, even if they did reflect something like an outfit he had seen her in before. But that had been when they were both working for the Lady.

Now, he wasn't certain who any of this was for.

Hating his life here, all he had been forced to do, he wondered for a moment if screaming would help. The humans certainly seemed fond of it.

But no. Humans were fond of many things which didn't seem to be the least bit useful.

Still, silence didn't change anything, either.

Their captor even had the spear now, his old weapon. Turning it over to him had caused a nearly-physical pain.

The thing was part of him, like his sword, had even come the instant he had willed it when this woman had confronted them with it earlier. It wasn't that he minded Gabriel . . . Gabriela wielding it—or, at least, he wouldn't, if he could be certain that she hadn't done herself any harm.

From what Isis had apparently seen, though, this hadn't been the case. He couldn't personally spot the spell they had her under, Isis' own magical abilities quite powerful, but he could see that, whoever had had Gabriel, they'd done something awful to him.

It wasn't just her current form, either—which, though it disturbed him to admit it, was lovely enough. But how had they gotten him into it?

When their captor had summoned him, he had appeared in the way he had most often appeared before, when incarnate. Gabriela, though . . .

Had she been summoned like he had—or had they managed to find a way to actually implant her soul into a human form from birth?

If so, she was currently more a creature of flesh and blood than he was, which also meant that she could be more easily hurt. The fact that she had been waiting for them, had seemed to have been given orders to attack, argued that she had been trained for something awful, as well. If they had started such a manipulation from her birth in this life—and her current body was . . . what? 18? 20 years old? It was difficult to remember just how long Gabriel had been gone using human terms like time. Still, it would make her captors' compulsions even more powerful.

Enraged, he ground his fist against his leg. If they had been brainwashing her all this time . . .

There were too many questions now, what would happen when she woke up just one among them. And that said nothing of what their captor might plan for her.

Trying to think of any plan to save her—just letting her go to return to her own probable captors less than enticing—he saw an ethereal head stick through the door.

"Oh, you're here." He was soon joined by the Terminally-Confused Ghost, but he wasn't exactly the greatest company he could have.

Michael had resigned himself to their ghostly entourage quite some time ago, even conversed with those who noticed him occasionally. None were evil, just lost, and it seemed rude to ignore the Lady's creations if addressed.

Still, this time, he only nodded, having little to add.

Looking back to their unconscious guest, the ghost seemed worried. "They said you had brought someone back with you."

Still watching Gabriela, Michael nodded again.

The ghost reached out toward her but couldn't come very close because of Isis' spell. Pulling back his hand, he sighed. "Is she of this era? Is she alive?"

Michael opened his lips to answer but didn't really have any.

His confusion clear, the spirit went on.

"Is she dressed for *Julius Caesar*?"

Blinking, he stared off into the distance.

"I didn't think there were any female soldiers in that."

Despite himself, Michael smiled. This ghost rarely got anything right, but he was always kind-spirited. "There aren't." While Michael had never been a particular theater expert, he'd learned a great deal in his years of watching the ghosts.

The spirit almost scowled. "Modern productions can be so confusing. I saw one director once who cast a 50-year-old opera singer as Nora in *A Doll House*. Then, he made the rest of the cast sing their lines, while she had to speak all of hers." He shook his head. "It was the fact that he dressed her only in a trash bag that was most confusing, though."

This time, the smile turned into a small snort. The Lady's creatures could have that effect on him.

Entering into the conversation at last, he wondered, "Were you Helmer?"

Michael didn't think it likely, the ghost rather young and nebbishy with wire-rimmed glasses—not really the leading actor type—but there was no need to insult him. He had always been nice enough.

Probably not surprisingly, the ghost looked confused. It seemed to be his perpetual state—thus, his nickname.

"I'm not an actor. I just did the lights."

It was the first time the former angel had really focused on the ghost. Before, he had thought that their various spirit companions were the unearthly remains of disappointed thespians, still tied to the theaters which had driven them to their suicides—although why and how they then followed along, as the group left, was another unanswered question. For the few whose deaths he had heard discussed, they seemed to have enough, varying reasons why they had committed such a final act: not getting the part they were convinced they were born to play, having a play they had worked so desperately to put together close on its opening night, being outshone by a former protégée . . . the list went on.

How a lighting guy fit into all of them, he had no idea.

Wondering again at the ghosts' presence, he would take any clue to their situation he could find. "Then, why did you . . .?"

Not finishing the question, he was unable to comprehend why anyone would reject the Lady's gift. Every life had a purpose—although even he admitted that, in some cases, it would probably be very difficult to understand.

The Terminally-Confused Ghost tilted his head, trying to follow. "Die?" he finished.

There was a shrug when he saw Michael's nod.

"I don't know too much, really. A lighting rig fell on my head." The confusion grew deeper. "I thought I had it secure, but . . ."

This added a new twist to their situation, but Michael didn't get a chance to ponder it for long, their unwilling guest stirring. When her eyes opened, their terror pierced him, the ghost utterly forgotten.

"No, don't!" he cried.

Gabriel wasn't listening, though, her horror obvious, which he supposed was no surprise. The last thing she would remember was being trapped and overpowered—as well as in pain. There was no way to know if she at all understood how Isis had helped her by removing that sign from her neck.

Apparently, she didn't, her terror clear and made all the worse when she raised up her hand and saw Isis' ankh hanging from a band wrapped around her wrist. It was her attempts to pull it off which made Michael scream, but he needn't have worried. Thankfully, it stayed firm—not that that made Gabriel any calmer.

Struggling desperately, even as Michael tried to settle her, Gabriel managed to make her way out of the chair and halfway to the door. It was clear she believed herself in for torture, death, or worse, if she stayed.

Almost to the door, though, something seemed to happen to her, as though stabbing pains had taken her over, driving her, shaking, to her knees. For a moment, she sat there with her eyes closed, murmuring something tormentedly about werewolves and sirens, until, weeping, her hand closed over where Isis had removed that ugly brand from her neck.

When her words were finally clear, the cry came straight from her soul. "What have you done to me?"

There was a whimper before her voice returned, soft and hoarse.

"Why can't you just kill me?"

Oh, Lady save me. She thinks I'm torturing her.

And maybe, in some way, he was.

Kneeling before her, trying to get on her level to not be seen as quite so much of a threat, he wanted to make her truly see him, even as his confusion reigned. Her violent collapse made no sense, Isis' spell certainly not created to do her harm.

"Gabriela, please."

He tried to remember to use the name she was used to, wanted to hold her but knew that Isis had created the barrier around her to evaporate at his touch—and he feared too much for her safety to dismantle it just yet.

"Tell me what's happening to you."

Her gaze was deep, pained, and she didn't even seem to notice that he now knew her name.

"You don't know?"

She gave a little tremor, and he wanted to hold her so badly he ached.

"You don't know what you're doing to me?"

At that moment, he couldn't have honestly explained any part of his existence.

The Terminally-Confused Ghost didn't make things any better by peering in much closer at the woman, pressing his face right up against the barrier. "Is she all right?" He pulled back a little. "She looks to be in pain."

A little outraged, his shocked gaze fell on Michael.

"Are you hurting her?"

Michael was sitting on the floor now, his elbow on his knee, head in his hand. "No, I'm . . ."

Gabriela didn't let him finish, her gaze on the spirit—obviously in shock. "A ghost?"

She had pulled back to the far side of her barrier, her horror quite clear.

"You keep *familiars*?"

Michael sighed. Whatever she thought of them was becoming infinitely worse.

Pleading, he refocused on the ghost. "I'm not hurting her . . . What's your name?"

Smiling, the ghost seemed almost touched. "No one alive has ever asked me that. It's Gary."

Glancing back to the distraught woman, Gary apparently saw that his presence was only making a difficult situation worse. He pulled away.

"I'll go."

"Thank you, Gary," Michael sighed, and his eyes met the ethereal man's for a moment, before the latter disappeared through the door. He suspected there was more to be learned from him, maybe from all of the ghosts, than he had comprehended before—but he didn't have the time, at the moment.

Gaze returning to his oldest friend, who now seemed terrified of his very presence, he sighed. This would have been so much easier, if he understood anything at all.

Still, it was obvious that she wasn't going to reveal any details of her current situation, would never let him understand how to help, until she could trust him further.

He couldn't blame her. They had basically kidnaped her.

Like that doesn't make me feel like even MORE of a creep.

"My name's Michael. We used to . . ."

Trying a different path, he stopped.

"You used to know me."

Shuddering occasionally, shaking her head, she still seemed to be in pain but did appear to be listening. "I've never seen you before tonight."

Settling in front of her, sighing, he resigned himself to this taking a while.

Just as when he had had to work as a messenger for the Lady to explain to one of her creations that this particular body's lifetime was over, he knew this had to be broken to her gently. Whatever was happening, whatever had been done to her, they couldn't let Gabriela return to her former world.

"Not in this lifetime, no."

She looked at him as though he had just grown several extra heads, but he pressed on.

"But we've known each other since the beginning of time."

That makes me sound like the biggest psycho ever.

Still, the fact that it *wasn't* the one dressed in armored fetish gear who sounded the craziest here was just the story of what was becoming his life.

Chapter 4
Gabriela

The pronouncement the beautiful demon had made to her sounded like the worst pick-up line ever.

Still, Gabriela knew he wasn't lying—or, at least, that he didn't think he was—but that just meant that he was convinced of his insane story. She wanted to argue that he was a demon, and—at least as far as she knew—she wasn't, so that wasn't likely.

Somehow that response didn't seem like it would make her sound any less lunatic, but she suspected she wasn't really on a first-name basis with sanity. Growing up in the compound tended to do that to a person.

However, every time she wanted to contradict him, those terrible images of her victims pounded back at her, making it difficult to think, to care. They had already driven her to her knees from the moment she woke up here. As long as they were there, she couldn't crawl her way past them.

Drawing up her knees in front of her, she pressed her face to them—not the wisest move for a woman in a micro-mini, but she was far beyond thinking about modesty. It was very clear she was trapped.

"What do you want with me?"

There was a pause as though he were debating, which didn't entirely encourage her.

"I need you to understand what's happening. I, Isis, . . . none of us are human."

She shuddered a little. The fact that one of his companions referred to himself as "Isis" wasn't exactly an encouraging sign.

What in heaven's name are these demons mixed up with?

Watching her sadly, he pressed on.

"We're spirits, many of us considered deities in various religions." He looked into her carefully. "And none of us are here by our own free will."

Peering up at him over her knees, she watched as he went on.

"We were captured by a man who sends us on errands for him. The ghosts follow us."

His sigh lingered.

"There isn't really much more I know."

Keeping her knees raised defensively before her, she wondered over this. If he were a demon trying to manipulate her, that was an awfully odd way to do it. Of course, it did reflect her own situation, in some ways, which he might know, and it wasn't as though she were some normal civilian who had no idea about the supernatural world. The compound had made sure of that. But still . . .

A sudden thought occurred to her, gazing at the pendant which hung from her arm.

Isis.

It had been a while since anyone had associated that name with an actual Egyptian goddess, but the woman was beautiful enough to be one.

"Is this ankh hers . . . Isis'?"

He nodded softly, and Gabriela resisted the urge to try to rip away the bracelet again, having been trained from birth to fear any heathen religion. Somehow, that feeling wasn't as strong as it had been now, and, anyway, the thing seemed impervious to harm. As crazy stories went . . . well, it wasn't that much odder than many of the things she'd seen . . . and killed.

Swallowing heavily to try to silence the sounds of the dead which reverberated through her entire form, she made an attempt at refocusing. Certainly, he and the woman had power, and it was a weird story for a demon to make up.

"Why would someone want to bring a bunch of pagan gods together to do his dirty work? And who are you, anyway?"

Sighing, he wouldn't meet her eyes, and he did truly *look* like an unwilling captive. She'd caught that same look in her own eyes in the mirror once or twice.

His voice was very quiet, as though he did his best to hide his own power. "Gods are only pagan to nonbelievers."

Tapping his finger against his shoe, he stared at the floor. Oddly, his obvious uncertainty made her believe him even more. Somehow, she suspected that a demon would be far bolder with whatever tales he told—and she really didn't think one would start by explaining rather than torturing.

When his deep, quiet voice went on, she did everything in her power not to admit that the sound of it was rather soothing.

"Even The Lady isn't believed in by everyone, and we have her to thank for everything there is."

The name made Gabriela shudder, that spot on her neck hurting again, but it also started up a sort of yearning deep inside her for a time when all the world had made perfect sense.

Blinking, she just couldn't remember such a time in this life.

Still, she realized a moment later that this man hadn't answered her question.

"Who are you?" she pressed.

She didn't remember the great god Michael in any of the mythologies she'd heard of.

It took him a while to answer that one. She would have thought he was using the time to make something up, except that he looked so intensely sad.

Finally, he sighed, his eyes closing, before gazing into her—his expression so deep with memory and pain that she didn't even know how to begin to process him.

"My name is Michael," he said again. "I used to be an archangel."

As he reached out toward her, she nearly thought she could see a tear in his eye.

"And you were the other half of my soul."

Wanting to reject him outright, she didn't know what to say, except that she had no idea what was real anymore. Besides, when he touched her cheek so gently, there was a brief vision of wings, and she startled, pulling away, eyes wide.

While part of her yearned to believe, she had been trained too well that demons had many powers of deception. If she just accepted him now . . .

Once his hand was gone, she winced, his look so sad—the memories of the eyes of all those she had killed flashing back at her accusingly. If his touch kept that away, she would have been happy for it alone—but she couldn't fight her own memories. Those, at least, she knew to be real.

"How can I trust you? How can you prove that anything you say is true?"

Sadly, he didn't seem to have an answer for this—and, even worse, wasn't allowed to find one.

The door opened, a tall, gray-haired man entering. Michael—if that were actually his name—let out something like a hiss, moving to block her from his sight.

It just made the visitor laugh.

"Oh, how noble of you, Michael, trying to protect your old playmate."

His gaze ran past the man, taking in what of her he could see, which prompted the most horrible leer, and she remembered suddenly that she was showing off *way* more of herself than she ever would have chosen. Lowering her legs and sitting up, she glared into his eyes.

"So this is your old friend?"

There was a chuckle which was anything but encouraging.

"My competition has good taste."

Gaze probing in the most disturbing ways, he started to kneel down.

"Or did they just screw up, when they intended you to be born a boy?"

This statement made both his prisoners blink. Gabriela was both furiously pondering whether he actually knew the people who had trained her and also wondering exactly what he meant.

Michael half looked at her. His back nearly touching her, he had moved even closer, and, if she had wanted to, she could probably have caught him in a chokehold, could have tried to bargain her way out as her trainers had taught her—but the look in their captor's eyes said that the life of this man meant far too little to him to have such a ploy work for long.

Besides, Michael—as she guessed he really must be called—did seem to actually be worried for her, which made the plan impossible. Despite all her training, even with those she had killed, she had never had to work such an active betrayal, and she had no desire to ever begin. Her distaste for them was no surprise, as she'd been hurt far too much by all those in the compound to want to inflict such pain on others.

"You were born?" he asked over his shoulder, but his question only furthered her confusion. She didn't even notice that whatever spell had isolated her before seemed to have disappeared.

"Uh . . . yes?" she answered, confused.

Wasn't everyone?

Their captor moving closer, his look was evil, even if his voice seemed so reasonable. "Now, Michael, you know I need answers."

His horrible laugh returned.

"Not the same ones you do, of course."

Taunting, the grin widened.

"I already know those."

The man was leaning forward, Michael clearly doing his best to block Gabriela from his sight, and she suspected his protectiveness was not an act. Between that and this visitor's extreme sleaziness, she was starting to believe Michael's story more. Despite herself, he reminded her a bit of Father Deacon back at the compound—and, for the first time, she wasn't certain whom she was insulting more with the comparison.

Their captor's smile spread like an oil slick. "Now, tell me, my dear. What have they gotten you to retrieve for them? Who have they made you kill?"

Her protector stiffened before her with this question, looking back at her uncertainly, and, in some ways, she couldn't blame him. She wasn't clear on anything much lately, either. Still . . .

The compound had always trained her to be formal. "I have no need to tell you anything."

Her captor's look mocking, her resistance wasn't rewarded. "Aw, what a shame. You mean you want me to teach you what happens when you disobey?"

The words struck a hideous sort of chord in her, left her vibrating to all the torment she had been given her entire life, any time she even thought of pulling away. Even Michael seemed to sense it, shuddering in front of her.

Not wanting to give him the satisfaction—and utterly determined to share nothing with him—she didn't answer. It occurred to her for a second that her protector's position might even be a front, all of this some sort of weird version of good cop/bad cop. Maybe Michael was just here to earn her trust, before he got her story out of her.

It was certainly possible, but his disgust with their captor, his terror for her, seemed very real, even left him shaking.

Despite Michael's attempts to block her, their captor held her gaze perilously. "So, what is your lever, my dear? Not the safety of your trainers or family, I see. You won't betray them, but they've done nothing to win your love."

Neither had he, which was clearly why he continued to look for a way in.

"Mm," he murmured, leaning back, and Gabriela actively attempted not to pull away.

"Perhaps the same lever as your old friend, then."

Out of the corner of her eye, she could see Michael's nails cut into his palms, his knuckles white.

"How would you like me to dispose of a few passersby each hour, until you decide to talk?"

Gabriela's eyes widened. "You're insane."

Even the compound hadn't done that. Yes, they'd destroyed all possible joy in the world around her and taught her to kill, but they hadn't just threatened random people, until she went along. There was no way that he would . . .

This wish wasn't answered as she would have liked, Michael glancing back at her, his face grim.

"Please," he ground out, and she saw for the first time that he wasn't at all afraid. He was furious. "He'll destroy the Lady's creations, if you don't tell him."

She wanted to believe that this was all a trick, but Michael seemed anything but insincere. She had no idea what he meant by "The Lady," but sensed that he at least believed that their captor wasn't bluffing.

"He'll just kill random people?"

It seemed far too crazy. Even the compound had had some reason for assigning each of her missions, even if they had never bothered to explain them to her, and all of them had been against the unnatural. Why would he . . .?

Her protector sighed, his gaze angry and tortured, even if he only half-looked at her, keeping one eye on their captor.

"He'll choose the first happy person who comes along, and he won't do the dirty work himself." His gaze became desperate. "But the Lady's creations *will* die."

Not understanding any of this, she could still see something about the man which told her that he wasn't trying to fool her.

"And if I tell him what he wants?"

She had the distinct displeasure of seeing their captor's grin grow, as he answered for himself.

"Then, those people get to live their pathetic lives for another day."

It hadn't taken much to make Gabriela hate this man, and she could clearly see that she wasn't the only one. She wanted to think that their captor was bluffing, but Michael's rage told her too obviously otherwise.

Sighing, she gave in, not actually seeing any harm in it. For all she was supposed to keep the compound's work secret, there was nothing she had done for them which should tell any outsider very much.

Still looking at Michael, she answered. "I'll tell you anything you ask, except where they're located."

Her back stiffening, she tried to draw some sort of internal line—even if she was well aware none of them would have returned it.

"I won't give them away."

More and more lately, she was beginning to wonder whether they should be, but she didn't think any mortal police or federal agency was really up to taking on the magic the leaders used. Besides, she couldn't focus on this question now.

To make the moment worse, her current captor did her the disservice of laughing in her face, before standing up.

"Like I don't already know that."

Starting to walk away, he left his orders with Michael.

"Debrief her. I want to know everything she's collected, everyone she's killed, and why." His hand circled dismissively. "At least as much as she knows."

Abandoning them, he opened the door.

"I'll figure out what to do with her later."

And, with that, the die was cast, and she had apparently chosen a side.

Chapter 5
Michael

Once their captor was gone, Michael let out a long shudder. Repressing the need to destroy him was taxing his strength.

As he saw the man's departing back, he wished for his sword, wanted to shove it deep into their captor's heart—but he knew that wouldn't really be the end. All of those the man had captured were missing something or someone he had stolen. Well, all except him. If the man were dead, there might be no getting them back.

Even after the man was gone, Michael's eyes narrowed. Their captor had other ways of keeping him in line. Just the thought of him harming some creation of The Lady's who was blithely ignorant of the danger they lived in . . .

He turned back to his old companion, however little she remembered him. Looking her over, he moved to sit against a nearby wall, enough away that she didn't feel any more endangered than she already must. Even if he didn't want to question her, didn't want her to connect him to their captor in any way, it was inevitable. Sadly, at the moment, he was all too much under the other man's control.

Still, he reminded himself that she had agreed, which was unfortunately for the best. He didn't want to know what his captor would try—or what he might do to the man in response—if she had continued to rebel.

But that didn't make it any easier to begin. Even in that ridiculous armor, she was so beautiful, looked so lost. He wanted to hold her, to assure her that everything would be all right. But he had no real guarantee of that for any of them—and, given her situation, any physical closeness he could give would not be a comfort.

Sighing, he began his questions at a spot which was more for himself than his captor. "Were you really born?"

Whatever Gabriela had been expecting, it clearly hadn't been this. "Isn't everyone?"

That alone told him a good deal. Either she had never seen the captors she had been born to incarnate someone or the rest of those in her former life were more normal humans, as well. Whether they too had been intentionally brought into human form as she had been, he didn't know, but her previous captors didn't make the fact that they were bringing the immortal and demi-divine into the world obvious.

"No," he responded simply. "Our captor brought us into being in physical form from our other worlds. How he managed it is just one of many questions I don't have answers for."

Resting her head on her raised knees again, she looked very lost, and he wished he had a blanket to cover her, as that short skirt hid little. It wasn't what preoccupied him just now, but he disliked the fact that she was dressed like a slave.

Dear Lady, please don't let that be a sign of other ways they've harmed her.

"People can just come into being?" she murmured against her bare legs, hiding from him like a child. When she glanced up over them, her naked need for reassurance broke his heart. "You seem to be real. If you're not really here, why can't you just disappear?"

Before she had arrived, he had thought about it once or twice, only his sense of duty keeping him in place. "I can't. The Lady wants me here."

Saddened, he shrugged—an all-too-human move he had come to appreciate.

"I just don't know why yet."

Somehow, this only served to frustrate her, although he wasn't certain why.

"Who is this 'lady' you keep talking about?"

Too shocked for a moment to answer, his confusion let her go on.

"If you're really the Archangel Michael, I know you're mentioned in Judeo-Christian beliefs, maybe in Muslim ones, too. I can't remember. But what does some woman have to do with you?"

Sadly, all his suspicions about her upbringing were being fulfilled.

I hate fundamentalists. They tend to forget all the actual fundamentals.

"The Lady created this world and all the beings in it."

He could hear the hurt in his own voice and saw that she didn't believe—had been made to forget. His heart ached for all of them.

"The Lady makes us whole."

Opening her mouth, she was clearly going to argue—but then seemed to decide against it—although whether that were because she'd decided there was no point or that he was crazy, he didn't know.

"What is it I need to tell you now?" she asked wearily.

The ache took him over, his hand in his hair, as he leaned forward, trying to hold himself together. How one of the Lady's archangels could forget her he couldn't understand. Why would she ever allow that to happen?

"How did you end up like this?"

There was a plaintive tone to the question, and she looked like she wished she knew the answer.

"I was born into it. I've been trained for this work for as long as I can remember."

Trying to encourage her, mostly because he needed to understand, he nodded.

"What work?"

Not meeting his eyes, she looked a little ashamed. "To seek out the devil's handiworks and put an end to them."

As she made a bit of a face as she said this, he suspected that even she was starting to see that this was crazy, and he was grateful to whatever unraveling spell Isis had used. Still, she put her hand to her head an instant later, looked to be in pain. He only wished he knew how to stop it.

His soft, hoarse voice pressed on. "And how do you do that?"

Watching her wince, he ached.

"They tell me where to go, who to watch. I've only been doing it for six months now. Some of the . . ."

She pressed her hand hard to her head, and he could see that, whatever pain she was in, it was growing.

". . . kills required a lot of tracking. Others were . . ."

She whimpered lightly.

". . . simpler."

The more she went on, the less she would look at him. "It's work which needs . . ."

He had nearly heard the lines she had been trained to say and also saw it when she edited them.

". . . which I have to do."

She had both her hands in her hair now, was actively holding onto her head, as though it might explode otherwise. Michael ached for her, for all that had been done to her. He wasn't certain exactly what she was going through, although he suspected that her current state had a lot to do with Isis' charm. She had said that it would start to break up the compulsion which had been put on her, would let her see her own, uncompromised emotions.

While he might hate seeing her suffering, then, he didn't interrupt the process. If he did, she might never be able to return to herself—and he couldn't bear to see her lose her soul.

He didn't want to ask his next question—partly because he hated doing their captor's work, partly because he simply didn't want to know. "Tell me about the . . ."

His finger tapped on the floor, as he tried to force out the thought. ". . . kills."

Watching her obvious torment, his whole being ached. They had turned her into a killer—this bright, beautiful soul—and, if his suspicions were accurate, they had made her destroy some of the most vulnerable of the Lady's creations, too.

For whatever reason, Gabriela answered, telling him at length about her ordered murders of a vampire, two ghouls, a zombie, a siren, and, as she put it, "that damned suicidal werewolf." By the time she finished, she was weeping, and he suspected that she was going to be haunted by all of this for far too long to come.

Letting her cry, even as his heart clenched, he allowed her to take in all she had been brainwashed to do. But his fists were clenched, the rage at all their captors unbearable.

"Were any of them harming anyone?" he wondered softly.

Still weeping, she shook her head. "I thought they were but . . ."

Sighing, Michael closed his eyes, understanding too well. Yes, she had been trained to believe this from her first breath, trained that these beings just going about their normal lives—tending their day-to-day concerns, loving, laughing, surviving—were somehow an abomination. Sometimes, it amazed him, in the worst of ways, the myriad boxes The Lady's creations put themselves and each other into—always with themselves on top as the only "true" ones.

As much as he hated her pain, then, he let her weep. The only way she could reclaim her soul was in fully understanding what she had been forced to do. If even a tiny part of her still excused it, she was headed for a very bleak path, indeed.

Moving a little closer to give her some sort of comfort—within reach should she want him but far enough that she could move or push him away easily—he looked into her sadly. "I know." He sighed. "I'm here."

While it took a moment or two, she eventually responded, putting her head on his shoulder, and he put his arm around her as he would for a wounded comrade and let her weep against him without a word.

For several, long minutes, they just sat there, his hand rubbing warmly over her shoulder, but his embrace loose. While he wanted to give her more, he couldn't. She was human and young and damaged by those who had raised her—and he was lost on where to even begin.

Still trapped by this conundrum, he was caught unaware by the arrival of Isis.

Pulling back from his altered old friend, he felt a great guilt on many levels, not the least of them his relationship with the goddess. While he knew that Isis was simply amusing herself with him, they had been fairly faithful lovers for a while. Even if nothing was—or was likely to—happen with Gabriel, Michael wasn't really used to the concept of two-timing.

Nevertheless, he wasn't entirely surprised to see Isis hiding a smile. It was her usual look with him around, and it had occurred to him more than once that she might well see him as just a child.

The look became more apologetic a moment later, as she pulled up a chair, settling herself to gaze down at their prisoner with the knowledge of several thousand years in her eyes. It was a calm Michael often envied, but it hadn't been possible for him without Gabriel . . . Gabriela at his side.

Poor Gabriela stared up to their visitor, her look half-terror, half-longing, and her question surprised him. "What can you tell me about my life?"

Isis just smiled, leaning elegantly back in her chair. She had changed out of her mission clothing into a golden dress which helped to offset the sheen of her black hair and the dusky perfection of her skin.

"I'd like to hear what you have to tell *me* first."

And he knew then that Isis was here partly as their captor's representative but was also trying to reveal the rest of what he needed to understand.

Chapter 6
Gabriela

Accepting as inevitable that she would have to tell these people everything, Gabriela sighed. While she knew that there was undoubtedly magic in the ankh hanging from her wrist, understood she was a prisoner, she found her comfort with these two people difficult to fight.

Partly, this was because, every time she had a flash of the eyes of those she had killed, saw more terribly the evils she had done, she knew that she couldn't trust the people who had raised her. All those only half-thought questions had finally come entirely to life, and now she was left to wonder how she could ever have believed.

Michael had stopped holding her, but his shoulder still touched hers, and the feeling of it was oddly familiar. Maybe it was just his own apparent honesty when he had explained his unhappy position here, but he felt like a friend she had forgotten—as insane as part of her told her this was. If he suddenly started making moves on her, she would have fought, but absolutely nothing about him said this was coming.

Weirdly.

Of course, her entire existence had been insane, so that she had simply fallen into a new vat of crazy shouldn't have been a surprise. While she still ached at being a captive, that was more a general complaint about her life. To her, freedom had always been a myth.

Giving in to the questions, then, her fingers rubbing over her elbow, arms around her raised knees, she stared at the floor. "I don't know where to begin."

Kind, maternal, the beautiful woman whose ankh she wore smiled. "At the beginning is always good."

Isis glanced a smile over to Michael, which Gabriela noted with some discomfort. Breaking her from her curiosity, Isis prompted her again.

"Were you born to these people?"

"My parents are part of the group, yes." She spoke a truth she had known for sometime. "I think they had me solely so I could be trained to follow their orders."

This clearly fulfilled Isis' suspicions, even if it was territory Michael had already covered. When he filled in the rest of what he knew, Gabriela suspected that he was doing it to shield her, and she was grateful.

"She's been trained to kill on command."

Thankfully, he then went on to relay the rest. While hearing wasn't easy, Gabriela didn't think she could have actually spoken it twice.

Nodding as this list of horrors ended, Isis' deep gaze was still on Gabriela. "Was there no other explanation given?"

Restating the sum of her training, Gabriela shrugged. "No. No one at the compound ever saw those as necessary."

Isis and Michael stared at each other, and she suspected it was the term "compound" which had done it. Even she heard it as code for "the bunch of crazy-eyed wackos I was raised by" for the first time. She tried to give their oft-repeated phrase.

"They were the devil's . . ."

"No," the other woman interrupted, and Gabriela looked back to her, wondering. "Was there anything you had to retrieve?"

This question made her uncomfortable—as had the act, as much as she had argued all of her training back at herself at the time. She couldn't meet the woman's eyes.

"I had to bring back a . . . souvenir from each . . . kill."

No matter how deep her training, it had *always* seemed ghoulish. She didn't like recounting it any more now.

"What were they?"

Gabriela didn't answer. She didn't want to.

"Did they specify what they wanted you to bring?"

More uncomfortable by the second, Gabriela nodded, and Isis had to prompt her once more, before she'd reply, her voice so soft it was a wonder they could hear it.

"It was different every time."

But she told them, nonetheless, the details difficult to forget. With the two ghouls, she had brought back charms they had been wearing or carrying. With the vampire, it had been the necklace he had had on. But the zombie, werewolf, and siren were by far the most unsettling. With them, she had had to recover body parts: teeth or nails or scales.

She felt Michael shudder and couldn't blame him, even as Isis's questions went on. "What will happen if you return to them?"

"They'll kill me, probably." True, that mostly didn't happen in public. It was more that someone just wouldn't return from a mission and anyone who asked would be very definitely encouraged not to inquire any further. While it was vaguely possible that she'd be retrained, death really was much more likely.

Of course, that said nothing of those who came back when they shouldn't. Watching for intruders, the patrols were always out, their vans and pickup trucks indistinguishable from the various "good ole country boys" in the areas the compound tended to inhabit. If someone were caught by them . . . well, there had been a few gunshots in the night she would never be able to stop hearing.

Accepting all of this as disturbingly normal, she looked down to her wrist. "Can I take the ankh off now?"

The woman who wore a similar one tilted her head slightly, but Gabriela just shook hers, too tired to argue much. "I think whatever spell it was meant to weave is already complete."

Sadly, as though she were a little hurt at having been misjudged, Isis smiled at her. "It's an unweaving, not a weaving."

Beginning to disconnect the bracelet, she really did look like she was on Gabriela's side—which was more than anyone at the compound ever had.

"I had hoped the truth would give you strength."

Uncertain how Isis could think such a thing, Gabriela tried to smile. While she did see the facts of her life more clearly now, knew she had been raised to destroy those who had done no harm only because they were different, how that was supposed to cheer her up, she had no idea.

Unfortunately, too, Gabriela soon couldn't ponder it, as she felt the horrible effects of the departing spell.

Despite her training, she let out a whimper, nearly collapsed. Without the bracelet, the pain, the memories, were all too much.

Somehow, Michael caught her just before she was about to curl up in a ball. She had never thought that she would be so grateful for some heathen charm.

The thought was half her trainers', she knew, could feel their old persuasions so much more strongly with it gone. But, at the same time, she knew much too clearly that she did not wish to hear them, could never believe again.

Only Michael's soft stroking of her hair, her head now in his lap, gave her any sense of peace. That alone let her know that the story he had told her might well be true.

His every action supported it, as well, his horror at her collapse obvious. Staring up to Isis, he seemed to be pleading. "Give it back to her. Please. Magic isn't my strength."

But Isis just looked at him sadly. "Try giving her something of yourself, Michael. She isn't sympathetic enough to my magic to have it help."

While Gabriela partly wondered over this—after all, who had magic, if not an angel?—she could see Michael's torment, even if dimly through her pain.

Finally, he looked down to a ring he wore, a gold signet, with an engraved fleur-de-lis. Quickly removing and pressing it toward her, he looked desperate to end her suffering.

It was making it really difficult to question his stories.

Gabriela wasn't able to help much, though, the memories of her murders feeling as though they were being projected onto and etched into her bones.

Holding her up, Michael pushed the ring onto one of her fingers.

For a second, it rattled there—much too big for her. But then . . .

Looking up in surprise, she saw Michael's own, as the ring adjusted itself to her, now fitting her left index finger snugly but not painfully. So surprised was she that she barely noticed that much of the agony of the memories had dissipated, now just a soft roar of guilt and despair somewhere in the back of her mind.

Staring at it, she only half-heard Isis' sighing, "Good. Now open your mouth."

Confused, Gabriela did, and she soon saw Isis pull a black oil-like ball of evil from her lips.

Choking a little, her eyes wide, as the apparent goddess glared at it, Gabriela could barely find her voice. "That was inside me?"

Isis shook her head but enclosed the black ball in a golden light, and, with a flick of her wrist, disappeared it somewhere. "Compulsions are ugly things, yes." Smiling at her, she seemed to be actively hiding her anger. "At least you're free of it now."

Sadly, none of them were able to explore this small miracle further, the door opening to let in their captor.

"Aw, how sweet."

Just his mocking tone made Gabriela hate him, and she was well aware that she wasn't alone in that sentiment.

Glaring at the man, Michael didn't let go of her hand, while, stiffening slightly, Isis rose to go lean against a distant wall.

"Have you learned everything there is to know?" the man wondered.

Something about the way Isis let out a breath let Gabriela know that she still was repressing her fury.

"We know everything she does now, which isn't much."

Holding Gabriela's hand more tightly, Michael glanced at her, and she suspected that it truly wasn't his captor's side he was on.

Gaze relishing cruelty, the man nodded. "And what do you suggest we do with her?"

Michael's lips opened but nothing came out, and she saw a struggle in his eyes. Clearly, part of him wanted to say to send her away, but away to where? Not even Gabriela had an answer to that.

Instead, Isis went on, and her glare at the man was hard to deny. "She may be mostly human, but she's been trained for missions. She could help us."

The man's eyes landed on the picture Michael and Gabriela currently made—both of them on the floor, clutching each other's hands tightly. While it embarrassed her, she didn't let go.

He MUST be the angel he says. That's the only thing I can imagine being able to cut through the torment of what I've done. Well, that and the fact that I somehow don't want to kick him repeatedly in the crotch for bringing me here.

Still, this wasn't good news for quite the same reason for her new captor. "Yeeees." That terrible grin widened. "She could be very useful, indeed."

That horrible look held for longer than any of this captives could appreciate. Still, chuckling to himself, he did finally leave.

Michael gazed back at Gabriela with a look which said that he would do whatever it took to keep her safe. He, at least, seemed to believe his stories.

Finally, she asked him worriedly, "What do you think he meant by that?"

Seeming to know all too well, the angel sighed, as Isis studied the dusty floor.

"I'm afraid it means I'm no longer the only one here without a hostage to keep me in line."

Chapter 7
Michael

It was turning into a tumultuous day.

Trying to cast off his regrets, Michael helped his partner up. At least they were together, and she wasn't actively trying to kill him anymore. Whatever the Lady wanted of them, he would be able to look after her at last.

Before he could bring his mind back into line to suggest it, Isis smiled at him, then focused on Gabriela. "Why don't we find you some more comfortable clothes?"

Her gaze ran along the Roman-legionnaire-by-way-of-armor-fetishist outfit.

"I don't think that look is very practical for the day-to-day."

Gabriela nodded but glanced at him tentatively, still holding his hand. He didn't want to let her go.

"You'll be safe with Isis," he smiled.

She didn't seem entirely certain, but she did release his hand.

The separation gave him a nearly physical pain, and he really couldn't decide whether he liked this whole "physical form" thing or not.

To his surprise, Isis was staring at him, one eyebrow raised expressively. "And just whose room should I take her to?"

It was a good question. The theater—like all the theaters they went through—was attached to another dimension, one where they were housed in a building where the rooms were serviceable if not comfortable and they never saw the outside. The only time they really did was on missions. There was probably room for more there, but he didn't want Gabriela too far away from him. If she was, their captor might just steal her away completely.

He didn't want to say this, though, partly because—while his intentions were honorable—his physical form apparently had dreams which definitely weren't.

No, he had no desire to ravish some unwilling girl who'd been raised by zealous morons, one who no doubt had Lady-only-knew what kind of mental sludge still cluttering her mind from them, as much as he and Isis had tried to dismantle their compulsions. But he did want her close. And this darn new body of his was making it all too clear that it would be more than happy to go much further than that.

That absolutely wasn't going to happen, probably ever, but it made him feel his own creepiness to an uncomfortable degree. He wondered if that came as a set with the body.

Sighing, he decided to give the power over to her. "Gabriela, I'm sure our captor can find you a room of your own, if you'd like."

"Probably far away from Michael's," Isis chipped in, apparently playing his wingwoman.

Suspecting he was blushing, which was just embarrassing in an archangel, he moved on. "Isis would probably let you stay with her, as well."

The woman's raised eyebrow seemed to answer that, but her look was entirely for Michael.

He wanted to suggest his own room as an option, but, while he wanted to watch out for Gabriela, his physical form's interest in her was not anything he was comfortable with. Having her too close would undoubtedly get extremely embarrassing quickly.

Besides, "the compound" she had been raised in had taught her to say "yes" to any demand. He could imagine nothing worse than having her feel she had to give into desires he hoped to hide away for good.

The poor woman looked back and forth between them, seeming just as uncertain as she probably should be. Still, when her eyes met his, he wanted to moan.

"Can't I just stay with you?"

It was asked in the sweetest innocence, made his whole body shake, and he began to wonder whether The Lady hadn't put in a few design flaws.

Before he could answer, though, Isis turned her away. "Of course you can, dear child." She gave him a knowing look over her shoulder, as she led the girl away.

Oy vey.

He sat in the nearby chair, his head in his hand. Just what the Lady was up to allowing *any* of this to happen, he had *no* idea. "Mysterious ways" was putting it *mildly*.

He only took a moment to be thankful that his own captor hadn't demanded the sort of sickening trophies Gabriela's apparently had—hadn't even insisted that he kill to get his prizes. So long as the religious and mythological objects he wished for were brought to him, he was satisfied.

Until the next time, that was. Then, the demands started all over again.

This was the expected rhythm of their lives by now. Just what their captor—and hers—were doing with all these objects was a mystery he wished he didn't need to uncover.

In some ways, he was starting to empathize more fully with The Lady's creations who gave into despair. The fact that there undoubtedly *was* some purpose behind it all, as incapable as he was of seeing it, did little to encourage him. For those who could not even clearly remember having known her, the hope must have been even harder to find.

He wondered briefly about the various ghosts upstairs. Apparently, many of them had fallen into a similar state, incapable of seeing the larger picture the Lady had created for them. It was what had led each of them to give in.

Well, except for Gary, but he was a conundrum all on his own.

Of all the ghosts, the terminally-confused one seemed least to understand why he was here. The rest got along with their eternal, in-between existence as best they could, amusing themselves with their productions, but Gary had obviously been left in the middle.

It was his addition which made the whole issue of why the ghosts appeared and followed them even more confused. Were they just curious about the only incarnate beings who could see them? Or was their permanent entourage even with them of their own free will? If they weren't . . .

Thinking into any of this was getting him nowhere, though, except increasingly frustrated. Forcing himself out of the room, he wandered back up past the abandoned props of a million old plays to the theater.

When he got there, a few of his fellow prisoners were watching a fairly passable rehearsal of *Julius Caesar*. In a strange casting choice, the Lady in Red was playing Caesar. As in any role, she was spellbinding.

Ghosts and gods both watched silently. Michael took a seat beside two of the newer recruits.

They were odd ones, weren't exactly friends—not that anyone here besides Isis really was. Instead of spiritual beings, they were the children of them—a teenage girl whose long blonde hair seemed to exist as its own living thing and a young man in his twenties who seemed to always have a black cat prowling around his shoulders.

Michael had been told that she was the daughter of Thor and the head of the valkyries and he was the son of a disgraced demon. Although they submitted to their imprisonment quietly enough, they also seemed to make it very clear that they would fry beyond recognition anyone who tried to part them from each other or their cat.

They could do it, too. Michael had been on a mission with them once. They could both conduct enough electricity to bring down a major power grid.

They were a strange pair to work with, then, especially since they always brought their cat along. They had been sent to retrieve a golden dish from the British Museum with him. While it had been hidden in a case in the basement, along with a few hundred years' worth of other looted treasures from around the world, it apparently had a connection to an ancient goddess of love. She was one of the few their captor hadn't managed to bring back, even if Michael didn't know the details.

Although keeping some attention on the performance, he could see the Terminally-Confused Ghost—Gary, he needed to remember that—and the Silent Ghost watching from the wings.

The last one was new to the company and rarely talked except to the other ghosts, at least not loudly enough for Michael to ever hear. He didn't seem to be particularly interested in performing, either. He tended to be only caught out of the corner of the eye, like a traditional ghost should, a speechless young man, dressed all in black.

Michael was just pondering him further when he heard a "mwerp," as the couple's black cat landed on his lap, staring up to him in classic, Egyptian guardian cat pose. When Gabriela returned in one of Isis' blue silk dresses, he had to hold his breath, staring at her.

The cat was giving him a profoundly knowing stare.

Great.

Even the Lady's non-human creatures could see his every thought.

Until he heard her warm, low chuckle, he hadn't noticed Isis herself.

Thor's daughter—who refused to go by anything other than her apparent last name, Thorschild—spoke softly to the cat. "Leave him be, Pie. He'll figure it out in his own time."

It wasn't the first time that Michael had thought that "Tweetie Pie" was a *terrible* name for a cat.

If the feline had had them, it would probably have raised just as expressive an eyebrow as Isis could. Still, it jumped back over to Thorschild's lap eventually, still looking scornful, and then back to Cain, who put the cat on his shoulder.

"I think it's because you didn't pet it," Gabriela whispered to him very quietly, as she sat down beside him, and he nearly moaned when he felt her soft breath on his ear.

But he knew that hadn't been the cat's message at all.

Still, he couldn't say he was paying a great deal of attention to anything which happened right now—even more so when Gabriela tapped him on the arm and crooked her finger for him to follow her.

He did, but following her in that clinging silken dress was a menace. She was a sturdily-built girl in this form and it had a *lot* to cling to.

Nearly groaning, he slide a look to Isis, but she was just smiling knowingly. Sighing, he followed Gabriela up the aisle.

They got to the theater doors before she stopped, turning back to him. "Um, can you tell me a little about who all these people are?"

She shrugged when he just looked at her.

"Somehow, I don't think I'm going to get a formal introduction."

She was probably right, their captor not exactly well-versed in manners.

Wonderfully, Gabriela was different, as she was trying to keep her voice down so as not to distract from the Lady in Red's soliloquy.

Pointing around the audience and stage, he tried to fill her in. "Not everyone's here, but of those who are, you've met Isis. The young blonde and the red-haired young man with the black cat . . ."

"It looks more brown to me," she interrupted.

"The cat?" He was thoroughly confused. It was definitely a black cat.

"No, his hair."

She had a very nice smile, and he wondered how often she'd been able to show it.

"Fine, auburn, then. Anyway, that's Thorschild and Cain, the daughter of a Norse god and the son of a demon."

She winced at this last piece of information, but at least she wasn't trying to go after him with a knife or something.

"And the cat?" she asked.

Lost in memories, he smiled. Trust Gabriela to want to know even the cat's name.

"Tweetie Pie."

She frowned. "That's a terrible name for a cat."

Tiredly, he shrugged. "Humans and their companion animals. We're probably just lucky he isn't named Puddingwiggle McStinkyton the Third."

She raised an eyebrow, and he couldn't really blame her. This day was making him punchy.

"Anyway, the large man down by the stage . . ."

"The one dressed all in gray?"

He nodded. "That's Hephaestus. He makes or repairs pretty much anything we need. The thinner man in the golden shirt two rows behind him is Hermes."

"Let me guess. He's responsible for sending any messages."

Michael nodded. "And occasionally for rounding up transportation. The rather operatic-looking woman in the middle of the aisle is Loviatar and the sort of scarecrow-looking man in the middle is Hastrman."

Gabriela looked at him strangely.

"Trust me, you don't want to mess with either of those last two."

Critically, she scanned over them. "Other than Isis, they're a pretty European bunch."

He'd noticed that as well, lowered his voice.

"Apparently, our captor needs something which is connected to the person to summon them. He found my sword in a private collection, and there are European and Egyptian treasures in museums all over, many more valuable than their handlers realize. In other parts of the world, those items have often been destroyed or hidden, and sometimes there's a person or people charged with keeping them safe."

Well, what hasn't been looted to Western Europe, at least.

He shrugged.

"Basically, their followers are just smarter about the potential dangers of magic."

Sadly, Gabriela was looking over the crowd before her gaze moved to the stage. "And the ghosts?"

For only the second time, Michael realized he hadn't much noticed. Smiling sheepishly, he said, "I can tell you what I call them, but I only know one of their names."

Eyebrow raised, she stared at him but listened, as he told her what he knew. Finally, she shook her head.

"You don't take enough time to notice individual people, do you?"

Heart aching, he shrugged. She had accused him of that in heaven *many* times.

She was looking down, playing with the ring he had given her earlier, her gaze confused and tormented. He didn't know how to help her, beyond giving her the ring—not that he really understood it, either. It had appeared with him when he had been brought into incarnation by their captor. He had always thought it some sort of symbol of the man's dominance, but, now that he thought it over, none of his fellow captives had one.

"Are you going to be all right here?" It wasn't like she really had a choice about it—either from their captor or the ones she would return to—but he worried.

She just shrugged. "Apparently, everything I was raised to believe in is a lie. The creatures I killed were entirely innocent, and now you tell me I'm really an angel and your partner. Oh, and if I was raised by madmen, I'm now in the hands of another one, and there's no point in fighting again."

Looking up to him at last, she sighed.

"If you know an easy way to process all of that, I'd like to hear it."

Smiling sadly was all he could do in response.

He didn't get the chance to say more, either, their captor—who had the sense never to give them the power over him of his name—interrupting the play at just the moment Caesar was about to be stabbed.

"Attention, attention, my little gods."

As several of them bristled, he grinned. Loviatar and Hastrman, especially, were looking as though they were pondering ways to eviscerate him.

"It has come to my attention that some of you are a bit bored. Well, good news. I have some assignments."

That awful grin deepened.

"Thorschild, Cain, go with Hephaestus to retrieve the golden bough."

Speaking softly, Gabriela looked to Michael. "Isn't that a myth?"

Glancing back to her, he nodded at the crowd. "Aren't all they?"

Apparently, there wasn't much she could say to that.

Besides, their keeper soon had new orders. "Michael, take Gabriela and go back to her family. Don't make contact but watch them. See what they're up to."

Possibly, he saw their looks.

Shrugging, he added, "You can take Isis, if you want some backup."

Oh, gracious Lady. When will it end?

Staring back at Gabriela, Michael mourned her obvious torment. He had only known her a couple of hours, and he apparently couldn't help but always be part of her pain.

Chapter 8
Gabriela

Sometimes, no matter how prepared you think you are, life just out-weirds you.

Gabriela learned this first by taking what her forced companions referred to as a "portal" to just outside the compound. Having been used all her life to being driven around in the back of an airless van to wherever she was next going, it was a truly odd experience to just step in a doorway and end up somewhere else.

This particular somewhere else was much too familiar, if not at all comfortable. Gabriela wasn't really used to comfort, though, so that was nothing new, but the way Michael and Isis exchanged glances with each other was putting her into an awkward position. At least she had been allowed to change out of Isis' much too beautiful silken dress in-to some more comfortable jeans and a t-shirt, which Thorschild had let her borrow.

As much as she tried to fight it, the long-trained part of her wanted to defend the people they were watching from behind some bushes, wanted to tell them that the fact that Gerald and Edgar were patrolling with AK-47s was because they needed to. Their enemies were many, and it was always best to be prepared.

But the part of her which had had its eyes opened in the last few hours now thought they looked like the most stereotypical, redneck hillbillies anyone could ever hope to not see.

While the sun was only just starting to rise, she knew everything it would reveal once it did—and, besides, it didn't mean anyone was sleeping.

The one thing which probably would have surprised them most was that the group was not all white. True, most of them were—everyone in command was—but there were families of all colors there. For her entire life, the compound's basic policy was "Humans = Good, Everything Else = Spawn of the Devil." The skin tone and background didn't matter as much as any potential member's rigid adherence to this rule.

Aside from the ones who, like her, had been born to it, there were always a few new converts, as well. Having a werewolf or vamp chomp down on a family member tended to change hearts and minds.

"Is anything unusual or out of place?" Michael prompted her.

Sadly, nothing really was. "That's my family over there in the corner."

She nodded toward the last camper nearest the fence. All of the group's campers were dirty, huddled together suspiciously, some of her old colleagues and even her family occasionally wandering in or out of them.

"If they've been told I'm not coming back, they don't seem to mind."

That thought depressed her only a little, because she'd always known that was how it would be.

Why fight the inevitable?

Michael stared at her sadly. "Do you think they've been told?"

"Well, I've been gone for several hours now without communication. That's usually a sign that someone's not coming back—and, if they do, they'll probably be killed, anyway." She shrugged. "I think they've already moved on."

Those sad, deep, hazel eyes of his kept staring at her mournfully, making her go on just in hopes that he'd stop. She was happier not thinking about her miserable life.

"Other than that, it's pretty much just a normal Tuesday." She pointed. "Border patrol. Training. Some schooling for the younger ones."

It occurred to her now that the primers she'd been taught from would probably seem fairly lunatic to any outsider. How many others would have had "W is for Werewolf, a bane to mankind"?

"Anyway, I don't think knowing that I failed my mission's upset anyone particularly."

"Do they look like they're planning something bigger?" Isis asked.

It seemed blatantly clear to Gabriela that they weren't, and she had to remind herself that her companions did not have her background. True, most of the people there were dressed in fatigues, but that was pretty standard, since they were fairly comfortable and didn't require a lot of thought. It wasn't unusual to have everyone up this early, either. About three hours a night was standard.

Her eyes scanned the scene. No, nothing there said that anything had changed, except . . .

Even as she thought this, she saw Fatima emerge from the recruits' trailer in the same kind of outfit Gabriela had had on earlier—the one they wore when they were sent out on a hunt. She looked like a warrior goddess, which wasn't surprising. It was an outfit intended to make a statement, not to blend in.

Fatima definitely did. Her long, dark hair was braided into a thick twist running far down her back. Her dusky skin gleamed against the bronze sheen from the armor, her body thin and shapely—although Gabriela was well aware how misleading that last fact could be.

For a few years now, she and Fatima had been sparring partners, and the girl could use her pure muscle to knock aside Gabriela's spear, grab it, and have it at her throat before she could blink. Even though at least 80% of Gabriela's definite girth was muscle, she had never once bested Fatima in a fight.

She felt Michael startle beside her, as the girl emerged, coming to Father Friar, one of the heads of the community, for her orders, her helmet in one hand, sword in the other.

"Is that . . ."

Looking astounded, he peered through the bushes further.

". . . Uriel?"

Isis was crouched on Gabriela's other side, and she knew very well the goddess was there as a guard.

"Your heavenly brethren seem to be getting into all kinds of new shapes these days, aren't they, my dear?" She sounded supremely amused.

Michael just stared.

Because it was clear denial was going to get her nowhere, Gabriela sighed. "So, you're saying that Fatima is also an angel?"

Still clearly stunned, Michael didn't answer.

Isis asked instead. "How long has she been with you?"

Pondering, Gabriela grabbed her fire-red braid, twisting it around in front of her to play with the ends. It was a nervous habit they had long tried to break her of. "Maybe two years?"

Isis' silence somehow demanded more, and Gabriela hated herself a little for giving in.

"She wasn't born into the group. Sometimes, we pick up a recruit or two from the homeless or drug addicts or prostitutes when we come into a town."

"Sounds like your leaders enjoy a certain lifestyle," Isis said sourly.

Gabriela wished she could disagree. The men in charge, Father Deacon and Father Friar, often took off for several days at a time when they came to a new place. Sometimes, they took one of the newly-teenaged boys with them. Sometimes, the boys didn't come back.

She had learned early not to ask questions about this. Maybe once upon a time she had believed their tales that they were "ministering" to the fallen, but, the older she'd become, the more some barely-acknowledged part of herself admitted that they were probably just out whoring. If they happened to pick up a new recruit, well and good. If not, their followers knew what happened when someone asked too many questions and were all too terrified to try.

"Were you camped here when they found her?" Michael finally managed to come back to himself enough to ask.

"No. Iowa maybe?" She'd spent most of her life travelling in either the back of a van or a camper with cardboard taped over the windows. Half the time, she barely knew *where* she was, except for what others said—and, as she was starting to discover, that might not always be the truth she had believed.

Isis looked around them. "Where are we now, by the way?"

Gabriela stared at her.

"I hop in a portal, I'm one place. I hop through it again, I'm back at whatever new theater we've taken over. None of it makes that much difference to me."

Wondering, Gabriela watched her. "Do you even know where anyplace is nowadays?"

Isis raised an elegant eyebrow. She was dressed in a black leather catsuit, her dark hair flowing around her in a way Gabriela had never thought possible outside of a comic book. It was really clear she wasn't human.

"I mean, you're an ancient Egyptian goddess, right? If I tell you we're somewhere on the outskirts of Lynchburg, Virginia does that really mean anything to you?"

Isis had her fist on one hip in a perfect superheroine pose. "I can read an atlas, dear. And I prefer 'seasoned' over 'ancient.'"

Gabriela swallowed. It occurred to her that pissing off a deity from whatever religion might not be the best road to a long life. "Sorry," she shrugged.

"Children," Isis rolled her eyes, then looked back at the encampment, speaking to Michael. "So, was Uriel in heaven the last you knew?"

They watched Fatima, or Uriel or whoever anybody was anymore, nodding, getting ready to board the van to be taken on her next mission. As always, she looked both obedient and grudgingly resigned to her life. She had never been their most enthusiastic recruit—not that Gabriela could blame her. She'd been born into this life, and she still hated it.

"Yes, the last I saw of him . . . her. . ." He made an annoyed noise.

"Human words for gender are so weirdly specific, aren't they?" Isis mused.

"The whole gender thing is bizarre," he grunted, voice lowering. "I sometimes wonder what The Lady was up to with it."

Isis nodded toward the now moving van. "I think the time for sociological debates is later. Whatever they're up to, that girl is the one doing it."

Gabriela wondered for a moment just how the heck they were going to follow her, as they had nothing like transportation, but Isis wiggled a finger in the air, leaving a little trail of silver sparks.

"Hermes, one pick-up, please," the goddess spoke into the sparkles. "Three people."

A moment later, Michael grabbed her hand. "Sorry."

His eyes were warm and soft, and his touch made her feel things she didn't understand at all.

"This can probably be a bit odd if you aren't used to spirit form."

As Gabriela definitely wasn't—and hoped not to be for some time—she forced herself not to let out a loud scream as what felt like a whirlwind picked her and her companions up, spinning them in the air.

She found herself yelling above it in hopes of being heard. "Isn't this going to make us a bit obvious?" Somehow, a tornado with two exangels and a goddess being spun around inside it didn't seem like the height of stealth.

Michael's voice was still soft, but she could hear it. "It's not visible to anyone besides the supernatural."

She didn't question him on this, as he had been right about one thing. The whole feeling was utterly disorienting. Still, with an effort, she found she could make herself stay still, even as the whirlwind continued around them. It didn't make it any less strange, though.

Apparently invisible, they moved along in their own private tornado behind the van which held Fatima.

They were following for quite sometime. After what had to have been an hour or so of green hills and valleys and way too many cows, Gabriela spoke up. "I think they're probably taking her to D.C." After all, it was where she had been when Michael and Isis had found her.

"It's times like this . . ." Isis mused. ". . . that I think our captor really should invest in some good travel games for us. Some Scrabble would go a long way to cutting down the boredom."

While Gabriela wondered how an ancient . . . okay, "seasoned" . . . Egyptian goddess knew about twentieth-century board games—Gabriela had an only notional idea of them herself—Michael looked at the woman admonishingly.

"No more turning the cows into giant statues of Bast. I can't stand to hear the way they moo anymore."

Isis rolled her eyes. "No one enjoys a good joke these days."

Well over three hours later, they finally followed the van into D.C. and down an alley in a mostly rundown neighborhood but with a few signs that it was changing. One of them was a huge, closed theater but with a sign saying it was being renovated and would open soon.

Michael and Isis looked at each other worriedly.

"What?" Gabriela wondered. It was a lovely old place with lots of cracking gilded wood and burnt-out bulbs on its front but would be amazing if someone put some time into it.

Still, Michael's serious glance pulled her back from speculating. "I think we discovered what your family is up to," he muttered.

"Yes," Isis watched, as the door to the van was opened, and Fatima emerged. "They've found us."

Chapter 9
Michael

Michael's heart was beating loudly, and he wondered how the humans dealt with such odd sensations all the time.

Bodies are a PERPETUAL distraction.

As Hermes' transport hovered nearby, Michael watched Uriel hopping down from the van. Her sword looked as deadly as it always had.

While there was part of him which wanted to let her go wild in hopes of taking out their captor, he couldn't let her. Maybe the other gods and goddesses with him were immortal in their current forms, and maybe they weren't. Even putting them aside, there were the all-too-human offspring, Thorschild and Cain, to consider. Maybe their lightning magic could take on Uriel, but anyone mortal against an angel was a bad bet.

Nodding toward Isis, then, he heard her give an order to Hermes, their whirlwind starting to settle them onto the pavement. He did notice that she didn't pass on a warning, though, and knew she was letting him take this chance to bring Uriel in without hurting her.

Uriel had two guards with her, her outfit every bit as ridiculous and revealing as Gabriela's had been. As they came back into the mortal world nearby, her guards were giving her instructions on a pickup point after her mission was done.

Once they were fully apparent, her head spun toward him, and she surprised Michael by giving him a giant grin.

"About time you discovered me, you old slowpoke."

The two guards near her were bulky white guys in fatigues, and Michael suspected the transport people were not chosen for being the sharpest tools in the shed. It didn't matter anyway, because, before he could move, Uriel beheaded them both.

"No!" he screamed.

Beside him, Gabriela cringed. "Fatima, what are you doing?!"

Supremely uninterested in the consequences, Uriel shrugged. "Getting rid of eavesdroppers. Trust me." She rolled her eyes. "They are *not* gonna be missed."

When she pointed her sword at the bodies, it seemed to smoke slightly. A moment later, the bodies just disappeared.

They were all staring, although Isis more interestedly than Gabriela and Michael's horrified shock.

"D.C.," she explained, shrugging. "If you think those are the only bodies buried here, you're crazy."

"Fatima," Gabriela whispered in a strangled voice which let Michael know all her feelings matched his own.

"Ugh, 'Fatima.'" Uriel looked over her nails which, between one second and the next, were suddenly painted a deep red. "'Uriel' is fine. It suits me more."

Michael really didn't know where to begin. While he had brought an end to the lives of some of The Lady's creations, he had never done it so casually. "Uriel . . . you . . ."

She just blinked, glancing down at herself. "What? Is it the skin suit? Does the female thing bother you? Because personally . . ."

She started doing some odd dance which waved her lithe but sinewy arms in both directions.

". . . I find the female form *way* easier to move in. All those dangly bits . . ."

She waved toward Michael's pants.

". . . make walking *such* a pain."

Still too stunned to speak, he just stared.

"Is she always like this in heaven?" Gabriela wondered. He looked and saw she was staring, too.

"Hi, Gabi, I forget sometimes how much you can't remember when you go full incarnate. Sorry about the whole, 'Grr, arrgh. I'm a tough chick' nonsense back at the compound. I'd like to have told you any of this sooner, but it wasn't the right time. By the way," she rambled on, looking down at herself, "am I the only one who finds all of this a bit . . ." She raised an eyebrow. ". . . breezy?"

She pointed at Michael's trousers again.

"It's a good thing I forewent the dangly bits. It'd be serious public exposure time, otherwise."

Isis was the only one of them who didn't look wholly shaken. "I take it you're here to join up? Because I'm sure our captor will be only too happy to have you." The speculative look she gave made it clear she wouldn't mind that herself.

Uriel grinned. "Absolutely. By the way, if you're not as fond of the female form . . ."

She moved in on Isis.

". . . I'm not entirely adverse to the dangly bits."

Suddenly, Uriel's body started to transform, all the softnesses turning into the hard planes of a *very* attractive man. Even for Michael, it was difficult not to notice.

"I'm a fan of The Lady's work in all its forms," Uriel smiled at the goddess.

It was only when Michael saw Gabriela staring determinedly upward and turning slightly pink that he noticed that Uriel's speculation had definitely come true.

One hand held up to block the sight of said dangly bits, Michael rolled his eyes. "Uriel, do you mind? Some decorum, please."

Uriel giggled and transformed back to female. "Whatever you say, Michael dear." She chucked him on the cheek, as she walked toward the theater's back door. "You always were a traditionalist."

They followed in her wake, uncertain what to tell their captor or what was really going on.

Certainly, the newcomer made it difficult to ignore her, yelling up into the top of the theater, which still had impressive acoustics, "Yo! Lord Head Muckety-Muck! Mr. Big Cheese! Get out here and meet an old friend, wouldya?"

There was a deafening silence for a moment. Even the ghosts had entirely ceased their rehearsal. Just for a second, Michael thought he spied the theater's most traditional ghost fade in and out in the corner.

Finally, their captor stalked down the aisle. "Uriel! You miserable bit of baggage."

Michael nearly started to leap to her defense when their captor grabbed her and put her in a headlock, but when she started giggling insanely, as he noogied her head, he just stood and stared.

"Where's your lady been hiding you?"

He let her go while she still giggled.

Gabriela leaned in to Michael. "I have to ask. Is this normal?"

Agog, he focused on her for a second.

"For them or for anybody? And the answer's still no."

He returned to watching his old colleague giggling like a schoolgirl.

"Oh, here and there. You know how it is," Uriel answered at last. "And look at you."

She poked their captor in the chest.

"The last I saw of you it was all butch black leather. What's with the formal suit and letting yourself go gray?"

Michael looked over to Isis to see if she had any better idea what was going on, but she just shrugged.

"Hey, a god's gotta have a change every once in a while. Besides, today, black leather gets you only so far into a biker club or an S&M bar, and neither one's really my scene."

"You're kidding." Uriel stared. "I figured you'd be all 'Mr. Gray will see you now.'"

Carelessly, he waved a hand. "Been there, done that, sold my fetish gear to an extremely enthusiastic couple in Chicago. You know how it goes."

Michael had entirely no idea what to think. "Um, Uriel?" he prompted.

If she were here, surely The Lady had some sort of plan for them. It was just that he was beginning to wonder whether his old companion had any intention of letting him in on it.

"Oh, sorry, Michael."

She swatted their captor on the shoulder with the back of her hand.

"I am *so* gonna blow your cover. Everyone!" she raised her voice. "This is Ares. And he is a total, total *brat*!"

Chapter 10
Gabriela

To Gabriela, "brat" somehow didn't translate to "I've forced a dozen or so spirits and gods into human form and taken them hostage by stealing something precious from each of them," but maybe angels just worked on a *whole* different level.

If they did, Michael didn't seem to be among them, clearly agape. After a moment, he looked far more formidable, folding his arms to glare.

"Would you care to tell us how you came to know the Greek god of war, Uriel?"

It occurred to Gabriela for half a second that she had always loved Michael's formality. It was the sort of random impulse from the back of her brain which let her know that their stories of what she and Michael had been might well be true—as overwhelming as that thought still was to her.

Deadened from following soulless orders—that, she was used to. *Look, I'm an angel!*—not so much.

Uriel, still immune to any frosty glares or open shock, let out a "pfft" noise.

"How do any of us get to know each other? You do a little work for The Lady, you come across an old goddess of the harvest running an organic hemp farm here, a god of the underworld guiding subterranean city tours there."

There was an eloquent shrug.

"You know how it is."

Michael's continuing glare seemed to say otherwise.

Some impulse from deep in Gabriela's brain told her she had missed that look and kinda wanted to kiss him. She told it to be quiet.

"Do you know what he's been doing to us?" he questioned her, one eyebrow raised.

"Eh, so he's been having a little fun at your expense. No one's been hurt, have they?"

When Michael was clearly about to explode, Gabriela put her hand on his arm, hoping her look told him more than she was about to say. After all, either Uriel was here on some sort of mission—in which case she would break cover no more here than she had at the compound—or she was truly as unreachable as she seemed. Either way, having a fit at her in front of Ares, who was clearly thrilled at their reunion, wasn't going to do any of them any good.

"We're here now," Gabriela shrugged.

She watched Michael's nostrils flare slightly for a second and marveled.

How in God's name is it possible I find even that attractive?

Between her weird, half-conscious feelings for him and her bizarrely quick transition from where she'd been last night—when she'd been questioning her orders just a little but definitely hadn't been seeing everything she was always raised with as some sort of weird cult—it was clear that these people had to be telling her the truth.

'Cause I reeeeally don't think Stockholm Syndrom happens quite this quickly, especially with someone as thoroughly indoctrinated as I was.

"Fine," Michael agreed at last, starting to walk away but with an air which said that it was intended to be with Gabriela by his side. "Have your reunion."

Following him as he stomped down the aisle, she looked back to see Isis hanging out with Ares and Uriel and suspected that the goddess was really good at information gathering. Of course, as there was nothing she could do about it even if the goddess did end up siding with Ares, she let it go.

A little of her hated that she was running after Michael like a well-trained puppy, but she couldn't see any good in staying behind, either. So far, everything she'd seen—as well as those random, internal impulses—backed up exactly what he'd told her. Insane as that was.

And, given my childhood in the compound, I have a pretty high threshold for "insane."

Whether Michael had a destination in mind was unclear, but they were greeted near the stage by Loviatar, who obviously didn't do subtle. She was dressed in some outfit out of a superhero movie—skintight, black, and exceptionally revealing—kinda Emma Frost in bootie shorts going through a goth phase. She even had the short, frost-blonde hair to go with it. Superhero movies had been one of the few bits of pop culture the compound had approved of, even if they'd reinterpreted them to fit their own ends.

"Are you telling me . . ." the formidable goddess confronted Michael, her gaze burning. ". . . that we have been taken prisoner by some puny god of war?"

Michael just shrugged, the king of understatement. His expression didn't change, even when she began, quite literally, to smoke with wrath.

"Loviatar, honey."

One of the pair of ghosts Michael had pointed out to Gabriela earlier as the Bickering Twosome approached the goddess.

"Margo and I were having a disagreement we thought you could solve."

Loviatar turned to them, her gaze flinty. It was amazing the two spirits hadn't disappeared in a cloud of smoke.

"You know how we were asking about ways to do the best fight scene? Do you think this would work?"

A moment later, the two ladies simulated some truly unconvincing fisticuffs.

Clearly distracted if still irate—which seemed to be her default mode—Loviatar's gaze burned brighter.

"I have told you before. When you eviscerate someone, you must do so quickly. Otherwise . . ."

Gabriela tried very hard to stop listening at this point, as Loviatar was even more graphic than the compound's "How to Disassemble a Zombie" classes.

Still, she didn't really know what to do with herself—and, apparently, neither did Michael. Glaring blindly at the stage, he just stood there.

Feeling a bit like a wallflower, Gabriela dawdled uncertainly till they were joined by Thorschild and Cain, who had just returned with the golden bough and presented it to their captor. They looked curious, even though their cat was now sitting backward on Cain's shoulder spitting in the direction of the god of war.

"I get the feeling we missed something," Cain told her. He had a very nice English accent and was stroking the cat soothingly, for all it seemed to notice him. For demon spawn, he was pretty friendly.

Gabriela noticed that Hephaestus had quietly taken the same seat in the theater again, looking thoughtful.

Putting a hand on Michael's arm, she drew him back from whatever dark reveries he was caught in, as she answered. "Apparently, our captor is Ares."

Cain turned back to take another look, accidentally bringing Gabriela face-to-face with his cat. Tweetie Pie stopped hissing immediately and stared interestedly at her.

"Not the traditional iteration of him," he noted.

Smiling at the loving look Thorschild gave him, Gabriela decided that she apparently wasn't the only woman who enjoyed a little formality.

When he turned back to Gabriela, Tweetie Pie turned around, his head cocked as he stared at her.

"Who's his old friend?" Thorschild wondered.

"The angel Uriel, apparently, although she's spent the last couple of years in the compound with me."

Thorschild, Cain, and their cat all stared.

"Sorry," Gabriela sighed. "Raised in a cult. Long story."

She almost thought she heard Cain muttering, "Tell me about it," definitely saw Thorschild smile, but wasn't sure what to make of any of it.

Shrugging, she went on. "Anyway, she seems to know Ares and told everyone who he is."

Thorschild crossed her arms over a fairly expansive bosom and looked to be pondering. Tweetie Pie distracted Gabriela from questioning their situation further by standing up tall and sticking his nose out toward her.

An instant later, Thorschild glanced over, her voice calm. "Oops, cat attack. Look out."

Suddenly, Tweetie Pie did a sort of sideways flip and ended up catapulting himself at Gabriela, back down. She let out a little cry and pulled out the shirt Thorschild had loaned her, thankfully catching him in her arms.

Tweetie Pie purred.

"Um, sorry." Gabriela stood holding the cat awkwardly in some combination of her arms and the shirt, looking up to Thorschild. "I don't mean to damage your clothes. You were nice to lend them to me."

The woman whose blonde hair seemed to be everywhere at once just laughed. "Trust me, if those shirts could be damaged by cat attack, they'd all be in shreds by now."

She glanced down at the purring black bundle of fur lovingly.

"Pie seems to like you, anyway."

He was certainly purring. Gabriela would grant her that.

Trying to reposition the beast—who, she had to admit, was oddly comforting—she put his front paws on her shoulder, back paws hooked in the waistband of her jeans. Still purring, he made no complaints.

As she stroked the cat, Michael was just staring at her, but she had no idea what he was thinking.

Thorschild had been looking at her, too. She had taken up Cain's hand, their fingers entwined, as though it were their natural resting pose.

"Would you like me to introduce you to the ghosts? Some of them are fairly friendly."

It was an odd offer, but what else did she really have to do? Whatever was going on with Ares wasn't going to be solved instantly, and everybody else was just sitting around. Being immortal, they probably didn't have to worry about things like eating and sleeping.

"Sure," Gabriela agreed, adjusting her new cat friend slightly. He was relatively thin but still rather hefty.

Following Cain and Thorschild around to the side and onto the stage, where the ghosts were still milling around after the entrance of Uriel, Michael silently at her side, Gabriela wondered. Why Ares would collect the various gods and angels made sense, in a selfish way, but the ghosts were a little harder to figure out.

Thorschild pointed, and Gabriela tried to hear her over the mad purring of the cat.

"The two ghosts talking to Loviatar . . ."

The ones Michael calls the Bickering Ghosts, Gabriela remembered. They seemed to be getting quite the lesson in disembowelment now from the formidable goddess.

". . . that's Margo and Eve. They were society rivals in Charleston, South Carolina in the fifties. Apparently, they both wanted the same part in a local play but were killed by a passing car when they were standing in the middle of the street arguing about who would be best for it."

The pair of them seemed to have continued their old ways, although they were now much too fascinated by Loviatar's detailed decapitation explanation to be saying much. Both white ladies of a certain age, they were dressed in what was probably politely high fashion for the era. Margo even had on a rather complicated hat.

"That one there, the rather sweet but out of place one," Thorschild went on. ". . . is Gary."

There were several ghosts gathered around just staring, but Gabriela nodded toward the one she thought Thorschild meant, the one who had so badly surprised her last night. Still, she wanted to be sure.

"The tall, thin African-American guy with the glasses, the kinda pudgy white one with his hands in his pockets, or the hot Asian guy in black who only ever fades in for a moment or two before disappearing?"

Michael had pointed one of them out to her the other night, but there could always be more than one by the same name.

"The African-American guy . . ."

Looking oddly confused, Michael had been watching. "What is it which makes you humans so obsessed about race?"

Gabriela looked at him, then at Thorschild and Cain, who made it clear they were equally lost.

His head now underneath Gabriela's chin, Tweetie Pie stopped purring and stared at Michael as well.

A small part of her thought about challenging him on the nonsense of claiming "I don't see race," as everyone who claimed that tended to see nothing but. Even at the compound, there had been a possible new recruit or two who had said that but decided against joining when they saw that everyone wasn't solidly white.

Still, he was an angel, so maybe he really didn't, whatever outer form he was currently in. After all, Fatim—. . . Uriel was . . . well, something middle eastern and Michael himself sorta Sephardic, so . . .

When no one answered, he seemed a little annoyed.

"The Lady said she only started making the lighter-skinned humans because she'd gone through all the darker colors she could think of. Apparently, she tried a blue-skinned one once but decided it didn't really belong so sent it into one of the other dimensions."

Especially since he was probably right, there wasn't much to say to this. *It's a human thing. Don't expect it to make sense* would probably have been the closest Gabriela could get, but it didn't seem worth the effort. It would require a several decades' long master class in sociology, psychology, and history or no answer at all.

"Anyway," Thorschild picked up, apparently having decided the same thing. "He's the only non-actor here."

She went on to tell Gabriela about a few dozen others, most of whose names ended up in a big pile of goo somewhere in her head. It was only hours later that she realized that Thorschild had never mentioned the Asian ghost who was more not there than there. But maybe she couldn't see him very well. Who knew?

The only one which stood out in all of these was Gerta, the one Michael had referred to as The Lady in Red. She had been a German Jewish refugee in the late 1930s who, despite her talents, hadn't quite been able to succeed. Apparently, she had died of tuberculosis. Because of it, half the other ghosts referred to her as Camille.

Gabriela didn't get it, but it seemed to make sense to Thorschild, so she figured it was something she'd missed because of the compound and let it lie.

Somehow, Gabriela thought, as she allowed Tweetie Pie—or just Pie, according to Cain—to wander back to Thorschild's keeping, she had hoped that knowing more about the ghosts might tell her something she needed to know. She wasn't certain it really had.

Still, Thorschild and Cain were nice enough. And she kinda liked hearing Pie purr.

As nothing else seemed to be happening just then—Uriel and Ares still involved in a long session of playful reminiscing—Michael suggested that she try to get some sleep.

In many ways, this sounded like a wonderful notion. As used to exhaustion as she was, it wasn't like she enjoyed it. And all the multiple shocks and changes of the day had left her feeling pretty lost.

Still, what this meant was that she had to go to Michael's room, where she could either sleep entirely unprotected or with the angel himself watching her.

She wasn't sure which idea freaked her out more.

It wasn't that she thought Michael would try anything, as he was proving fairly assiduous in attempting not to even touch her. It was more that she had no conscious memories of their past and wasn't at all sure what she wanted with him.

As far as she could tell, Michael felt exactly the same way, at least if his worried glances were anything to go by.

Moving through the tunnels of the theater, she would never have known when they shifted into a different dimension if he hadn't told her. It was still a long walk from there, but one more unattended-looking door did eventually lead to a room with a bed in it, if very little else.

For a moment, Gabriela just stood there, taking in the bleak scene. Of course, it was better than any of the compound's trailers, but that wasn't saying much. She'd seen what was supposed to be normal on TV, and this definitely wasn't it.

Then again, most of the characters on TV weren't displaced angels.

There was a bed, a dresser or two, a couple of black suits on hangers, and a small bathroom—although whether an angel required any of its uses was a question she didn't feel she could ask.

"Do you actually sleep?" she wondered, looking at him finally.

Holding many layers she could only guess at, his gaze was deep.

"I can, but I don't have to."

Before she could ask more, he shrugged.

"It's kind of the same with food. This body wants certain things, but since I wasn't born to it, I can ignore them without particular harm."

Uncertain whether that were a good idea or not, she just stared at him. There was part of her which wanted to ask for a separate bedroom, but that would mean being left all alone. Whatever the uncertainties, she found Michael's presence soothing, and she was certain he wasn't going to do anything to her she didn't want.

Any basic consideration of her feelings was a welcome enough change to calm her even more.

Still, it did unsettle her slightly to think about a few of the looks which had passed between him and Isis. Up to now, she suspected that this bed had mostly been used for one thing.

He caught her look and shrugged, going to stare out the window. She couldn't see much through the curtains but a flashing red neon sign which said "Eat at Joe's." Weird, but what did she know? Maybe those were standard, wherever they were.

Apparently, he picked up on her worries.

"Like I said," he sighed. "I can ignore what this body wants, and I would never do anything to hurt you."

Somehow, she knew this was true, and that truth soothed her further.

Lying down, she gave in to the feeling.

While part of her wanted to get out of these clothes and be more comfortable, she wasn't going to do that around him. Even if he had no designs on her, he was an angel dealing with human form. It would be rather cruel to tease him any more.

Chapter 11
Michael

As an angel, Michael understood eternity, but he had never truly comprehended how overwhelming such a concept must be for humans till he sat watching Gabriela sleep for several hours.

It was a time of many worries and very little he could do, but his mind probably wouldn't have let him sleep even if he had wanted to try. For one thing, he knew that—if Uriel and Ares ever stopped having their prolonged reunion party—they needed to discuss with their captor what to do about Gabriela's earthly family. The insane rubes who were dedicated to destroying innocent extranormals were not going to take it well when three more of their people disappeared, especially since they apparently knew where Ares and his captives were hiding.

Of course, the relationship between Ares and whoever was running the fools Gabriela had been born to was just one question now. The war god certainly seemed to know a good deal about them, and Michael was starting to worry over just who might have been informing on them.

To say that Uriel seemed changed since Michael had last seen him, as well, was ludicrously understated. The angel was altogether too chummy with their captor. Had he gone rogue and was now working with a god of war to . . .

. . . what? That was really the plaguing question.

Unfortunately, it was only one he had no answer for. He just knew that the last situation with rebelling angels hadn't worked out well at all.

Of course, he would like to believe that Uriel was some sort of double or triple agent for The Lady, but he had watched the angel behead two of The Lady's creations without a second thought. True, they were working for an evil group and he had no way of knowing what horrors they might have committed on their own, but it would have been far better to at least *attempt* to change their minds. Just killing them made him . . . her—he now officially hated pronouns—seem far more likely to side with whatever madness had made Ares bring them here to begin with.

As Gabriela finally began to wake, he sighed. Her nap had been something like ten hours long. True, he had created a small pocket dimension to allow her some extra time, but he rather worried about what was happening back in The Lady's world, even if only a half hour or so would have passed there.

As Gabriela's gray eyes opened, he saw a moment of terror there and wanted to touch her to calm her.

But he wouldn't.

She had no memory of all their millennia together. While she had adapted remarkably quickly to the many changes of the last day, he had no intention of throwing himself at a woman, especially one for whom he was essentially a stranger.

"You're safe," he assured her, although he wasn't entirely certain how true that was. Not with Ares bringing them all together—including some truly bloodthirsty specimens like Loviatar and Hastrman—for a larger plan he had no idea of.

What if we're all here to help him with some sort of terrible war on The Lady's creations?

What that would have to do with the assorted artifacts they'd collected, he didn't know. But, then again, Hitler had tried to collect many sacred and magical objects too, so the whole "trying to destroy every-one" element wasn't exactly off the cards.

As he stood beside the bed, she looked at him, and Michael began to feel a bit like a moony teenage, vampiric stalker.

Great. All I need to do is sparkle.

"Have there been any other orders?"

Michael shook his head. "It's only been a half hour or so."

Clearly uncertain, she stared at him.

"I changed things a little so you could get some more sleep in that time."

This didn't entirely wipe the look off her face, but she didn't seem to be objecting, either. He hoped that wasn't simply because she was too worn down by a lifetime of taking orders to even think of question-ing anymore.

She lay there for a moment before sitting up. "I need to ask you something."

He could imagine many things she might need to know. He just wasn't certain he had the answers to any of them.

"Of course," he nodded.

If he was going to be an *I watch you while you're sleeeeeeeepiiiiing* stalker type, he could at least be a useful one.

"It's about you and Isis."

Without meaning to, he tensed a bit. He had already felt guilty enough for the relationship before she had arrived.

Clearly, she saw this, looking at him quietly. "If you don't want to answer, you don't have to. I have no rights to you."

He suspected his inner rage over this statement was probably ev-ident in his eyes, since Gabriel had always had a right to everything which made Michael who and what he was, but he took a deep breath, trying to calm himself.

"I'll answer whatever you want to ask."

It was difficult to make out her expression, as he was sure it couldn't be disappointment over his not claiming such rights. In her world, she was 18 and had just met him. Perhaps there was some sense of him somewhere deep inside her, but he was uncertain how much of that she could truly access.

"You're sleeping together," she said after a moment, and he suspected she'd had trouble knowing where to begin.

He couldn't keep her eyes. "We have been. It's been . . ."

How do I explain this?

". . . comforting."

She just nodded. "Are you in love with her?"

When he looked back to her, she shrugged.

"I wouldn't blame you if you are. She's exceptionally beautiful."

Smiling, he wondered if his formality were wearing off on her. "You're much more beautiful."

"I wasn't asking for compliments, Michael. I just want to know."

He realized he *hadn't* actually answered her, but there were several things he wanted to explain at once. "No, I'm not in love with her. She's a friend and having her as my lover has been a pleasant distraction for both of us."

Somehow, that made it sound rather cold-blooded, but it was the truth.

"She's stuck here without the person she loves and needs most, and for small moments at a time, I can make her forget about that." Shrugging, he looked at her. "It's the same for me, too."

"I don't remember you, Michael." She seemed frustrated. "I mean, there are these flashes and these random feelings, enough to let me know that you're telling me the truth, but I can't remember anything about our past or . . ."

Rolling her eyes, she seemed to find the idea ludicrous.

". . . being an angel."

"I know. I wish you could, but I know."

Sighing, he sat on the very far edge of the bed from her.

"There is absolutely nothing which could make me try anything with you without your complete permission and desire."

She smiled at last. "You are so sweetly formal."

The ache started in him again. "You used to accuse me of that in heaven, too." He smiled back. "I kind of liked it."

It was a tender moment of understanding in a sort of non-relationship, but even it didn't last for long.

A small silver ankh appeared in sparkling magic before him, a message from Isis. He touched it and heard her voice.

"Ares needs to see you and Gabriela. I think you better make it quick."

Sighing, he stood, offering a hand to his old partner. Apparently, whatever way they could find to go forward would have to be discovered at another time.

Chapter 12
Gabriela

Given all the labyrinthine hallways out into other dimensions, Gabriela was impressed at how quickly they made it back to the main part of the theater. Then again, angels could probably be anywhere they wanted, so it shouldn't be a surprise that Michael was capable of getting a move on.

For one of the first times, Gabriela was really awake. Even if she didn't know how long he'd let her sleep, she could tell it had been at least eight hours or more.

She wasn't certain she'd ever been allowed to sleep that long—at least not since the time when she'd been hurt on a hunt she'd helped out on when she'd been 13 and had ended up sleeping for several days before they could get her to wake.

It was an odd state. She sorta felt like she should be more aware and perky. Instead, she really just wanted to take a nap.

Still, she was also more fully processing the things around her, which she thought was probably for the best. Whatever the heck was going on lately, she would need to be able to think to deal with it.

They arrived back to see Ares standing on the stage, commanding his troops. The ghosts were still milling about uncertainly behind him.

"Finally, the ones we need arrive."

Ares looked slightly annoyed. Although he was still wearing the same silver suit, his hair was a dark black now.

"Choose a better time for a nooner, wouldya, Michael? We've got things to do."

Seeing Michael's anger over this, Gabriela touched him briefly on the shoulder to let him know the small god's words weren't affecting her. Clearly Michael had wanted to let her sleep. She had never seen a man try less to get in a girl's pants.

Sitting back down beside Thorschild and Cain, then, she resigned herself to wherever this was heading. Making things a little better, Pie wandered from their shoulders over to hers and flopped down around her neck like a furry scarf.

She had to try not to giggle. Only a few minutes into Pie's acquaintance and now she *really* wanted a cat.

"As I was saying before . . ." Ares glared at them. ". . . the Coven of Michael knows where we are."

He grinned at Gabriela.

"But we have one of their own."

She just blinked. *Coven of Michael?*

Shaking her head, she decided to speak up. He wouldn't like it, but since when did anyone actually like her?

"If you're talking about the compound, I think you have the wrong people. They've never called themselves that."

For all of her experience, it had just been *us* and *them.*

"No, they've never told *you* that. That is *definitely* the name they go by in the outer world."

She let out an "ummm" but then shut up. Ares was glaring at her, making it clear that he didn't really care what she had to say.

"Gabriela is going to go back and spy for us."

While Michael looked thunderous, Gabriela objected for other reasons, shaking her head. "There won't be much spying done before they kill me, you realize?"

Looking over to her ex-colleague, she prompted.

"Tell him, Fatima. You know they don't tolerate failure."

"Oh Gabi, sweetie, you haven't failed."

She pointed at Michael.

"You're bringing them back the biggest prize of all, the angel they quite literally kill for."

So it was that, only a few hours later, she and Michael were close to the compound again, taking the van which had been abandoned near the theater back to them. Gabriela had been a little surprised that they wanted them to go in such a mundane way and not just transport them and even more surprised that Michael didn't know how to drive, but she knew when she was stuck, so she let it go. At least driving lessons had been an essential part of her compound training—right after "here's your spear" and before "twelve fabulous ways to disembowel a ghoul."

Her mind was reeling, though. She could not remember in the entirety of her life having the Archangel Michael's name particularly mentioned by her leaders. True, she'd learned about angels and he among them but not as a particularly special entity.

It was all very confusing.

But this wasn't even all. Every time she looked in the rearview mirror, she could swear that she saw one of the theater's ghosts—the shy, Asian one in black—shimmer just in and out of existence. She suspected that he was trying to tell her he was there.

She wondered if Michael knew.

The closer they got to the compound, the more nervous she became, the reason for it all too horribly clear. "Michael, I need to tell you something." It was a confession she hated to make—and one she should have revealed hours ago.

When he looked at her quietly, she felt extremely guilty—not that she had known about him before or had had any kind of choice in the matter but still . . .

His hazel eyes were beautiful and trusting, and she had to remind herself to keep watching the road.

"You can tell me anything you'd like," he whispered, and she felt a tingle she'd never known before.

She was just opening her mouth to try to explain when she realized they were out of time. Unfortunately, she hadn't noticed just how close they were getting to Lynchburg, and the patrols were out.

Chalk one up for my trainers' old message, "if you forget, you die." When AREN'T the patrols out?

At first, it was just two vans following at a discreet distance, but, as they got closer and saw that it wasn't Clive and Rafe who were doing the driving, they sped up.

Crap.

"Hold on," she instructed to both her angelic and spirit passengers. Maybe neither one could be hurt, but this was still going to be a bumpy ride.

Pushing the pedal all the way down to the floorboards, she roared off down the road, thankful that the traffic here was fairly light. Already, she was having to make some pretty precipitous curves around much slower cars, sometimes straight into the path of oncoming trucks. She didn't want to know what she'd have had to do if there'd been a lot of people around.

"What are you doing?" Michael wondered, and she didn't know whether he were eternally calm or just trying to sound that way.

"They know it's me. If I let them catch me before we get to the compound, they'll kill me. The only way this works is if I can get to Father Deacon and Father Friar first."

She made a mad swerve around a tiny car.

"They're the only ones with the authority to stay my execution."

"They'll kill you without asking questions?"

"Do not listen to the devil's voice, lest you be tempted by it," she quoted.

Michael let out something which sounded like a whistle. "Every time I think I've discovered the limits of your family's insanity, you prove me wrong."

"Trust me, you ain't seen nothin' yet."

Barrelling down the road at a good 120, which was sadly about the best this old van would do, she didn't have time to talk, although part of her could see that Michael was holding onto the panic bar pretty firmly.

Smart angel.

Their spirit hitchhiker wasn't in evidence.

Even smarter.

She wasn't wholly certain Michael was breathing, as they took a spinning, mud-spitting turn down the dirt road which led to the compound, very nearly rolling over in the process, but she wasn't entirely sure that was necessary for him anyway. Noticing some light sparkles coming out of his fingers, she suspected that was the only reason they were still on the road.

The other two vans were closing in fast.

"If you have any prayers or spells or whatever to make us bulletproof for the next hour or so, now would be a *great* time."

To a stranger, she probably would have sounded calm, but she had long ago learned how to hide her terror.

She didn't know whether he performed any of them, as she was busy braking with both feet just before they would have hit the compound's outer wire fence.

Michael let out something which really did sound like a gasp, as the van spun around crazily before stopping, and she suspected angels didn't do car chases as the normal course of business.

It was only a few seconds before both of the other vans were on them, as well as half of the compound.

"*Don't* make any sudden moves," she warned, getting out of the van with her hands well up. Thankfully, Michael did the same.

As soon as she was out, she started yelling. "Mercy! Mercy on the Children of God! I ask to speak to the fathers!"

Of course, there was zero way to know whether the traditionally-worded plea would work, but she had to try. Either that or hope that Michael really did have anti-bullet spells.

They were quickly surrounded by at least 50 men, women and children. The men who'd been chasing them grabbed them roughly, pulling them around and slamming them back against the front of the van, one in particular glaring at her.

She had known he would be there. He always was.

"How *dare* you plead for mercy, traitor?" he growled. His long brown hair was pulled back into a rather greasy ponytail, his light green eyes furious, and he had a knife he enjoyed sharpening late into the night at her throat.

Out of the corner of her eye, she could see that Michael had at least three guns on him, but he was still looking at her worriedly.

"Michael," she just managed to say around the press of the blade which was very close to cutting her. "Welcome to my family."

The man near her glared.

"Let me introduce you to Edgar."

Edgar stared daggers over to the angel.

"He's my husband."

Chapter 13
Michael

Even with the press of dozens of humans threatening the life of his current physical form, Michael had very little attention left for anything besides what Gabriela had just revealed. Still, he managed to keep himself from saying anything, as any reaction he could think of was either entirely inane or would only sound like he blamed her.

While he was only not going mad with worry over Gabriela because he had tossed a blessing over her to keep her temporarily safe, he couldn't help but obsess over the fact that she was married. Still, his reactions boiled down to three quick things.

One—given the look in her husband's eyes, as he growled out, "Summon the fathers," which someone in the back ran off to do while everyone else continued to guard them with serious hair triggers—it was clear this was no love match. Whether Edgar even tolerated his wife was questionable. It only made Michael mourn for the terrible existence his beloved had endured.

Two—this was the same man who had been patrolling the compound earlier that day as they watched, and Gabriela had said nothing about him. Her entire reaction to him seemed to be vaguely-resigned sorrow. Given this militia of horrors she'd been born into, he suspected child brides were a normal part of them—and such girls were never given any say in the choices made on their behalf.

Three—and possibly most significantly—he and Isis had essentially kidnapped Gabriela yesterday, and she had no working memory of him.

It was amazing she hadn't tried to kill all of them. She certainly owed him nothing like fidelity—and, given his own dalliances with Isis, he couldn't claim to be wholly faithful, either.

These thoughts pressed in on him, even as he saw some tall men in fatigues coming through the crowd—no doubt the "fathers," as the crowd pulled back to let them through.

Of course, this also said nothing of the fact that, while Gabriela and he had always been closely entwined with each other, the subject of "faithfulness" wasn't really one which existed in heaven, as there were no physical bodies to cheat with. Those there understood that love was shared among many other spirits. Jealousy only came into being once there was a form to want to possess.

These brief truths flashed through him, right up until a grizzled and unwashed lunatic in fatigues and an army-green beret was staring him in the face.

This did refocus Michael, if just a bit. The "father's" eyes were a washed out sort of blue, and whatever madness motivated him was nearly visible there—especially with how close he was. It didn't surprise Michael that this particular madman felt the need to carry the biggest gun of all.

Having been a holy warrior for several centuries, Michael knew his kind. He was not a fighter but a coward, taking on the mantle of the soldier for all the world to see as a way to cover his many fears. Making it even more evident was the fact that he'd started an entire organization to try to kill the terrors which stalked his soul.

"What do you have to say for yourself, you prick?" the "father" growled at him. "What makes you think you can come here and live?"

Michael sighed. Even his breath was terrible.

It must be hard having chosen to live as such a stereotype. You can't break from it without being killed by the dangerous madmen you've nurtured.

Despite his natural empathy, Michael had no true love for this man, who had made his own poor decisions to come to this point. It told him everything that this man had immediately come to question his male prisoner, ignoring the woman he'd had to have known all his life as entirely insignificant.

Michael's arms were only half raised, but he lowered them, meeting the man's look evenly.

"I know I can come and go as I please, especially among those who follow in my name."

The thought made Michael a little ill, but they'd created a role for him, and, to get anywhere, he was going to need to fulfill it. Timidity was not useful.

Through it all, he half-noticed another man dressed in much the same clothes as the "father" but with a red beret, standing with his arms crossed about twenty feet away in the crowd, whom he took to be the true leader. This was just his attack dog.

"Oh yeah?" the attack dog sneered.

Stepping away from him, he retreated well back into the crowd—out of the line of any future bullets.

"Kill them both."

Michael had known this was coming but saw Gabriela close her eyes, clearly waiting for the end. He hoped she would understand his decisions soon.

Responding quickly to the order, obviously all-too-ready to murder on command, four of the men and one woman surrounded him with shotguns—an impromptu firing squad—and he saw Edgar draw his knife along Gabriela's throat with a sneer, slitting it without a second thought.

Despite his knowledge of his blessing's strength, this body's heart lurched at the thought of her being harmed, and he wondered if this were some small measure of the fear that humans faced all too often.

Still, there was no time to think about it, as five shotguns fired at close range. Apparently, this group was into some seriously messy kills.

There was an audible gasp, as the shells crumbled to dust as they neared him, and Gabriela opened her eyes, her head still well attached.

Someone in the back of the crowd screamed, "It's the devil! Gabi's brought back the devil to destroy us!"

They were about one second away from every gun in the crowd firing in a mass panic.

As much as he hated the showy stuff, Michael took his moment. Rising taller than this current body's usual height, he let his glare fall on the assembled masses, allowed his voice to boom and echo off the surrounding hills.

"You dare?"

The wings of light unfurled from his back and seemed to hover over the crowd, lifting him into the air. Knowing it would be the last concern for the terrified group before him, he let one touch Gabriela for just a second. He even allowed slight blue flames to surround him.

"You dare to try to kill the Archangel Michael?"

Some interior, very human part of him made a vague gagging noise in response to such over-the-top nonsense, but this was one of those moments where there was nothing to do but live down to the crowd's lowest fears and expectations.

He carried on the "Avenging Angel" charade while watching the group carefully.

"You dare to try to hurt the one you serve and the woman I've claimed as my own?"

When he heard Gabriela's voice in his head, he knew the touch of his wing had worked.

I've been claimed by him? Yuck.

It made it exceedingly difficult not to laugh.

Still, he kept to his character, watched everyone before him about to panic and flee, except for Gabriela and the red-bereted man who was truly in charge. That particular "father" continued to watch with arms crossed, gaze assessing, as though judging the merits of this show.

Gabriela's husband and guard was definitely panicking too. He kept drawing his knife across her throat, trying to slit it while she just stood there passively.

While Michael wasn't entirely certain whether her calmness were resignation, a knowledge that Michael wasn't going to let anyone harm her, or simple bemusement at what he was up to, he still couldn't let Edgar's murder attempts go on.

Nothing like a good smiting to win hearts and minds.

Pointing toward the knife imperiously, he sent a blue flame toward it. A second later, it started to dissolve, the metal suddenly molten and burning Edgar's hand.

Even as Michael made a small blessing not to hurt the idiot too severely, settling on a good second degree burn he'd eventually mostly recover from besides the scars rather than destroying the hand for well and good, Edgar screamed. The second-in-command attack dog ran over to him in concern and clearly wanted to scream something up at Michael but was way too much of a coward to try.

Michael flapped there for a moment or two on wings of light, wondering how long it would take the actual leader to break. The man's arms were still crossed, and he had a vague smile on his lips.

Gabriela was staring at him, too, and he heard her thoughts again. *Enjoying yourself, are you?*

Michael continued to look severe and flap but answered her.

Honestly, I feel a complete fool. I hate playing to expectations. Did you feel it when I connected with you?

She looked a little uncertain. *I'm not entirely sure I like the sound of that. But I've been hearing your thoughts for the last minute or so.*

The leader . . .

That's Father Deacon. Get the names right, or they'll never believe you.

. . . grinned at him finally. With a snap of his fingers, Michael saw the red sparkling lights descend upon the crowd. The guns lowered.

"Okay, you've made your point," Father Deacon grinned. "Why don't you come back down to earth, and we'll talk in my trailer?"

Casually, he turned away, as the crowd rather nervously parted and began to mill back to the main part of the camp.

Starting to descend, Michael felt it necessary to make one point before he returned to earth.

"The girl is mine."

"Yup," Father Deacon acknowledged, waving his hand in the air, his back still to him as he walked off. "Heard that."

Well, whee. I've been claimed. How nice of you, he heard in Gabriela's rather dry tones in his head.

Sorry.

He came back entirely to earth, and several of those around him scattered like rabbits.

I just didn't want Edgar to start trying to stab you again.

Gabriela gave her husband one glance, as she took Michael's outstretched hand and started to follow Father Deacon into the camp. Edgar was still being comforted by the second-in-command attack dog, although now the man he had been patrolling with earlier was tending gently to his wounded hand.

That's Father Friar, and he's Edgar's actual father. The other guy is Gerald. I hope you didn't completely destroy Edgar's hand. He needs it to play at his nightly knife-sharpening.

Michael blinked. *Why would you care? He tried to slit your throat.*

Though it was very quiet, he heard Gabriela sigh.

I could tell that you'd put some sort of spell on me. Besides, Edgar is a coward and a wannabe bully, but he's got his own problems. He never much liked me, but we developed a live-and-let-die policy with each other. He's not a fun person to share a trailer or a life with, but he really didn't hurt me in any of the ways you're fearing. Thankfully.

Michael kind of knew but asked nonetheless. *I'm guessing you didn't have much choice in marrying him.*

Oh, sure, because every 16-year-old girl's dream is to be married off against her will to an inbred loser. Which part of "I was raised in a dangerous cult" are you failing to understand?

Sorry.

This brought to mind another issue, however. As they were getting close to what seemed to be Father Deacon's trailer, Michael needed to know.

Is it common knowledge here that Father Deacon is a sorcerer?

He saw Gabriela blink. *From the way you say that, I take it that's some sort of specific term and not just used for someone who likes long robes and guttering black candles?*

Yes—and not as a rule, no. It's basically an incredibly strong witch.

Somehow that didn't seem to be enough of an explanation, as Gabriela didn't seem to know much about magical communities.

A witch is just someone, male or female, who's born with magical abilities.

Trying to figure out what she did and didn't understand about the supernatural world was daunting—although he guessed it made sense that Father Deacon hadn't wanted to share enough to let his followers figure out what he was.

He could see the Salem Witch Trial type images in her head but said nothing, especially as she started answering his question.

I've never seen those sort of sparkles like I did today and never realized he could control us like that. But our orders on a hunt often come through magic, so I sort of knew it existed. I just never thought into it in any depth before, which I guess was probably a spell, too.

She sounded a little sour over this, and he didn't blame her in the least.

When they came at last to Father Deacon's camper, a wary assistant held the door open and then closed it behind them, with just themselves and Father Deacon inside.

Gabriela's voice came to him again.

Yuck. I haven't been in here since Father Deacon and Father Friar announced I was going to be marrying Edgar.

You mean every girl doesn't dream of being put into a forced marriage to a knife-mad lunatic?

Her small but warm laugh was thankfully internal. *He's not actually crazy, just terrified and very thoroughly brainwashed.*

Michael wasn't entirely happy with this.

Why do you defend him?

Trust me. You don't know his secret. And no, he never raped, beat, or even raised his voice to me. Ignored me a lot, but I was fine with that.

This kind of left aside the whole "tried to slit your throat" issue, which made Michael worry that she was still suffering from Stockholm Syndrome, but they'd run out of time to talk.

Father Deacon took off his beret and scrubbed at his much-cleaner-than-Father-Friar's hair. It was a kind of salt and pepper color and held in a ponytail down his back. He looked like a seedy Eric Roberts.

This wasn't a comforting thought. Ares had occasionally had "movie nights" to keep them amused in captivity, but his taste was lacking. *Star 80* still gave Michael waking nightmares.

"Okay, so you caught me taking your name in vain."

Father Deacon looked like he was admitting to stealing the last brownie, not creating his own private, brainwashed army to kill on his command.

"Mea culpa. Other than the girl—which you can have, she's always been a bit of a bust—what do I need to give you to keep you from giving away my game?"

At that moment, some good smiting seemed like a really wonderful idea.

Chapter 14
Gabriela

Gabriela couldn't have agreed more. Even though she knew she should be letting Michael do the talking, she couldn't help herself.

"You have us all trapped here, killing on your command, for some kind of game?"

She had a real desire to punch him in the face.

"Look, honey," Father Deacon leaned in toward her, and she supposed he was trying to sound reasonable. He only managed condescending. "I didn't force any of them to join me. They *like* my ideas, and I gave them something to belong to."

"Really? And what do you call those red sparkles you controlled them all with a little while ago—a persuasive argument?"

He shrugged. "They're clair-lumes, actually. Never mind. It's a magic thing."

Looking back to Michael, he tilted his head slightly.

"So, what's it gonna be?"

Michael was obviously caught between about fifty different reactions; Gabriela could sense them now. Several of them involved violence.

This is only a guess, he warned Gabriela, probably so she wouldn't react, *but it makes as much sense as anything else.*

"You and Ares have this bet going for what reason?"

Father Deacon looked cagey. "Eh. A bet's a bet. It doesn't need a reason."

That's not working, Gabriela noted, *although it does confirm part of why Ares took all of you hostage.*

Clearly, he agreed.

"Is there some sort of end point at which you'll know who's won?"

The Eric Roberts lookalike grinned. "You really don't know what this is about, do you?" He leaned back smugly. "I think I'll keep it that way."

Eric Roberts? Gabriela asked.

A moment later, Michael played some images in her head.

Her eyes opened a little wider. *You're right. He DOES look like Eric Roberts. And ew, gross,* she noted at some of the scenes.

Exactly.

Michael went on. "Why shouldn't I free every single one of your captives right now?"

Father Deacon sighed. "You can try, but it's pretty essential magic. Taking the compulsions away may cripple them or worse."

Gabriela had a feeling that he had intended them that way, and really wanted to pummel him. She only realized she was rising to do so, though, when Michael put his hand on hers. She tried to stay calm and watch.

"I could end you quite easily, sorcerer," Michael stared into him calmly. It was a simple statement of fact.

Father Deacon grinned. "You can try if you like, angel, but I'll have you know that I've made some pretty good deals with a demon or two. Anything happens to me because of you, it'll be serious 'war between heaven and earth' time. And somehow I don't think your 'Lady' will really appreciate you bringing on the apocalypse."

That can happen? Gabriela asked.

Ever heard of World War I?

Not much more than the name. Raised in a dangerous cult, remember?

She only just caught Michael's sigh, before he explained.

It started because various European countries all had treaties with each other, so when two countries ended up in a war, dozens of others followed one after another because they'd promised to fight along with someone else.

There was a pause.

Well, that and they were all really hungry to steal as much land from each other as they could. Still, tens of millions dead, years of conflict and chaos, and all entirely pointless.

Okay, so maybe not so good to start another one.

Agreed.

Michael started making his demands. "I'll risk it, unless you do the following."

Father Deacon grinned unbelievingly but listened all the same.

"No more killing to acquire anything—or for any other reason—either within the compound or out of it. No more forced marriages or any other types of rape."

Clearly unconcerned, Father Deacon shrugged.

"And you also give me a list of everything you've collected."

Why? Gabriela wondered.

Because it's something to take back to Ares. And maybe luck will be on our side and there will be something on it which will help us figure this out.

Father Deacon shrugged again, his hands folded in his lap. "Sure. Why not? I already know everything Ares has collected, and he probably knows all my acquisitions, too."

"And the killings and forced marriages?" Michael pressed.

"Stopping the killings just takes a small tweak in the compulsions, and there were only ever two forced marriages. The one with Gabriela here seems to have ended already. The other one would be hard to break up."

Michael glowered.

"Trust me, those two are happy enough."

The angel looked over to his companion, as she filled him in silently.

Angelina and Mordred. Trust me, those two go at it like rabbits about five times a day. They're both total sociopaths, but they're happy together.

We might be better off breaking them up.

Possibly, but it's probably not a primary concern at the moment.

Gabriela had nodded, backing her ex-leader up, and hoped that Father Deacon didn't know about the other communication going on.

Still, Michael's glower brought on more.

"Look, angel. I don't sleep with my subordinates as a rule, with or without their permission. You think I'm taking any chances with breeding some brat into this group? Then I've got an heir trying to unseat me? Forget about it."

Clearly Michael didn't like it, but he nodded all the same.

"Good," Father Deacon smiled. "We have reached an accord. Tell me, was it Uriel who gave me away?"

Not waiting for an answer, he laughed.

"I always knew I should never trust that little bitch. It's one thing to summon an angel into human form like Gabriel here, but bringing them into being full-grown is *so* much harder to control. You don't get the years of training from the cradle up, for one thing."

This time, Gabriela really did want to slit his throat. She was standing, Michael's hand on her arm holding her back from violence, but her eyes blazing.

"You mean my parents purposely pulled me down from heaven to be in this hellhole?"

"Aw, honey," Father Deacon said calmly, rising to meet her, his hand on her face, as much as she flinched away. "Just who do you think your real daddy is?"

Chapter 15
Michael

Michael had to act quickly to keep Gabriela from trying to kill the man. It wasn't so much that he thought "Father Deacon" didn't deserve it, but this place had already put too much blood on Gabriela's soul. More wouldn't help.

He sent up a shining gold screen in front of her, made up in a series of pinwheeling arcane symbols he doubted she understood. It repelled the man's hand off her cheek and left Gabriela standing there, glaring.

"See what I mean about brats," Father Deacon turned to Michael, grinning. "She didn't even know I was her daddy, and she still wants to kill me."

Slowly, Michael stood and put his hand on Gabriela's back, stroking over it softly, soothingly. "She is wise. I would happily end you myself."

Father Deacon let out a snort. "Angels! Always so formal. Look, sweetie."

He refocused on Gabriela, who still glowered.

"Don't blame your mama. She doesn't remember. Hell, with the kind of compulsions I've got on her and her idiot husband, they barely remember you exist most of the time."

Michael could feel Gabriela's many old pains, wanted to soothe them desperately, but didn't know how.

We must wait, he warned her. *Before this is over, we'll do all we can to free them.*

She stopped struggling somewhat but didn't answer. Unfortunately, there wasn't much else to say.

It was about an hour later when they were driving back toward D.C., the van now gifted to them by the compound. Michael had thought about simply taking a portal back, but admitting its location didn't seem wise. To do so would make it even easier to be followed, and he had no idea what either Ares or Father Deacon intended next.

Although this all appeared to be a game to both Ares and "Father Deacon"—or whomever that man really was—he wasn't certain there were any guarantees that the latter wouldn't just send in his troops to wreak havoc on Ares' prisoners. For the sake of Gabriela and their few other, more human hostages, it seemed safer to drive.

So Michael did, even though he never had before. It wasn't terribly difficult for an angel to learn something new. Besides, given the fact that poor Gabriela was so tormented by all they had just learned, it seemed safer to have a first-time driver than a highly distracted one.

There had been few interactions between the woman he loved and anyone at the compound beyond Father Deacon in the hour or so they had been there. After their stunning arrival, the man had clearly woven some spell which left the members barely noticing them.

Gabriela spoke aloud, although he wasn't certain whether she was just reverting to what was usual for her or avoiding such mental intimacy. "There was a mark on my neck when you found me yesterday, wasn't there?"

Michael nodded but kept his eyes on the road. "A tattoo, yes."

He could see her playing with the ends of her long braid out of the corner of his eye. "Do you think it was being used to control me?"

"I think it was part of that process, yes." He thought about it for a moment. "Did you know you had it?"

She looked flummoxed. "I had no idea any of us did. But walking through the complex today I saw them *everywhere*."

For a long moment, she sat there, looking disconsolate. Finally, she tossed her braid to the side, thumping it against the door. "Do you think it's *his* mark?"

He was well aware she meant Father Deacon's.

"Yes—or one he's taken up as his own, at least."

"What does it mean?"

She looked over to him, and he wanted to stop the van and hold her, but, well . . . no. Definitely not.

He drew his mind back to the question. "It's a trident, kind of a three-pronged fork. It's meant many things over time. Often it's a symbol of some sort of divinity."

Didactism, thy name is archangel, he noted sourly. But he went on because Gabriela apparently wanted to know.

"It's been used by everyone from sea gods like Poseidon to Shiva to Taoism. Many today mix it up with the supposed weapon held by Lucifer, though, so it's sometimes associated with demons."

Apparently okay with the sudden lesson in symbology, Gabriela seemed to think about this for a second.

"Is Lucifer real? Was there really a rebellion?"

He glanced at her curiously for a second, but there was no reason she shouldn't know. "He is, and yes, there was."

She seemed about to ask more.

"He was a whiny little snot, if you want to know, and The Lady had to eventually lock him up in the basement to give him a time out."

She blinked for a moment. "I think that description just blew out a few of my brain cells."

"Never mind. What did you want to know about the tridents?"

"Do you think it's the satanic interpretation Father Deacon was going for?"

"It's certainly the feeling yours gave off, but it's rather difficult to say. Perhaps he just feels that the humans he's assembled are easily caught, like spearing fish."

They could have asked the man, but he was unlikely to have given any real answers, anyway.

Gabriela rubbed over the side of her neck, where the skin was a little pink. "You did get that thing off me, didn't you?"

"Actually, Isis did, but yes, you should be cleansed of it now."

"Good." Huffing, she crossed her arms. "I can't believe that bastard's my father."

Sadly, Michael could. It was difficult to imagine a maniac starting a group like that and not using it to recreate the world in his own image.

Gabriela took after her mother, though, whom he'd seen briefly, barely looking at her daughter. She was a sturdy woman with brownish-red hair tied up in a messy bun and a look in her eyes which suggested that very little was happening behind them. In another time and place, she would have been beautiful. There, she was only a slave to Father Deacon's will.

This brought on another issue, though, one which still worried Michael.

"It does make more sense for why he would forcibly wed you to the son of his second-in-command."

Clearly, whatever his claims about "brats," Father Deacon was trying to create a dynasty.

All too easily, Gabriela picked up on his actual fear, leaning her head back against the headrest with a thud.

"I've told you before, Michael, Edgar's a rather disturbed jerk, but he didn't touch me."

It wasn't enough. To think of her forced to lie next to the man every night . . .

Obviously, she understood his silence.

"Like I said, he never *touched* me."

She was slightly hunched up now, as though protecting herself from something, but a certain truth had finally broken through to him.

"You don't mean . . ."

"I'm a virgin, Michael, pure and simple. There's no one in that compound I would have willingly touched, and thankfully not even Edgar tried to push the issue too far. In fact, being married to him meant that the other boys stopped trying at all, since I was now someone else's property."

"That's an entirely disgusting attitude," Michael noted, feeling a little ill.

She snorted. "Welcome to the mortal male mentality, angel."

Drumming his fingers on the steering wheel for a moment, he sighed.

"You've been raised in a compound full of lunatics under compulsion to . . ."

He let out an annoyed breath.

". . . well, I'm not sure what he is. But under compulsion to someone entirely soulless."

Looking over to her for just a moment, his gaze begged.

"Please don't paint all of The Lady's male creations by their insane attitudes."

She was about to say something, but he held up his hand in agreement.

"Yes, I know humans have made it harder for certain among them for very little reason, but that doesn't mean that every person alive holds to such malicious stupidity."

She gave him a quirking smile. "You really are ridiculously formal, you know."

"So I've been told."

Mostly by her. Which he missed.

Still, there was no way to know if she'd ever be able to fully accept him in her current form, so he resigned himself again to just appreciating her lack of argument over his presence.

Regardless, there were so many things he'd like to change here.

"I wish I could free them all," he whispered.

It was one thing to commit terrible sins of your own free will. That was a tragedy but at least one you had chosen. But to live like a puppet with strings . . .

Gabriela huffed. "I think Father Deacon would have to either be dead or done with them." She shook her head. "Wherever this is going, I don't think that's going to happen till we see this through."

That seemed only too likely, so he said nothing.

They rode in silence for some time longer, until Gabriela spoke again. "You know we've got a passenger, don't you?"

Michael glanced at her, having no idea what she meant.

"You don't have to give me, 'I fear you are losing your mind, strange human' looks."

Her voice had gone quite pompous for part of that, and he hoped that wasn't how she saw him.

"I mean that one of the ghosts from the theater came with us. I just don't know whether he's here for his own reasons or as part of Ares' plans."

Michael looked around the van through the rear-view mirror but saw nothing. While, as an angel, he could spot every spirit in the area, the ones which wanted to hide from this human form seemed to be able to manage it quite easily.

"Is this the one which only ever appears for a second and never takes part in the rehearsals?"

"Yes, the tall, thin, extremely attractive Asian one who's always dressed in black."

"Is he here now?"

Gabriela looked behind her. "I see a flash of him every now and then. I think he does it just to tell me he's still here."

She raised her voice.

"Anything you want to tell us, oh Spirit?"

A very soft "no" blew through the van. Both Michael and Gabriela shivered.

"Okay," she noted. "I think that's the sensation they refer to as 'someone walking over my grave,' although, for all we know, we've been walking over his."

Predictably, having a spirit eavesdropper brought the conversation to an end. Maybe there was more to be said, but they had no way to know that all of it wouldn't be taken back directly to Ares, so they decided not to try.

Chapter 16
Gabriela

An hour later, Ares was thrilled at the information they'd returned with and wasn't the least bit upset that they had learned they were all being held in captivity just to win a bet. "I'm a god, I'm immortal, and I'm bored" was his shrugging half-defense.

Gabriela was beginning to wonder whether Loviatar would give her eviscerating lessons.

Mostly, Ares went back to his flirtatious conversation with Uriel, which had gone on for something like a full day now, leaving the rest of them rather forgotten. But, just before she and Michael tried to walk away, he changed the subject.

Apparently building on something they'd been discussing, he gestured dismissively at Gabriela. "Tell me. You're vaguely a woman."

Gabriela put her hand on Michael's shoulder, as punching the god would get them nowhere.

Although it would feel SO good.

"If you could literally have anything, anything at all, what could a man bring you which would win your favors?"

The way he waggled his eyebrows and emphasized the last word made Uriel giggle and Gabriela try to stop her fist from curling up.

Answering the non sequitur truthfully, she sighed. "Devotion, empathy, emotional strength, and intelligence." It wasn't really everything, but it would have been a very good start.

Ares rolled his eyes, shaking his head to Uriel. "Like I said—useless."

Since she took this as a dismissal, Gabriela guided Michael back down the aisle. Otherwise, both of them were going to pummel the god.

They were met by Thorschild, Cain, and Pie, who pounced into Gabriela's arms from Cain's shoulder the second he saw her and started purring madly. Fortunately, she caught and managed to hold him.

That wasn't always easy when a full-grown cat insisted on lying on its back in her arms like an infant, purring insanely and rubbing his head against her arm. Fortunately, Gabriela was not a dainty girl.

"Your cat is *really* friendly," she noted, although she hadn't actually seen him do this with much of anyone else besides Thorschild and Cain.

Cain smiled. "He has a type."

Thorschild laughed, poked him in the ribs with her elbow, and then took his hand, as he smiled.

Gabriela wasn't certain she understood, as she and Cain's partner weren't really that much alike. Other than being around the same age and rather large with long hair—hers was a *lot* better behaved than Thorschild's, which was somehow making forays to trail over onto Cain's back—there was nothing else which might make the cat favor her. Thorschild had the sort of confidence which said that she knew she could take on the world, thank you very much, but had decided not to just at this moment. Gabriela always felt like she cringed.

Still, she let it go, as Thorschild looked her over. "I'm glad to see they didn't kill you."

"Not for lack of trying," Michael sighed.

Gabriela knew he wasn't going to be forgiving Edgar anytime soon. In some ways, she couldn't blame him. In others . . . well, her supposed husband was being controlled by heavy magic and was not the sharpest tool in the shed to begin with. What would she have done if the situation had been reversed?

You wouldn't have tried to slit his throat, Michael told her authoritatively, as though he understood her completely.

I've killed other innocents, she reminded him. They were going to weigh heavily on her soul for eternity.

But not ones you'd been raised with, lived with, and even been married off to, he pointed out.

Because she would have to admit that he was right, she focused back on the spoken conversation.

Thorschild winced at Michael's information but also appeared to see this as fairly normal. "How'd it go otherwise?"

"Well . . ." Gabriela stopped, as she didn't know how much to trust her, especially within Ares' hearing. "It went."

Thorschild just looked at her for a moment in a way which said she was summing up everything about her. Then, she gave a very brief glance to her partner and a small nod somewhere in the direction behind Gabriela.

Gabriela turned slightly but saw nothing except just out of the corner of her eye. There, she thought she saw the not-quite-there ghost who had been following them all afternoon. A moment later, very disconcertingly, she felt a spirit hand reach into the front pocket of her jeans.

She almost gave a yelp, not ready to be felt up by the spirit world, but a second later, the fingers were gone, as though they had slipped something in her pocket.

"For later," the invisible someone whispered in her ear.

Gabriela managed not to startle but only just.

The way Thorschild was looking at her made it clear that she knew about the message. Gabriela decided to play along.

"Come on, Pie," Cain said, and the cat focused on Gabriela with a look which practically said, *Later, my love.* Then she tried not to drop him, as he sat back up and launched himself back at Cain.

How on earth does he keep from getting scratched all over? Gabriela wondered, as she watched the cat climb the man, finally ending up behind him, with one foot on either shoulder, his front paws on Cain's head. She thought there must be some magic involved in keeping him from falling off.

As the pair gave a wave and wandered off hand in hand, their cat riding along on Cain's head, Michael didn't answer, and she supposed he didn't know either.

What was that about? Michael wondered.

I think I have an idea. Play along?

As she turned to him, he said nothing, but she felt his agreement. "I'm exhausted after all that. I could use another nap."

Heck, after all their adventures, it was nearly bedtime again.

Without a word, Michael nodded solemnly and led her down to his bedroom.

Once there with the door closed, she asked him, *Is there some way you can keep others from seeing or hearing us?*

Yes, but it would probably be noticed.

How about some sort of "forget about us" spell?

They aren't really spells but . . . never mind.

She saw a finger flick very casually and felt the air around her change just slightly.

It will last for maybe five minutes, but it's still safer to talk this way.

Nodding, she reached into her pocket. There was indeed a small piece of paper there. How a spirit could carry it around, she didn't know.

Opening it, she read instructions on where to be and when. They were vague, probably needed to be, but they were definitely directions toward a secret meeting.

Michael joined her on the bed to look at it. *Who gave you that?*

Our spirit hitchhiker, I suspect. I think Thorschild told him to.

She handed it over to him.

It might be safer if you destroy it.

Nodding, he held it between his first and second finger. A second later, it went up in flames. Not even dust was left.

Y'know, she noted, *if we ever get free and you want an earthly life, you'd make a heck of a conjuror.*

He just stared at her.

She smiled. *I'm just sayin'. I think Las Vegas has found its new act.*

He shook his head, but the look he gave her was loving. *We have a half hour before we go. Why don't you take a nap?*

Suddenly, she realized just how exhausted she actually was. Nearly getting killed and finding out about your bastard of a real father could do that to a girl, she supposed.

Without thinking about it, she lay down with her head in his lap. A moment later, she was asleep.

If he found a way to let her rest for even longer, she didn't notice, just the soft hum of his voice and his fingers stroking over her hair.

Chapter 17
Michael

A half hour later, in this reality at least—Michael had actually let her sleep for another eight till she woke on her own—he and Gabriela were on their way to Thorschild and Cain's room and hoping that Ares was still distracted enough not to notice.

When they got there, their knock was answered only with a soft "meowr." Deciding that was the best invitation they would get, they took it.

Entering, they saw Pie sitting on the floor, sitting up with his tail wrapped around his feet, eyes glowing in a way which only magic could create. Michael closed the door behind them, hoping no one would notice.

Still, Pie's eyes weren't the most magical thing about the small bedroom. Behind him, where the wall should have been, was instead a lovely beach with a huge old house perched upon it. Glancing over at Gabriela, Michael decided this was probably their destination.

Taking Gabriela's hand as a way to be near in case he needed to be, which, thankfully, made her smile, he cautiously walked onto the white sand shores of an entirely different dimension.

Glancing around, he held her hand tighter.

A perfect, clean ocean spread off into the far distance, the giant, three-story house with several wings behind him. When he turned, he saw a forest of soaring trees of every type, all of them in a riot of bloom, stretching away behind the mansion. There was even a waterfall to its side which seemed to start from and go to nowhere but roared away in a comforting way in between.

It was improbable and entirely, idyllically beautiful, but . . .

"We aren't on earth anymore," he warned Gabriela, holding her hand close.

Uncertainly, she looked around and then back to him. "Soooo, this is what? Mars?"

He laughed a little but turned to her. "No more . . ."

"It's Cain's private world," Thorschild said, as she walked up to them, her hand entwined with her partner's. "We're inside his mind."

Gabriela stared at the man, clearly pondering the magical physics at work. Michael couldn't blame her. While the place was lovely and somehow the perfect setting for the pair before them, he found it a little disconcerting. For all the old metaphor of an angel on a shoulder, he wasn't actually used to being physically inside someone's mind.

Cain shrugged off their obvious questions. "Please don't ask me to explain. I wasn't aware of what I was doing when I created it, so it wouldn't make much sense. Still, it's somewhere Ares can't reach unless I let him."

Gabriela assessed the pair curiously. "You two weren't really captured, were you? You came by choice."

This was a slightly terrifying insight to Michael, especially as the pair before him smiled.

Just as he was about to grab Gabriela and fight his way back, Thorschild held up her hand, her head shaking.

"We're not your enemies. We want to figure out how to stop Ares at least as much as you do."

Invitingly, she pointed back toward the house.

"Now, can we count you as allies?"

Michael would have expected this to be a threat, but it clearly wasn't. Thorschild seemed to have decided they could be trusted, whichever way this went. Taking this as a compliment, and only slightly warily, he followed the woman and her partner inside.

It was clear Cain had quite the imagination. The house was huge and rather Victorian, but anything but stuffy. Of course, this had much to do with the group of pirates playing Twister in the middle of the living room.

Gabriela stopped and stared, making Michael pause—but it wasn't as though he could claim to find it normal, either.

A very tall man in full pirate getup—complete with hat—had his hands and feet both on either end of the mat and his center parts raised in the air in a backbend which was only slightly wobbly. Between his legs were the legs of a woman in full pirate wench outfit, but she was then bent over to his side and was touching colors underneath him in a way which didn't look either natural or comfortable, although she seemed to be under no strain at all.

Through their mental connection, he saw that Gabriela noticed the woman being African-American, as though that were important. He still didn't understand.

Another, very pregnant, woman was sitting in a chair nearby, spinning the dial. "Okay, left hand red. That's going to get interesting."

The pirate wench stared at them upside down from beneath the pirate's back. "Oops. Visitors, Billy. I'll give you a rematch later."

Then, instead of just standing up, she did a leaning handstand with her hands beneath him and her body rising to his side, before pushing herself off her hands, tapping down on the balls of her feet once and then doing a forward flip over the man to come up and offer them her hand.

It wasn't actually the wisest series of moves for a woman in a long, flouncy dress—and apparently very little else—but she didn't seem to care at all.

"Hey, I'm Tatiana." She poked her thumb back over her shoulder. "That's my husband, Billy."

Billy seemed to be struggling to get out of his current position. Finally, he stared upside down and pleadingly at the woman in the chair. "Arr, help a fellow, wouldya, lass?"

The pregnant woman let out a series of "oof"s as she stood up, but then helped him up with apparent ease. He went nearly flinging into a standing position and then aided her in sitting back down.

Tatiana seemed to notice none of this, just giving them a friendly smile. It was then Michael noticed the fangs.

"You're a vampire?"

He had to keep Gabriela from startling away, his hand warm and tight around hers. If she was going to leave her past behind, she had to get used to not stabbing someone merely because they were undead.

Well, unless they were wreaking havoc. He didn't think a spirited game of Twister counted.

This wasn't his immediate question, though, staring at the sunlight streaming brightly through the window.

Tatiana grinned at him. "It's one of the perks of being in Ev—..."

Thorschild held up a hand, her look a warning.

"Cain's world. We don't have to go to bed just because the sun is up."

Billy wandered over to meet them, shaking Michael's hand. Gabriela shook it only very tentatively.

"So you're the angels ..."

There was a pause, as he locked eyes with their hostess.

"... Thorschild is recruiting. Cool." He pointed his thumb to the woman in the chair. "That's Seraphina there. Her mate's away just now, or I'd introduce you to Patrick."

"Vampires have mates?" Gabriela wondered, although Michael wasn't certain whether her confusion were due to simple terminology or some lingering belief that vampires weren't capable of love.

Clearly confused, Tatiana and Billy stared at each other. "Well, we're married, so ..."

Thorschild stepped in, pointing everyone toward a chair. "Seraphina's mate is a gryphon."

Gabriela blinked at her.

"You know, half lion, half eagle, all cryptic mystery."

I just want to check, he heard Gabriela's voice in his head. *Have I gone entirely insane?*

The situation has, perhaps, but no, not you.

He sat beside her on a dark pink, velvet sofa with gold fringe. Somehow, the Victorian decorating scheme made all of it that much stranger.

Seraphina was staring down at her belly lovingly. "We're kind of wondering how that's going to work with me in the mix. I'm just hoping he doesn't end up with human legs, since that would probably be terribly uncomfortable for the little tyke."

Is any of this normal? Gabriela wondered.

It appears to be for them.

Personally, it had him fairly flummoxed. Most vampires he had known were extremely staid. But these . . .

There was a moment where the other people in the room just stared at each other, and Michael had to make himself wait. It was somehow clear that, not only had Thorschild and Cain—or whatever their actual names were, given the way their companions kept stumbling over the ones he knew—not been kidnapped, but they could also probably have freed themselves quite easily.

Of course, it wouldn't have stopped Ares from killing random people to punish them, but there was definitely more going on than he understood.

"Cain and I . . ." Thorschild started but was interrupted by Gabriela.

"Those aren't your real names, are they?"

Cain shrugged. Thorschild smiled. Somehow, it seemed odd not to watch the two of them being climbed on by their cat as though they were a kitty condo.

"How good are you at remembering to call someone by a different name than the one you've grown used to?" Thorschild stared into Gabriela kindly.

Gabriela sighed. "Good point. I suck at it."

Leaning back, she clearly gave in.

"I was raised to be an assassin, not a spy."

Their hostess went on with a nod. "Cain and I are trying to bring Ares' plans to an end."

"You know what they are?" Michael wondered.

"Not much more than you, at the moment. We came to try to figure that out and then free the various hostages."

This left several questions unanswered, Gabriela looking into her. "Who sent you?"

The pair just stared at each other before refocusing on her. "I think we'll keep that to ourselves for now."

Gabriela seemed uncertain.

"As you said, you weren't raised to be a spy. If you know too much, Ares might sense it."

Thorschild's eyes were angry.

"And I don't think there's much he won't do to someone who keeps him from getting what he wants."

This made sense of a god of war, so no one argued, as Thorschild went on.

"Here's what we know."

The "that we think is safe to tell you" part went unsaid.

"Ares made a bet with several other godly types to . . . well, that's just speculation right now."

Michael looked over to Gabriela and saw that she also knew when essential information was being left out. Still, he understood that they both trusted this pair. Whatever the larger picture here, Thorschild and Cain were trying to put things right. There was no reason to get churlish over a few hidden facts.

"Anyway, the bet involves trying to get the most or best divine or mythological objects they can find. Ares is serious enough about it to piss off gods and angels from any number of backgrounds. At least one of his competitors has established a following just to kill on his command."

Staring at Gabriela sympathetically, Thorschild gestured in her direction.

"I assume that's where you came in."

"Not that I knew it up till recently, but yes."

"Excuse me," Michael interrupted. "But you think the man who runs the group Gabriela grew up with might be a god and not just a sorcerer?"

"I think it's likely, yes," Thorschild nodded. "Tell me if I'm wrong." She looked into Gabriela.

"You were raised to kill anyone supernatural, although really just at your leader's request."

Gabriela nodded.

"Then he asked you to bring back souvenirs as proof of the kills." Another nod.

"What does he do with those who disobey or fail?"

"Kills them, as far as I know," Gabriela sighed.

Thorschild and Cain shared a look. "Familiar pattern," he noted.

"Small minded cult leader's handbook. It always covers for something else, doesn't it?"

Cain shrugged, but it looked like agreement.

Thorschild refocused on them. "Anyway, how long has your group leader been doing this?"

Gabriela seemed to be thinking. "My whole life, certainly, but I don't know how long before it. Apparently, he has spells to keep everyone from asking questions."

Thorschild looked curious.

"I only just figured that out when we went back a little while ago. Anyway, it's been at least 18 years."

Cain focused on Michael. "Do you know how long Ares has had everyone kidnapped?"

Michael was a little surprised to hear the man talk, as he seemed more than comfortable letting his partner do the communicating for them.

Maybe he thinks you'll respond better to a man? Gabriela wondered.

As it didn't really matter much, Michael focused back on the question. As much as he would have liked to be let in on some of the secrets they seemed to be holding, it was clear they were trying to help.

"I'm not certain. I'm not the one he's had the longest. I think that's probably either Hephaestus or Isis. It's kind of hard to judge human time, as well. Maybe . . ."

He tried, but it wasn't easy

". . . ten years or so for me? I'm not sure about Hephaestus or Isis."

Thorschild and Cain stared at each other, and Michael wondered whether they had their own methods of silent communication.

That's a long time, Gabriela broke into his thoughts.

For a human, he acknowledged. *When judged against eternity, it's only long enough to be a minor annoyance.*

The questions went on for a while. Michael and Gabriela told the pair everything they could about their recent journey to the compound, hoping for more insight.

When they finished, Thorschild and Cain looked at each other. "Think the rumors are true?" she asked.

"It does follow a familiar pattern," he nodded.

Looking back to Gabriela, they both seemed worried.

"I think there's probably something I should tell you. You see, gods sometimes breed with human women, and they don't tend to care much about the offspring."

There were enough tales of this from ancient Greece alone to fill a mythology primer. Michael just nodded.

Gabriela looked at them worriedly. "You think my father—the man who runs the compound—is a god?"

Thorschild nodded. "If the rumors are true, yes. But he's not just any god." Sighing, she leaned toward her. "I think your father's Poseidon."

Chapter 18
Gabriela

Gabriela startled at this new idea, and she felt Michael's shock, even as she heard his voice in her head.

It does make sense of the trident.

Gabriela wasn't as sure. "But the compound is almost never near an ocean—or even a river or lake. He pretty much always chooses somewhere completely landlocked, often in the mountains or desert. Wouldn't Poseidon be more interested in having us all by the sea?"

Michael's thought broke in. *They taught you about Greek gods at the compound?*

Clearly, he was surprised she even knew about him.

Well, my mother mentioned him once or twice, although mostly when she was muttering to herself.

Given what Father Deacon did to her, that's not surprising.

Good point.

Their hosts looked at each other for a moment, before Thorschild answered.

"It seems odd to us, too, but it's the rumor we've heard."

She gave another glance back to Cain.

"And I can think of a way to test it."

As that was more than she could, Gabriela and Michael followed Thorschild out of the house with the vampires in tow.

Despite the fact that Gabriela was trying to mend her old ways and dismiss the lies she'd been taught, she stayed well on Michael's other side from them. Even in pirate gear—why, she had *no* idea—or pregnant, those with sharp fangs freaked her out.

They ended up beside the ocean, Thorschild pointing at it. "Feel any special connection?"

Sighing, Gabriela stared at the sun shining off the waves. It was entirely beautiful, but she couldn't say she was getting any "Bow down before me, small ocean creatures!" vibe.

"I've never actually seen it before," she admitted.

"Is this truly the sea?" Michael asked, turning to Cain. "These vampires can be in the sun without harm here, so isn't this more of an illusion?"

"It's real," Thorschild assured them.

"It . . ." Cain started, then sighed, looking at Gabriela. "I was raised in a cult, too. It was a little different than yours, but there was a lot about magic I was never taught, so my own natural magic kind of went where it wanted."

Looking sheepish, he had his hands in the pockets of his jeans but calmed a little as Thorschild put her arm through his.

"It's real, but please don't ask me to explain. My magic's kind of wild, and I have *no* idea how I did it."

"Wild"? Gabriela wondered.

For witches, that usually means untrained.

Ah.

She looked back to Cain then the sea. Still, there was no flashing sign in her mind telling her how to harness it.

As she watched, Thorschild had her head on Cain's shoulder.

"I didn't know about my father being Thor, but his lightning kind of escaped me once in a while. When I started realizing that it was my power to conduct as I wanted, I found that there was this place inside me where it all connected. I can't really explain, but, if we're right, you may be able to access something like that, as well."

Gabriela knew she probably should try, wasn't certain if she were just attempting to avoid such a major shift in her world view by asking more questions, but they *were* ones she wanted an answer to.

"If you're the child of Thor but Cain isn't, how can he use lightning, too?"

Although she hadn't actually seen it, Michael had told her about it. Also, she was assuming that Thorschild and Cain weren't related, 'cause if they were . . . eww.

Thorschild shrugged. "I shared it with him."

She and Cain were holding hands again, and he was looking at the woman as though he were the luckiest person on the planet to have her love.

Somehow this seemed too private to delve into further. Besides, since she suspected she wouldn't understand the explanations even if she asked further, Gabriela looked back to the sea.

Okay, she said to Michael. *Being an angel is like Level 10 crazy already. Being an angel AND the daughter of the Greek god of the sea? I think I'd like to schedule a small nervous breakdown, please.*

He laughed in her mind, but the sound was soft and loving. *I understand your disconcertion, but I'm certain you can handle it.*

His faith in her was buoying, until she thought about the fact that he was an angel and faith was kinda what he did.

Please try, my love, he asked.

There was nothing for it. She had an audience of an angel, three vampires (one of whom was carrying a gryphon's child), the daughter of Thor, and the son of a demon. They were a little hard to just blow off.

Giving in, she tried raising her hand above the water and willing it to . . . *what? Form waves, maybe?*

The thought wasn't intended for Michael, although he probably heard it. She noticed that this ocean only barely rolled onto this beach and figured that was probably Cain's magic at work.

She was left standing there like an idiot, because nothing happened at all.

Taking a deep breath, she focused a little more, trying to call toward her some type of sea life.

About 30 seconds later, a crab wandered onto the shore and looked at her. She wasn't certain whether that were a victory or not.

Okay, time to get serious.

Thorschild had said that there was some connection to this inside her. It was the first time she'd ever seen the ocean and thought it was beautiful, but she couldn't say that she felt like she really had any power over it. Heck, she couldn't even swim.

Suddenly, she had an idea. Michael seemed to have picked up on it, as he looked at her worriedly.

"How deep is the ocean here, Cain?" It seemed to just be a nice, shallow beach.

"How deep would you like it to be?" he asked obligingly.

"Pretty darn."

A moment later, she was staring off the edge of the island into what seemed to be an abyss of water.

Well, here goes nothing, she told Michael. *Try to save me if I'm being an idiot, okay?*

Then, before he could shout for her to stop, she had thrown herself in and sank like a stone.

Chapter 19
Michael

A moment later, Michael was left screaming. The second she'd disappeared beneath the waves, he hadn't been able to hear Gabriela's thoughts anymore.

He was about to toss himself into the ocean to search for her, was about to go full angel in a command to the sea to bring her back, was about to part the waters, was about to . . . well, anything he could think of to make certain she wasn't hurt.

There was a very small part of him which pointed out that she was an angel and, even if this body died, her soul was not lost—but it wasn't enough to comfort him now.

It was only Thorschild grabbing his arm and staring into him, which stopped him.

"Please. Give her a chance, Michael. She needs to know this."

Only the distraction of her eyes made him pause. There was something there, something familiar . . .

"You're one of my kin," he whispered, certain that she had once been an angel. How she had become the daughter of Thor and a valkyrie, he had no idea.

She just smiled at him, Cain coming up to put his hand on her shoulder, and the look in his eyes said that he would not see her harmed. It also said that he loved her to the point of madness and far beyond and that he would do anything to make her happy.

Suddenly, the waterfall which started from and went to nowhere seemed to make sense. It was clearly there as some sort of present for her.

When she reached up and touched Cain's hand, Michael knew that Thorschild—whatever her true name in this life or in heaven—had found her other half. He also knew that, whatever the other parts of the story behind the two of them, she had come to earth to be with him, and she had no intention of being separated.

This was a momentary flash of recognition, however, most of his fears focused on the other half of his own soul, who now lay beneath the waves, possibly drowning. But there was something in Thorschild's eyes which said that she had as little interest in allowing anyone to be hurt as he did and that she would not willingly hold him back unless she were sure.

He forced himself to nod, and a moment later, Gabriela broke the surface.

To his amazement, she was riding a dolphin and yelling, "Whoo-hoo!" just before the dolphin arced and she disappeared again. She didn't seem to mind being submerged.

"Jealoooous," Tatiana and Seraphina chorused.

"Cooooool." Billy grinned.

Michael watched, as Gabriela whoo-hooed her way around the side of the island, her new dolphin friend clicking away in what seemed to be a happy conversation with her.

Michael had gone on many missions for The Lady, but he wanted to be sure.

"This isn't normal for humans, is it?"

Cain laughed, but his arms were around Thorschild, who smiled happily. "I think there are plenty who wish it was, but no."

They all watched, as the dolphin was joined by several friends, and Gabriela was switched off among them, as they clicked and whistled happily at her. Michael thought he saw a whale or two out there, as well, and possibly a narwhal, although it was kind of far away, and this body's eyesight, while excellent for a human's, wasn't that good.

Eventually, the show seemed to end when six of the dolphins stood on their tails, holding up Gabriela in a kind of arabesque pose above them. Then, with a cluster of clicks, they tossed her into the air where she did a full sideways spin and then arced back into the water beside them.

It took a while, but eventually Gabriela swam to the island and pulled herself on. She was no longer wearing the jeans, and the gauzy shirt she had borrowed from Thorschild hid little.

Billy and Cain looked away out of politeness, although all the women grinned at her. He thought he heard Tatiana say, "Niiiiiice."

As for Michael, his body was making very loud demands to be given permission to do many passionate things with this wonderful, wild creature, giving him a sudden realization.

Uriel was right. The dangly bits are DEFINITELY a problem.

Still, he didn't get the feeling that Gabriela was really into the other options, so dangly bits he was stuck with.

Sorry? Gabriela wondered at him, as she bent over to wring out her long red hair. She looked like a Pre-Raphaelite mermaid.

The dangly bits were making themselves known.

Nothing, he sighed. Her smile didn't help the problem any.

How do the humans survive all this—the fear, the yearning? No wonder it can be so hard to find true love. It takes up everything you are.

He tried to keep this thought from Gabriela but wasn't certain whether he succeeded.

Thorschild offered to get her some new, dry clothes, as Gabriela apologized about the loss of the jeans. She didn't seem to notice the dozens of sea creatures clicking and clamoring for her attention, as she gave him a smile, before following her hostess to the door. Still, whales, dolphins, sea turtles, and . . . *Is that a giant squid?* clustered around the side of the island.

He didn't blame them for wanting more of her.

She had nearly disappeared with Thorschild when she turned back, still laughing, and came to him.

For a moment, he wasn't certain what she wanted or was thinking, but her gaze stroked tenderly over his face. Then, she leaned in and pressed a soft, brief kiss to his lips. Almost before he could respond, she pulled back, smiled at him, and was gone.

The other women followed her in, Cain giving him a smile of sympathy before following.

To his surprise, it was Billy who came over and put his large hand on Michael's shoulder. The body Michael had now was tall, but Billy towered over him.

"It's difficult, isn't it?"

Michael assumed his look answered for him, as Billy went on.

"Loving someone so young. When I first met Tatiana, she had just crossed over after being attacked out of nowhere by a vampire. She was only 17, frightened, and entirely overwhelmed. The second I saw her I knew I wanted to protect and love her and never let her go." He smiled. "It took a year before I finally believed she wanted me."

Michael sighed at the fatherly confession from a pirate vampire but saw no reason to be rude. "How many centuries have you been together?"

Billy laughed. "Centuries? No."

He clapped Michael on the shoulder again, and the angel had to try to keep his knees from buckling. The combination of Billy's bulk and vampiric strength was even impressive to him.

"I've known her for three years now."

Michael just stared, wondering if one of Cain's powers was some sort of time travel ability.

"The outfit?" Billy wondered, looking down. "I and my family run a pirate cruise adventure. An hour or two every night sailing around a small harbor screaming things like, 'Aye, laddie! There be the wenches!'

some cheap beer in wooden mugs, and a passable roast beef dinner, and everyone goes home happy."

Michael had *no* idea what to say to this, except to marvel at The Lady's ingenuity in the sheer variety of humans she created.

"Give her time is what I'm saying."

Billy clapped his shoulder once more before leading him back to the house. The click of dolphins behind them sounded mournful at the loss of their playmate.

"No woman can be happy with a man till she finds her own place and knows herself first."

Michael knew quite well that he was right. He also knew that he was really going to have to work on hiding his emotions a bit better or risk more pep talks from helpful vampires.

Chapter 20
Gabriela

As she changed in what she guessed was Thorschild and Cain's bedroom, Gabriela was still riding high on the memory of impromptu dolphin rides. The waterfall to nowhere roared just outside their window. It was incredibly peaceful, if utterly inexplicable, and part of her just wanted to sit in the bay window which overlooked it and watch it all day.

"More magic?" she guessed, putting on a loose white t-shirt with a Mexican sugar skull design and long cranberry-colored sleeves over the new jeans she'd borrowed. She was going to need to be more careful, or she'd end up going through Thorschild's whole wardrobe.

"Mm?" Thorschild murmured, seeming to be off in her own little world. "Oh, yes." She smiled. "Cain created that as a present for me."

Gabriela hadn't known that being a demon's child could make a person adept at bespelling nature, but she supposed there was a lot she still didn't understand.

"Thank you for the clothes." She turned back to Thorschild. "I'll try to be more careful with these."

She had to say it twice before the woman actually seemed to hear her. Once she did, she smiled.

"Sorry. Was just thinking about how I need to brush up on my Greek mythology. The clothes are nothing." She waved a hand at her. "Don't worry about them."

That seemed to bring that conversation to an end, especially since Thorschild went back to her distraction. Gabriela turned to the two female vampires near her a little desperately but said nothing.

Tatiana grinned, which was a little disturbing, with a vampire.

"Don't worry about her. She gets that way when she's planning research."

Gabriela took their word for it. She'd never even been to a real school, just—what she was now seeing to be—the truly weird version the compound had dished out. It had left her with quite encyclopedic—if very one-sided—knowledge of some issues and a complete desert of information on others. She decided to see whether she couldn't learn a little more.

"Tell me."

She sat down on the bed, looking to the two vampires. Seraphina was now knitting an extremely complicated-looking onesie with room for four legs and two wings. Gabriela had to shake her head a little to get back on track.

"What do you know about angels?"

It was too embarrassing to ask Michael, and it was clear that she'd learned more the legend than the reality back at the compound.

"Not a huge amount," Tatiana admitted. "I mean, I had one present the options to me before I crossed over, but I can't say I've met any others before Michael that I know of."

She was still dressed like a pirate—why, Gabriela had no idea—and it made the moment even more surreal.

"Um . . ."

Gabriela hated to admit it, especially given some of her previous, fatal actions, but . . .

"I don't really know much about crossing over. Did you choose to become a vampire?"

Tatiana winced a bit.

"Not at the beginning. There was this out-of-control, or rather hypnotized, vampire and . . ."

She waved her hand.

"Long story. Anyway, I got bitten and drained without any real input. The part I got to choose was whether I crossed over to become a vampire or just died. That's where the angel came in."

Gabriela was glad she was sitting, or her confusion might have landed her on her butt anyway.

"Um, sorry, what?"

The vampire laughed. "Haven't taken Vampire 101? Here're the basics. Someone becomes a vampire when: One. They're bitten and drained or nearly drained. Just a casual bite or two between friends or lovers won't do it. The vampire has to be intending to kill and get pretty far along in trying. Vampires who aren't threat-level absolutely will not do it, unless the person is going to die anyway."

Gabriela blinked, as Tatiana barely stopped for breath—which made sense.

"That's because: Two. The person who's dying is presented by an angel with the option to either die and pass on or change into a vampire themselves. Either way, they'll lose their family, friends, and former life, so it's a choice of how to start over, as spirit or flesh. There's no such thing as someone being made into a vampire wholly against their will, since they can choose to die, instead. From what I've heard from a lot of my friends, the angel often tries to present dying as a better option, but I guess when you already live in the afterlife, it seems pretty normal to you."

Gabriela just stared for a moment or two. If this was Vampire 101, she was *not* ready for advanced lessons.

Still, she asked, although she was no longer certain it wasn't just from morbid curiosity. "So is there a hierarchy you become part of?"

"You mean some sort of, 'All hail the Vampire Queen!' situation?"

Although that wasn't quite how she'd have put it, Gabriela nodded.

"Well, yes and no. There are some vampire queens, and even some kings. Depending on where you live, as well, there may be families—groups where vampires live under a leader who protects, teaches, and occasionally controls them—or there may be more of an 'I rule this neighborhood or castle all alone!' situation. I've heard that's more common in Europe . . ."

Gabriela started to feel like she might fall off her perch. Maybe fortunately, she heard Michael in her thoughts.

Are you well? You haven't come back.

I'm fine, just . . .

How did she explain this?

I asked Tatiana a question about vampires, and I'm now caught in a Vampires for Dummies course. Thorschild is just staring off into space, apparently thinking about research, and Seraphina is knitting a onesie for a gryphon-to-be. I'm a little afraid I might be losing my mind again. You?

I'm being given romantic advice by the undead and the child of a demon.

There was a pause.

Although it's actually been more sensible than that makes it sound.

Um, glad to hear it? How do we get out of here? Or do you think they'll tell us something we need to know if we stick around?

She heard Michael's sigh in her head.

I have no idea. This day has been beyond confounding.

Gabriela had to agree, especially as she came back to the moment enough to hear Tatiana say, "And that's how I got a unicorn to agree to come to my wedding."

Uh-oh, she told Michael. *I missed something. Let me go.*

She tried to smile but had no idea what to say to the woman.

Tatiana seemed to understand. "I've been rambling, haven't I? I have that tendency. Billy loves it for some reason, but I have other friends who tell me they love me but that I occasionally make them want to have their ears removed."

Fortunately, Thorschild seemed to come back to herself and led them back downstairs again.

Gabriela was weirdly relieved to see that Michael looked every bit as frazzled as she felt. She sat beside him, taking his hand.

While he looked surprised, he was clearly pleased. She didn't explain.

Still, there was some sort of inner peace born out of her earlier swim. From the moment she had hit the water, it had felt as though she were diving into herself. While she had known that Michael was out there somewhere, he hadn't been her focus, although she had also recognized him as an essential part of herself. Now, after the awakening of that side of herself she had never known before, she didn't feel quite so much like either some freak or unwanted child Michael was taking pity on. She was something on her own. It might take her a while to figure out what, but she was determined to get there.

Thorschild was explaining some Greek legends she was going to research while Cain smiled at her adoringly, but Gabriela didn't follow very well. Michael's eyes were on her—loving, assessing.

Are you feeling better now? You seemed to enjoy your swim.

That's a bit of an understatement, and you know it.

Having him in her head was both comforting and disconcerting. While it told her the absolute truth of everything he felt—leaving her no room for doubts or fears—it was a little odd being on such display to him. Although, being an angel, he could probably have figured it all out anyway.

He was clearly about to say more, but there was a sudden, loud hissing sound echoing through the room.

"Crap," Thorschild muttered. "That's Pie. Ares wants us back. If we don't go, he might notice we're not where we should be."

They went, Gabriela and Michael saying a confused goodbye to the vampires and Gabriela giving a rather tortured farewell to her many new ocean friends as she passed them on their way back to the portal.

Then, they returned to find out what their kidnapper wanted of them now.

Chapter 21
Michael

Even as they returned to Ares' domain, Michael was rather amazed to find that Gabriela was still holding his hand. Part of him wanted to ask her about it—and the kiss whose ghost tingled along his lips—but he was afraid that bringing them to her attention might also bring them to an end. It was possible that she had just felt out of place in Cain's world and had wanted the comfort.

This didn't seem a likely theory, but he had decided to just enjoy the sensation while it lasted. When she wanted to end it, it would.

They arrived back in the theater just a bit before Thorschild and Cain, Pie—his eyes now normal again—riding on Cain's shoulder. Taking seats in different sections to try to avoid any appearance of collusion, Michael tried not to smile as Gabriela still held his hand.

They sat beside Isis who noticed and smiled at him, making it clear how casual their relationship had been. However, that thought didn't make him very comfortable. Angels and quick flings did not go together in his mind—which made him all the more disconcerted by his own actions.

Gabriela didn't seem as thrown, and clearly knew his thoughts.

Which part of "confused, sad, and lonely" are you failing to understand about yourself?

Ares strode down the aisle, followed by Uriel.

You aren't angry? True, they had never had bodies to be faithful to before, but he felt he'd broken that anyway.

I understand the need for comfort. If there had been anyone at the compound who hadn't made my flesh crawl, I might well have done the same thing.

Michael didn't know what to say to this. It made the new body part of him insane and the spirit part of him sad and all of him confused. Besides, Ares—now dressed entirely in black leather, as was Uriel—took a leap from the aisle up to the stage, which scattered several ghosts and made it clear that he wasn't truly human.

"I have a new task," he grinned, pointing at Michael and Gabriela.

Is it my imagination, or is he reverting to type? Gabriela asked him.

It's not your imagination.

Although whatever Uriel was turning into in a black leather outfit with several strategic sections left empty to reveal her skin, he had no idea. She had also cut her hair and dyed it bright silver—or possibly just reimagined it that way, incarnate angels being what they were.

Barely taking in Ares' words, he marveled. *What in The Lady's name is she up to?*

Gabriela clearly heard this, but mentally nudged him back to refocusing on their captor.

"Gabriela, Michael, and Loviatar will go to the British Museum."

Didn't you tell me you'd been there before? Gabriela wondered.

We all have, he agreed. *It contains sacred, profane, and mundane treasures looted from every part of the world, half of them in boxes in the basement. If you're looking to steal something precious, it's a good destination.*

Ares' orders went on. "You are after this gold ankh." He held up a picture on a tablet.

Somehow, Michael objected to Ares' adoption of modern human inventions. In his mind, if one were an ancient Greek god, he shouldn't be on Instagram.

"It used to be in one of my temples," Isis murmured, while supposedly covering her mouth to yawn.

Ares looked to both Gabriela and Michael then briefly to Loviatar and back. "Have fun, kids."

So we have to break into the British Museum, which I'm guessing might just have a guard or two, steal something made out of pure gold, and get back here, all while trying to keep Loviatar from murdering everyone in sight? Gabriela wondered.

That about covers it, yes, although the theft isn't really that hard when you're not fully mortal.

News flash! I'm fully mortal!

And an incarnate angel and daughter of a god. You've got a little more going for you than the average girl on the street.

He felt her grudging admission of this, as they stood. Still, she asked. *What time is it in London? Are we going to be dealing with guests as well as guards?*

He wasn't entirely certain what time it was now. It was a very human concept. Still . . .

Maybe around two or three a.m.? They'll be closed.

But he could tell, probably understandably, that this didn't entirely settle her.

Isis stopped them before they could leave. Loviatar—high heels, black leather bootie shorts, and all—tapped her foot and looked as though she should be carrying a very large axe.

"Take this." Isis slipped the same ankh she'd put on Gabriela earlier into her hands. "Being mortal makes things more difficult, and this will calm down some of the more irate objects you might meet."

The objects themselves are going to attack us?

Ever heard of the curse of the mummy's tomb?

He felt her blank confusion.

Sorry. Forgot about the "raised in a cult" thing.

Gabriela accepted the ankh willingly this time, holding up her wrist to allow Isis to attach it to her like a bracelet.

"Thank you," she smiled.

Although I'm still not happy about this "we're going to get attacked by objects" thing.

Not knowing what to say to this, Michael nodded his thanks to Isis, walked with Gabriela to Loviatar, and went with them toward the portal.

To his surprise, Gabriela stopped the formidable Finnish goddess as they neared it, although her obvious trepidation made sense.

"Loviatar, a moment, please."

Loviatar looked as though she should be fingering the edge of a blade, but she waited.

"Can we agree not to disembowel or eviscerate or . . ."

I'm going to have to name every possible way to kill someone if I go on like this, aren't I? she asked him silently.

No. Even if you did, she'd just come up with several more.

He watched Gabriela take a small breath, clearly deciding not to smile but to look pleasant as she went on.

"Can we just agree not to kill, maim, or otherwise wound anyone or anything mortal while we're there?"

Loviatar gazed at her all over, dismissively.

"You call yourself a woman with such attitudes?"

Gabriela gave her a small smile.

"Fine. I will satisfy myself with dreaming of ways to draw and quarter Ares. But you'll need to keep the mortals from attacking me."

Her eyes were nearly flames.

"I will not allow myself to be insulted by their touch."

Michael was impressed by Gabriela's consoling smile, although he also saw how wary it was. He doubted that she'd received many lessons in smiles at the compound.

"Of course," Gabriela assured her.

Know of any ways to keep us under the radar, so Loviatar doesn't murder anyone, big boy?

Her teasing made him want to kiss her, her growing comfort with him nearly too much for this body to bear. Taking a deep breath, he tried to focus on the mission.

Basic invisibility to mortals is probably the safest way.

It took some convincing, and enduring a few mild threats of disembowelment, but Michael managed to convince Loviatar to let him put a blessing over all of them which would make anyone mundane simply not see them. Then, he held Gabriela's hand as they and a murderous Finnish goddess stepped out to start their mission.

Chapter 22
Gabriela

Gabriela wasn't certain what to expect as they wandered through the portal, but miles of dark dust wasn't really it.

I take it we're in the storage area? she wondered.

One of the hundreds of them, yes, he agreed. *Did you think this was the way they displayed things?*

I'm mortal, remember? Gabriela sighed.

He still wasn't getting it.

I wasn't made to see in the dark.

Oh. Right.

He touched her forehead, and she saw a small shower of sparkles before the room came into focus.

Somehow, it wasn't what she had expected. Instead of an impressive treasure storehouse, there were just thousands of numbered boxes and dust.

"How do we find the ankh among all these?" she whispered, in case Loviatar had any ideas which didn't involve inflicting havoc.

Loviatar held up a well-manicured hand. Apparently, axe-wielding didn't mean she had to get grubby. "We wait and ask."

This was a worrying idea, considering what the goddess would probably do later with those she got the answers from.

Michael's voice in her mind refocused her, though. *Listen.*

She did, and suddenly she realized she was hearing odd, breathy whispers in the dark.

Creepy.

Still, she'd been hanging out on an island made by the son of a demon today, so she decided she better get used to it.

Attempting to figure out what the voices were saying, she realized the words weren't in English.

Any idea what they're speaking?

Ancient Egyptian, mostly, with a bit of Latin thrown in.

Clearly, he sensed her confusion.

Right. Raised in a cult. England wasn't the first country to try to colonize the world.

He touched her temple, and the voices came into focus, but that only made it stranger.

"Is she here?" "Is that her?" and some random giggling came from the direction of what she now realized were cases holding mummies.

Um, the mummies are talking? Is it okay to run? True, she'd been taught to kill all manner of the undead, but mummies hadn't been part of the lessons.

Hang on. I think they're counting down to something, Michael noted.

Sure enough, she heard whispers of "Three. Two. One." Then, with a group scream of "Surprise! Happy Birthday!" what had to be a thousand or so mummies rose from their boxes, spreading confetti.

Gabriela debated fainting for half a second but decided that, if she did, Loviatar might eviscerate her for failing on the part of womankind.

The mummies were holding a big banner and a huge cake with a mummy in a sarcophogus on it. Both read, "All hail, Nell! Great champion of the kingdom of the night!" Gabriela decided that the cake had to be that large just to fit it all on.

Any idea what's going on?

Michael shook his head.

At their visitors' blank gazes, all the mummies looked disappointed and started talking amongst themselves, but one in particular stepped out of his box. After setting the cake very carefully back inside with the help of one of his comrades, he came up to them.

"You are not our Champion. You are not guards, and you do not work for the museum."

He looked them over.

"You are also mostly not mundane. Who are you?"

Michael held Gabriela's hand warmly, and she appreciated the silent comfort. Instead of bandages, the mummy who addressed them was wearing some tan pants and a t-shirt which read, "Dead and Loving It, Baby!" Still, he was clearly a mummy and clearly undead.

Gabriela had no idea what to say, to any of it, even though the mummy was addressing and watching her. Meanwhile, Loviatar had wandered over to chat with a mummy in a corner box by herself who gave off an air of royalty. The mummy made it seem like a concession which she should be thanked for that she took out her earbuds. Gabriela thought she could hear old school rap.

This is another of those, "I think I've just gone insane" moments. Soooo . . .?

No, not yet, Michael assured her. *Although I agree this is surreal.*

He answered the mummy. "I am the archangel Michael. This is the archangel Gabriel."

She noticed that he almost stumbled over the name, having reacclimated himself to "Gabriela" in only about two days. She smiled.

It seems best to be formal, Michael answered before she could ask. *If I just say we're grave robbers . . .*

It will be "army of the undead" time. I agree.

Their mummy inquisitor looked at Gabriela curiously. "But you are not simply an archangel. There is something of the Roman gods about you."

"I'm the daughter of Posei—. . ."

Neptune, Michael corrected.

What?

Same god, different alias. Trust me.

"...Neptune," she finished.

The mummy looked her over. "A fascinating god. I congratulate you."

Gabriela wasn't so certain but kept her objections to the man to herself. "We've come on behalf of..."

Don't say Ares. Or Mars. Gods of war don't go over well with the countries they conquer.

Fair point, she agreed.

She didn't get to go any further, though, as the little man spotted the bracelet.

"You come on behalf of Isis?" he cried excitedly.

Gabriela and Michael nodded, because, really, what else was there to do? Loviatar wasn't helping much, except by being deeply involved in some discussion with a mummy who was probably a queen about the joys of power.

"I am Callahan," the mummy bowed.

Callahan? Gabriela wondered.

Okay, so she'd been raised in a compound. She still didn't think the Irish had taken over ancient Egypt.

"It is a name presented to me by my best frenemy."

Gabriela blinked but decided not to pursue it. Her life was weird enough as it was.

"What is it the goddess seeks from us?"

Feeling rather tired by the continuing oddness of her life, she left Michael to explain. Around her, mummies chatted, lounged, or occasionally cleaned up confetti to have it ready if their "Champion" ever came back.

She had vowed not to ask.

In standing over by the wall, though, she found herself near a very small mummy—*a child, maybe? A little girl?*—who was sitting on the edge of her box, swinging her feet.

"Who are you?" the child wondered.

"I've been asking myself that a lot lately," she muttered, before smiling at . . . well, maybe a girl. Hard to tell with a mummy, sometimes. "I'm Gabriela."

"You are divine and demi-divine," the girl noted with confidence.

"So I've been told," Gabriela sighed, looking back to her. The whole death/mummy thing was pretty creepy, but the girl had both an innocent and knowing air. "Who are you?"

"I am a child servant of Isis. I died before I could become a full priestess."

Looking a little sad for a moment, she then shook it away.

"You have met my goddess?"

"Yes," Gabriela smiled. "She's a beautiful and exceptional . . ."

She stopped, because "woman" seemed a bit sacrilegious to say to one of her followers.

". . . goddess."

"You wear her ankh. That means you carry her protection. She will not see you harmed."

Not knowing what to say to this, Gabriela just blinked. She'd barely met Isis, so this didn't seem likely, although possibly the goddess was looking after her as a favor to Michael, whom she seemed fond of after their affair. Of course, the protection could just be while they were on this mission. But something about the girl's words . . .

Shaking her head, she smiled. "I appreciate the insight."

Because what the heck else am I supposed to say to that?

To what? Michael asked, as he received the golden ankh from Callahan.

She also picked up on the mummy's words to him. "I wish you well in your efforts."

She didn't know what to say to that, either.

Loviatar distracted her from all of this, pulling herself away from her discussion with the mummy, who apparently went back to listening to her old-school rap.

"We cannot go yet. There are companions I've always wanted to bring back with me."

Gabriela had a vision of Loviatar dragging back a 20-foot tall statue which was prominently displayed, making such a fuss that they'd never get out without serious damage.

Um, there aren't any dangerous weapons in here, are there? she wondered to Michael.

If it could be looted from one of the corners of the world, it's in here, he assured her. *But I don't think Finland was one of their major spots for "acquisitions."*

They watched worriedly, as Loviatar put her fingers in her mouth and let out a whistle piercing enough to make certain that guards would come running. The series of loud crashes didn't make it any less likely that they would be found.

What came to her, though, wasn't guards. It was a hundred or so broken, marble lion statues.

Pulling themselves sometimes painfully toward her, they limped or rolled their way into the room. As they got to her, she petted each one lovingly. At her touch, the missing limbs regrew, until she had an army of marble lions growling and roaring and licking at her playfully.

"Yes, yes," she crooned. "I'll get each of you a golden collar and leash, my loves."

They rubbed themselves adoringly against her in response.

Gabriela had returned to Michael, if only to put her feet out of the way of a half ton of marble crashing down on it. The lions were each at least five feet long.

"Um, yeah," Callahan watched. "I think those guys are from a cemetery in Greece? Turkey? Anyway, they've mostly been shut up in boxes for a couple of hundred years. They seem happy to be found again."

The mummy queen—or whatever she was—closed her box's lid, possibly to get away from the commotion.

Even if it is by the Finnish goddess who birthed every disease in the world, Michael finished for Gabriela alone.

Um, she did what?

I told you. He smiled at her. *You DON'T mess with Loviatar.*

He looked back to the odd scene.

Although how she and some ancient cemetery statues from another part of Europe bonded, I have no idea.

There were some noises in a far room.

"It might be better if you go now." Callahan shooed them toward the portal. "We can handle the guards, but you three would be a bit much."

With some trouble, they got Loviatar's attention and the three of them, plus her new army of marble lion friends, went back through the portal.

Chapter 23
Michael

When they got back, Loviatar and her new marble minions were nowhere to be seen. Michael thought that was probably for the best and decided to give Ares his ankh and hope he forgot about her. If Loviatar was planning to put her new army to work, maybe she would only direct them at their captor.

He hoped.

One look told him Gabriela was thinking the same thing. There wasn't any reason to even discuss it mentally.

She did ask him something else, though.

How long do you think Isis has known Ares?

He just stared at her, as they walked back to the god. *Do you think she's been compromised by him?*

Given that she'd been a good friend, he really hoped that wasn't true. Still, Uriel now seemed to have taken on the mantle of Ares' best friend, and he'd never seen the angel do anything but serve The Lady before this, so maybe there was only so much he really understood.

Not really. But the museum got me thinking. If the Romans conquered Egypt, what happened to both countries' gods? Did the Egyptian ones become servants, too? Did they go away? Or did they and the Roman gods start to mingle?

Michael felt a cold chill up his spine and marveled for a moment at the in-built alarm systems The Lady had put into her creations.

Still, he tried to focus on the rather disturbing idea. While he absolutely didn't want to think anything bad of Isis, she had offered herself rather quickly to be his lover, which meant that he had also trusted her with his thoughts. If this had been a calculated move, it would both have worked to subvert any energies he might otherwise have expended on plotting revolution and given her an insight into any plans he might have the time to come up with.

Oh, dear Lady.

He absolutely *didn't* want it to be the truth.

Did anyone ever tell you that your thoughts become even more formal when you're angry? Gabriela noted. Still, the smile she gave him was tender.

He appreciated it but couldn't answer, as they were nearly to Ares again. The small god was still laughing it up with the now-silver-and-blue-haired Uriel, as well as Isis. It was going to take all his concentration not to get into a fistfight with the god of war. Well, or smite him. Smiting would be good.

He was somewhat aware that he was holding out the ankh as though he were a non-native New Yorker holding his first dead rat but didn't much care. Even as Isis raised an eyebrow at him, he held the object out silently to their captor.

"Ah, efficient as always, I see, Michael." Ares took it from him, grinning. "I have to say, of all the acquisition specialists I've recruited, you've definitely been the most satisfactory."

Michael's fist was clenched, and he was trying to keep calm. It wasn't working, especially as Ares tilted sideways to stare around him at Gabriela, whom he only realized now he was blocking from the god protectively.

"Your partner, though . . ."

Ares stared at her for a moment before a terrible sort of grin broke out on his face. Michael shifted further to try to block her from him, as Ares went on.

"Tell you what. There are a few other people I'd like to know more about. How about if your partner there makes use of that body she's been given and seduces a few?"

Ares looked back at Michael, still grinning.

"She really hasn't been earning her keep much, otherwise."

Considering that Michael was the only one to think of actually feeding her or allowing her time to sleep—which, admittedly, did make just a little sense since most of the beings here needed neither of these things—there wasn't much keep to earn, besides sitting around a theater Ares had already acquired.

Still, this wasn't the greatest part of Michael's rage. He couldn't help glaring over to Isis.

"She won't be your whore, Ares."

Michael . . . Gabriela warned in his mind, her touch soft on his back, and he knew she was right. He was furious, and that wasn't safe. But it didn't really matter, the thought of anyone harming Gabriela blinding him.

Somehow, Isis managed to look both sympathetic and sadly martyred at the same time, and he wasn't certain whether to apologize or yell at her. Instead, he refocused on the god of war.

"I'd destroy everyone here before I let her be touched."

In response, Ares presented him with a sarcastic slow clap which made Michael want to punch him even more. He noticed now that the god's beard was back and meticulously groomed.

He truly IS reverting to type.

The thought wasn't for Gabriela, although he was aware she'd know it, nonetheless. He couldn't focus on that through the rage, especially as Ares spoke in his usual mocking tone.

"Oh, bravo, Michael. Yes, you're the noble warrior. We're all *so* impressed."

He finally stopped the slow clap.

"Now tell me, angel, is your 'protection' of her real, or do you just want to keep your plaything for yourself?"

Michael felt Gabriela's fingers digging into his bicep even through his clothes, warning him to keep control—which was the *only* reason why he hadn't punched Ares' jaw loose, especially as he wouldn't stop yammering.

"Because we all notice the two of you sneaking off for a nooner every chance you get."

He peered around Michael again.

"Not that I blame you."

Grinning back in the angel's eyes, Ares' look said that he knew how well-placed his attacks were.

"I've always been a fan of the sturdy ones myself."

Michael, stop it! he heard Gabriela yell at him mentally, her fingers tight on his arm. *He's just needling you. I won't whore myself for him, which he probably knows. He's only testing how far you'll go and which buttons he needs to push. Don't give him any more power over you than he already has!*

In many ways, Michael knew all of this was true. Still, Ares' grin didn't help matters.

"Smoking, Michael, really?"

A second later, he realized the god was right. There was a light searing of flame outlining him. It occurred to him suddenly that every single entity in the theater—god, mortal, and spirit alike—were staring at him worriedly.

Through it all, Gabriela's hand held onto his arm, thankfully unharmed by the flame. Even if he hadn't known her on sight, that alone would have told him who she was.

"What's next, a lightning bolt or two?"

Admittedly, Michael could feel the smiting in the palm of his hand, really wished he could use it to reduce this god to a jelly.

He took a very deep breath.

But no.

This was bigger than just getting revenge on Ares for being a jerk. There was the entirety of the compound Gabriela had been raised in to think of, might well be other players in this little bet, too. Even if he could kill Ares—and it would just be blatantly ironic to try to kill a god of war with violence—that wouldn't actually end this.

"Is there anything else you'd care for me to loot at the moment?" he asked, somewhat calmly. At least the steaming had diminished a bit.

Ares laughed. "You can't steal what's already stolen, Michael. After a certain point, it's just a matter of which thief possesses it."

He gave a knowing wink and a leer to Gabriela, and Michael had to try very hard not to punch him.

"It's kind of the same thing with women and sex, too."

Michael said nothing, as he had no idea where to begin.

"What's the matter, archangel? Cat got your tongue?"

Michael sighed.

"I was just wondering whether that were the least intelligent thing I've heard you say, but, on reflection, I don't think it is."

For a moment, he thought about it.

"It's exceedingly close, however."

He heard an internal laugh from Gabriela and knew she was amused by his formality again. So long as it made her love him, he didn't much care.

For once, Ares looked a little irritated at losing the upper hand. Michael moved on the small, if pointless, victory.

"Now, until you require us again, our time is our own."

Stepping back, he put an arm around Gabriela, which she allowed without visible protest, even if her words made her feelings clear.

Careful there, big boy. Treat me like the bone some dogs are fighting over, and I'll punch you in the stomach.

Good. I'm fine with you keeping me in line, but I'm also going to make damned sure Ares stays away from you, and the only way toward that with men like him is to make a prior claim.

He felt her grudging agreement, as he led her down the aisle, well away from Ares. The small god was staring a bit too interestedly at her posterior, and he had a reputation as an "ass slapper." Michael shuddered. If the god had tried it, Michael really would have cut off his hand.

Thankfully, they made it down the theater aisle without further incident. When they took seats in the front row near Cain and Thorschild, Gabriela noted, *I'd say that was a very clever way of deflecting attention from the missing Loviatar and her new marble army, but I don't think you planned it.*

Sighing, Michael took her hand, looking her in the eye.

I'm sorry. Partly, I don't want Ares to harm you. Admittedly, the other part is that this body is sort of clamoring for you, and it makes it difficult to think.

To his surprise, she grinned at him.

Lets you know where the word "testy" comes from, huh?

Sighing, he stared at the stage, where the ghosts started rehearsing a Harold Pinter play, which meant there were a series of significant pauses.

I sympathize more and more with The Lady's creations by the day. Bodies are a nuisance.

Rubbing her thumb over his hand, she smiled. *But they have their advantages, too.*

Just the feeling of her fingers twined through his made him feel almost too much. He tried very hard to hide the thought from her: *Tell that to the dangly bits.*

Still, a moment later, he smiled at her. After all, his dangly bits weren't her problem. And if they made her stop holding his hand, he would never forgive them.

Chapter 24
Gabriela

Gabriela actually rather enjoyed herself for the next hour or two, sitting there watching the ghost actors perform—and occasionally, even she could tell, mangle—some rather long play which seemed to say all the right things but was also dreadfully depressing. Mostly, though, she just enjoyed holding Michael's hand.

She was aware that his body was "making demands" of him again, which he manfully ignored. Appreciating all this, she thought back to the compound. There, she had never known a man to ignore any demand his body made. The only reason she was a virgin was because she'd gotten good with a knife early on and they'd believed her when she'd threatened to geld them.

This said nothing of her enforced husband, but she was happier not thinking about Edgar.

Instead, she was amazed at the way her body reacted to the softest touch of Michael's hand. For a while, their fingers were entwined—and that was nice enough—but then he'd let go and started tenderly exploring first up her index finger then down into the dip between, until she noticed her breath catch.

That one had gotten Thorschild's attention, but she just smiled at her. Pie was sitting on her lap, staring at Gabriela and Michael as though they were a fascinating play themselves.

The soft explorations had gone on until she'd really wanted to take Michael's hand, lead him back to his room and ask him to explore many other parts of her with the same meticulous tenderness. It made it very difficult to concentrate on social satire.

There was really only one reason she didn't take this opportunity, and it wasn't the virgin thing. The more she was beside Michael, the more she realized she wanted to continue to be, for as long as this body lasted and then into the spirit—or angelic—centuries beyond. And she didn't really want all of them to just be about sitting beside him.

Weirdly, it had been her voyage into Cain's world which had made up her mind about this, in a few different ways. One of them had certainly been her swim with the dolphins.

She hadn't told Michael about this yet, not only because there hadn't been much time, but both because it was still too new and she wasn't certain she could come up with words for an experience that profound. From the moment she'd sunk beneath the waves, she'd felt at home, felt like herself—for the first time, really. Everything she'd done for the compound, everything she'd been forced through meant nothing. She was free and in her element. When the dolphin had swum up and she'd understood the sounds it made to her, she wasn't even surprised. She'd just known that everything would be okay.

She couldn't even clearly remember every detail of her swim, all of it a bit of a dream. Still, she did recall the dolphins holding her up together in what they referred to as a "Neptune's fountain moment."

She'd both wanted to stay there forever and to swim back and pledge her devotion to Michael for good.

This was another odd part of the experience. For the first time, she had truly known herself—and what she had found at her center had been Michael. And she had known absolutely that she was what lay at the center of him, as well.

From that moment, she hadn't even questioned that they would be together. He needed that as much as she did, so there was nothing anyone could do which would convince her otherwise—and no amount of pressure which would make her agree to let him go.

But this still hadn't been all. There had been something in those moments in Thorschild and Cain's room, in every aspect of that world of Cain's that Thorschild belonged in absolutely. His devotion to and love for her was in every corner, the mysterious waterfall only its most showy aspect. Even the vampires who had taken over his home were there because Thorschild loved their company. If what she had needed were an island of giant pink pachyderms, there would have been a rose-colored elephant parade a moment later—and her love and support of him was every bit as devoted. The things they were hiding from Michael and herself might be many, but there was no act they were putting on, instead. They belonged as one—and neither would allow anything to come between them.

While this was a lovely and inspiring romance, though, it hadn't been that alone which had convinced her. It was the fact that Michael had recognized Thorschild as one of their heavenly kin, as he had told her once she'd finally emerged from her dolphin swim. The woman was here to be with Cain because he needed her. Somehow, Gabriela was certain, Michael and she were both here for the very same reason with each other.

When the play ended, they all clapped politely, but she heard Michael in her head. *You want to talk?*

She just nodded to him once, and a moment later—since Ares was still yukking it up in the back with Uriel and Isis—they said goodnight to Thorschild, Cain, and their staring cat and headed back to their room.

Locking the door behind them, she turned to where Michael was watching her, waiting, but took him by surprise by pretty much throwing herself into a kiss and then pushing him onto the bed.

Michael caught her, moaning, but she felt his surprise.

What's the matter, Michael? she thought at him, as she ran her hand down his side.

His moan grew louder.

Never had an angel make moves on you before?

He was groaning now.

The only angel I want that with is you, and again, we're only spirits over there.

Catching her hand and pushing her gently back from the kiss, since she was pretty much on top of him, he panted.

Oh sweet Lady. Please stop.

He looked wild and desperate and beautiful, and she really wanted to devour him.

Are you sure?

She started to lean back down, but he held her away, still panting.

Yes. Have mercy. I think The Lady put in some design flaws. I'm afraid the dangly bits might explode.

She laughed aloud at this but gave him a bit of a break, lying down beside him instead, her head on his shoulder. When she tried to run her hand over his chest, he caught it, looking at her desperately, his hazel eyes so beautiful.

I'm more than willing to . . . well, do whatever we want together, she assured him.

She gave him a look inside her mind to the array of very explicit images, and he let out a strangled noise, covering his eyes.

Mercy. For the love of The Lady. Have mercy on me, Gabriela, please.

Mostly, she gave him a break, propping her head up on his chest.

All right, cowboy. I'll try to stop thinking about riding you.

He groaned.

But want to tell me why?

It took a few more seconds to get his breathing somewhat right, and his pleading gaze was focused firmly on the ceiling, but he did finally answer. *Because there's not enough time.*

Tilting her head at him, she wondered, but he just groaned.

Ares might give us an hour or a day or even a week. I could even take us to a different dimension and give us maybe a year.

Shaking his head, he looked back to her.

But it's not going to ever be enough while we're under someone else's control—or while we still need to find a way to stop what's going on and free everyone.

Since she suspected he wasn't finished, she said nothing, and he went on.

Once we vanquish him, and we're free, then I'll find you our own private paradise where we can be together, and I'll lose myself inside you repeatedly for at least three years.

Smiling, she kissed his chin, trying to give her agreement without turning him on. Given the images in his mind, she didn't think it entirely worked.

I'm still human, remember? I'll need to eat and sleep.

Okay, five years, then. No, maybe seven. Then you can have two years to swim in your ocean, as well.

Sadly, this led her mind away from these more pleasant paths.

Are all oceans that beautiful? In the compound, we were told that the earth and the seas were full of trash.

She thought about it.

It does fit a lot of the earth I've seen, too.

Sadly, that's true.

Clearly distracted, he looked at her curiously.

They gave environmental lessons at the compound?

Well, sorta. Mostly it was "The hellish sirens dirty our oceans. They and all mer-people are a scourge upon the world."

Michael just stared at her.

That was S in my childhood alphabet primer.

I am deeply affronted on behalf of all sirens everywhere. I've never met a single one who wasn't trying to keep the seas alive.

Gabriela raised her eyebrow at him.

What, you were expecting sane pronouncements from the lunatic fringe?

Good point.

For a moment or two, they just lay there before Michael sighed, looking her over.

Do you want to be with me, Gabriela? The last thing I'd ever want to do is make you feel like you have no choice.

Her eyebrow rose higher.

Do I need to make your nether regions try to explode again?

His hand went up.

No. No, please.

Laughing, she let him see into her mind.

When I was in the water, I felt you. You were with me. You were part of me I'd never realized was there but always relied on. Once I came out of the sea, I couldn't think of any future which can make me happy if you're not with me in it.

She kissed the tip of his nose, and he smiled.

But if you insist on taking your time with me, I'll wait. Just so long as you don't let me go.

Pulling her to him, he gave her a slow kiss of promise—and, even if it ended much too soon, as she lay down to nap upon him, she knew without doubt that they were both each other's alone.

Chapter 25
Michael

For one of the few times in an eternity, Michael slept. It was both peaceful and odd, full of strange dreams which ranged from terrors over losing Gabriela, to a glorious lifetime here on earth by her side, to some series of weird images he couldn't understand, including Gabriela riding a giraffe into an arc. Still, as he woke, he began to wonder. Even if they could end this god-plagued bet and free all the prisoners, was The Lady actually willing to let them have a lifetime together? Or were they both here merely until they could solve this puzzle, then intended to return to her side?

He had no answer to this and also wasn't certain what time it was or how long they'd been gone from the theater. All he did know was something seemed to have crawled into his mouth and died—and they'd sprinkled some sand in his eyes while they'd been at it.

He sat up to find Gabriela watching him, smiling. Apparently, *she* was now the moony teenage vampire.

Um, what? she wondered.

Seeing her totally blank incomprehension, he decided that Poseidon's tastes must not match with the god of war's.

Nothing. Ares has a thing for the Twilight movies.

She just stared.

An eternal teenage vampire who sparkles becomes obsessed with a dull girl and spends far too much time watching her sleep every night.

Yeesh. Stalker, anyone?

That's kind of what I thought.

And why sparkling? Did he roll around in glitter?

Don't ask.

Remembering, he blinked.

I thought that Loviatar was going to slit Ares' throat after 15 minutes of the first movie.

For a second, he felt her pondering asking just how many there were but then deciding to drop it, moving on.

How are you feeling? You actually slept for once.

Blinking, he pondered. *Yes. It's a very weird experience, rather comforting and exhausting all at once. Any idea how long we've been away?*

Possibly about ten hours.

His eyes widened, and she smiled at him.

I was only out for six or so of it. I haven't seen any signs that Ares wants us back. When we're not needed, he sort of forgets we exist.

That was very true. Still, Michael just lay there, propped up on his elbows, blinking. He supposed this was what humans referred to as being "groggy."

How are you doing? she wondered.

Well, my eyes seem to be full of grit. Something apparently died in my mouth, and . . .

He thought it over.

. . . is it possible I need a nap to recover from sleeping?

Welcome to humanity, kid.

Trying not to glare, he looked at her and enjoyed her happy laugh. That was a sound he could grow used to.

You'll also find that your perfect hair has been smooshed all over.

There was a part of Michael which wondered how he had let himself get in this condition. Apparently, he was allowing this body to win more and more lately. Still, while it was a little odd, these new experiences weren't entirely unpleasant—but he did continue to wonder whether The Lady was going to let them go on in these bodies after this was done.

Gabriela smiled, but he wasn't certain whether she understood, as she had no memories of The Lady. But, as there was no way to know what was intended at the moment, he focused on sorting through the various daily indignities of being human.

Some of them were more annoying than others. For one thing, he couldn't get his hair right. It either sprouted curls in just the wrong places or started some little dippity-doo thing at the back of his head. If he managed to get those in place, he'd suddenly be facing a follicle re-bellion on the other side.

Amused, Gabriela watched from the bathroom doorway.

Finally, he grew annoyed and just blessed it into place, although he still had a feeling that it was up to something when he wasn't looking.

He was entirely uncertain why his body seemed to be asserting it-self more today. His blessings still worked, and he didn't feel any less like an angel. When he heard his stomach rumbling, he was annoyed. He'd had perfect control of this physical casing for his soul for years now. Why on earth was it fighting him today?

As an angel, he wasn't used to facing many questions he couldn't easily answer. Since he'd been brought into incarnation by Ares, he'd had too many.

He didn't like it.

Gabriela shrugged away the issue. *If Ares doesn't need us, we could probably go find some food somewhere. Well, if you can bless us up some money.*

Michael wasn't entirely happy with the idea but gave in. While he had blessed up a meal or two to keep Gabriela going, it had never oc-curred to him to try one himself.

They went back into the theater, meeting Thorschild and Cain and their cat on the way. Pie sat on Cain's shoulder like some pirate's parrot, his head tilted as he stared at them. After a brief conversation, the four of them decided to go look for lunch. Well, five, if you included Pie.

Making a stop by the theater to see if they had missed anything Ares wanted, Michael was relieved to see that nothing had changed. Loviatar was back from wherever she had been and, to their surprise, demanded to come with them. Isis waved a goodbye to a shrugging Ares—who seemed to know they'd return when called—and a chattering Uriel. The angel was now literally half male and half female, some sort of invisible dividing line running down her—or his or their—center. Ares barely seemed to notice, although it was possible he liked it.

Michael left them to it, as he was no more likely to decipher Uriel's motives if he stayed behind.

While he'd assumed that they'd just go out into D.C. to find some food, Isis assured him that everything in the neighborhood was "fusion," which she defined as "a purposeful assault on the cuisine and traditions of two or three cultures at the same time."

Not exactly being a food expert, Michael took her word for it.

There was some vague arguing by the portal over where they were going, everyone except Michael and Gabriela weighing in on some favorite place. Finally, though, Loviatar spoke up, pointing.

"We consume Philly cheesesteak, or we consume nothing."

Then, since she was already through the portal and they'd lose her otherwise, everyone else followed.

Michael soon found himself in what he was fairly certain was Philadelphia, on a street with cheesesteak stands on either side. Loviatar marched confidently up to one, and Michael created a small blessing to convince those waiting to let them go first. He was worried that Loviatar might infect them with one of the diseases she'd released or start eviscerating to get what she wanted otherwise.

The blessing had the effect of making everyone cheerful. Still, this being Philadelphia, feeling cheerful just irritated everyone. They did start chatting with their neighbors about how annoyed they were, though.

They watched Loviatar remind the slightly greasy server that "if you do not give me the amount of cheez whiz I require, I will eviscerate you."

As there wasn't too much talk of "eviscerating" these days, the server seemed to think that this was some sort of sexual overture. Still, Loviatar got her cheez whiz and chucked the server lovingly under the chin for being a good boy. The server seemed to be in heaven.

As Thorschild and Cain made their order, with a third, very plain one that Michael assumed was for their cat, he heard Gabriela's voice again.

Do you eat meat?

Understanding her concerns, he examined the menu.

Animals and vegetation are all The Lady's creations, and all can feel when alive. That she made it so that nothing much can live without consuming something else living is one of her more ineffable decisions.

The truth was that he didn't really eat much, although he had a few times in the past. Some of it had been lovely and others quite disgusting. Still, he had no knowledge to order from, so he ended up getting a version of what Thorschild and Cain had gotten for their feline friend.

After they had gotten their food, it was decided by all that they'd go elsewhere to eat. After what proved to be a rather long debate—Michael threw a surreptitious blessing over their food to ensure that it stayed fresh, as he didn't want to know what Loviatar would do otherwise—they decided on eating with a view of Niagara Falls from the Canadian side. Isis assured him the American side was a "petrochemical dump."

The Canadian side, however, appeared to be a tacky tourist playground.

As they found a clear area with a picnic table to watch the falls from—put there with a combination of their various magics—Michael wondered to Gabriela, *Why do humans always take the most beautiful of The Lady's gifts and turn them into the least natural places possible?*

No idea, she agreed, biting into her sandwich, which she was clearly enjoying. *Still, this place kinda looks like fun. I'd love to explore some of those tourist traps.*

Silently, Michael gave in, watching those around him. All of them seemed to be enjoying themselves, and the falls were calming, although they also had a strange presence to them.

Just do me a favor and don't jump in the water. Whatever's already in there would be only too happy to drown a few more.

Trust me, I noticed that too.

She was already halfway through her sandwich and didn't seem to be slowing down.

Still, no one's jumping in at the moment, so why don't you just eat and try to enjoy yourself?

Not knowing what to say to this, he gave in. In an odd way, this was the closest he'd ever been to having a day out with friends.

So, in the company of his beloved, an ex-lover he wasn't certain he could trust, an angel who was also the daughter of a Norse god and her half-demon boyfriend, as well as their cat and a murderous Finnish goddess who now proudly wore cheez whiz all over her face, he made an effort at enjoying the world The Lady had made.

Chapter 26
Gabriela

Lunch was astonishingly good. Gabriela hadn't expected Loviatar to have such excellent taste, but she was definitely planning on asking Michael to take her back for more cheesesteaks in the future.

Still, she had noticed that Michael mostly picked at his. When she'd tried to prod him mentally, he'd just said, *It's odd. And it's greasy. And I like cows.*

Apparently, she'd be trying to find some vegetarian options for him in the future.

Thankfully, the group was surprisingly convivial, even if there were only a few people in it she trusted. While she really liked Isis, there was definitely the question of how much she was in on Ares' plans, and Loviatar was, well, Loviatar.

The Finnish goddess was still in her bootie shorts, which Gabriela had to admit, she was rocking, although her hair was now in at least the third style and color she'd had since they'd met. At first, it had been a short, ice-blonde 1920s style. When they'd gone to the museum with her, it'd been long, red, and in a high ponytail—a little like Gabriela's, in fact, although she tended to wear hers in a braid. Now, luxurious waves of black hair—a little like Isis', although the Egyptian goddess's had more curls—fell down her back and followed her every command.

Thorschild and Cain were arm-in-arm near the back of the group with their cat riding on a combination of their two shoulders. Thorschild's hair, as always, was long and wild and had a will of its own and covered not only her back and her partner's—but now the cat as well. It looked as though Pie had on a long blonde wig.

It didn't make the day any less surreal, but Gabriela was enjoying it, nonetheless.

Wandering through the town, she had to repress her giggle several times at the sheer touristy oddness of the place.

It was probably good that it was summer, as she'd heard that Canada could get cold. Certainly, the compound had chosen some chilly spots to hide in before—although she wasn't quite sure, she thought she'd been born in Idaho in mid-winter—but she wasn't really a fan of freezing temperatures. Spending a few years running around in a gladiator outfit would do that to a girl.

Now, though, children ran through the streets with ice cream cones. Lovers walked arm in arm, barely noticing that others existed, and their truly odd group took in the sights as though they were on vacation with absolutely no one even noticing them.

After two museums which claimed to have the same, true balls or barrels or whatnot that some crazy people had tried to go over the falls in—although whether for fame, fortune, or to satisfy the hungry voices at the bottom, she didn't know—and a fascinating arcade of games, where Loviatar won both admirers and a very large, stuffed minotaur with her rather viciously-accurate skeeball technique—they had had a truly fascinating game of mini-golf in the dark.

The place had had everything in black light so that the displays of wizards, dragons—a whole undersea world, including Poseidon—as well as the balls and putters glowed in a weird variety of dayglow colors.

As they had agreed at the beginning not to use magic, and as no one wished to even try to compete with Loviatar—who had magicked her stuffed minotaur to ride along on her shoulders—they all played for second place. Cain won that, to his own surprise, as far as Gabriela could tell. Then Isis, then Thorschild—occasionally helped by Pie batting a ball into a hole—then Michael.

Gabriela brought up the rear, as she found that she either put way too much muscle into hitting the ball, so that Michael had to make a quick blessing to ensure both that it didn't hit anyone and that it came back to them, or far too little, so that the ball would only roll an inch or two and stop. Pie stood on the side of each small, dayglow fairway looking at her sympathetically. Thankfully, no one commented on him, as he'd been made invisible to anyone who didn't know he was there.

As she accepted her last place mantle graciously, Michael smiled at her. *You're having fun, aren't you?*

Yep, she admitted. *Is this what childhood is supposed to be like? Surrounded by a family of two formidable goddesses, an angel, a former angel, a half-demon, and a cat while doing just ridiculously silly things?*

I think it's the theory, yes. How often it turns out this well, I'm not sure.

Although she had lost pretty much every game they'd played, except one at the arcade where she had to stop a circling light at exactly the right point—which she was weirdly good at and from which she'd won enough points to acquire a small plush toy black cat which "purred" when its string was pulled—Gabriela was weirdly, fabulously happy. She felt like a kid, especially since Cain and, bizarrely, Loviatar, paid for everything.

Admittedly, she was too afraid to ask where the goddess had gotten her funds.

Several funnel cakes, some ice cream, and a bit of cotton candy later—the former of which Michael seemed to take to better than the cheesesteaks—they were wandering back down Clifton Hill and were approached by a man dressed as Nosferatu who tried to give them flyers for an attraction called, Hades' Underworld. It was only as she took one that she realized his fangs were real.

Michael . . . she prodded.

I noticed.

Cain and Thorschild and Isis were staring, as well. Loviatar was pondering the merits of the flyer.

They had been at their entertainments so long that night had fallen, although it was only early evening. The vampire—who was clearly wearing a baldcap and a badly-fitted jacket as well as the fake front fangs gracing his usual ones—looked uncomfortably hot. He also looked rather young.

Isis moved toward him sympathetically. "Are you well, young fanged one? Is the day too warm for you?"

"The heat'th a bleedin' nuithance, if you mutht know," the vampire lisped around his fake front fangs in a distinct cockney accent. "I hate thtreet duty."

Loviatar had been paying no attention to any of them, just staring at the flyer.

"I had a small fling with Hades once. Only a decade or two."

She sounded pleasantly reminiscent.

"He was fascinatingly freaky."

Gabriela and Michael stared at each other.

Another bet participant, you think? she wondered.

Well, either that, or he's found an odd new way to make money by scaring people. With humans, anything's possible.

Gabriela rather agreed. Personally, she didn't see the point of going out of her way to be terrified, as life did that all too much on its own, but she supposed she wasn't exactly normal enough to count.

Everyone seemed to have made the same silent decision, but only Loviatar spoke.

"Excellent. There is a two-for-one coupon on the back."

A moment later, she seemed to notice their looks. Her hair had now settled into a long, silver-white braid.

"What? I dislike giving old flames money. It gives them the wrong idea."

They left the young vampire to continue trying to entice the tourists—although Isis left him a spell to keep him cool—and made their way to a three-story building which looked a little like a backlot Dracula's castle.

An older woman with dyed orange-red hair saw them staring, as she came out with two children who seemed oddly reflective.

"What? The decorating? This place has been a different scary attraction every year I've been here."

She had a distinctive New York accent, the type that turned the second word of the city into "yawk."

"Still, Frank and I drive over here once a year with the kids and now the grandkids just to have some fun."

Staring at the building, she looked reflective.

"I will say, though, this Hades guy don't go for the traditional scares. There's a ton of mirrors in there. I didn't see nothin' in 'em. I don't know what the kids saw, but they've been quiet ever since."

"Don't *wanna* be a bus driver," the boy near her moaned.

"See? Weird?" she soliloquyed, then led the silent children away, answering. "Then ya gotta work on yore math more, don't ya?"

Gabriela's group—or, really, she thought of it more as Loviatar's group, as they were just following the goddess around—said nothing but paid and headed inside.

The lady had been right. There were a *lot* of mirrors.

True, there were some skeletons hanging in cages, an occasional reaper or two, along with a surprisingly-realistic three-headed dog, but a lot of the interior had the appearance of having been left over from something else, probably whatever the haunted attraction before this one had been.

Still, it was the mirrors which drew everyone in—and they were far scarier than any typical haunted house.

In one room, Gabriela saw all her past crimes, the things the compound and Poseidon had brainwashed her into. She saw Cain nearly crumple and have to be supported by Thorschild, his cat purring and rubbing its face against him to try to comfort. A random woman she walked behind had gone incredibly pale, as the reflection showed her stealing a check from the purse of a very old lady she was supposed to be tending. Whatever Loviatar saw, though, she was just grinning with her arms crossed, as though she were watching a highlight reel of her greatest triumphs. It took a while to convince her to leave.

In the next room, there were images of Gabriela losing Michael—and, for Michael, she noticed, of him losing her. She saw Isis gasp and touch the mirror, muttering, "Osiris, no."

When Gabriela walked behind Loviatar's mirror, she saw her marble army of lions all broken and writhing on the ground.

Another room on, Gabriela witnessed the check-stealer looking into a mirror to see both the older lady dead and then herself killed by the hands of the man she was with. She took only one look at him, as he was smiling evilly in another mirror, and ran away as fast as she could. Thankfully for her, he didn't seem to notice.

Gabriela didn't even need to look. She knew what her worst fears were, and all of them involved being separated from Michael.

No, this one isn't the fears, he corrected her. *The first one was our worst deeds. The second our fears. This one is a warning of what we'll become if we follow our worst instincts.*

Gabriela stood behind him, looking in his mirror. There were two images there. One was of a life where he simply watched her but had no contact. The other was him as an avenging angel with the bodies of everyone near him turned to dust.

Touching his shoulder, she drew back his attention from the ghastly scene.

Are you that angry, my love?
Not now. But losing you . . .
He shuddered slightly.

. . . losing you could drive me to a madness which might cost MANY lives.

As she looked at him, his fear was so intense that she came around and held him, putting her head on his shoulder. Through their bond, she could feel that he was as warmed by her embrace as she was by his, his sigh a breeze against her hair.

I'm always with you, Michael. I'll do my best not to let anything happen to me, but even if it did, you will still never have a day without me near you.

Having had very little experience with actual love, Gabriela was a little surprised that she was as comforted by that promise as she meant him to be.

Chapter 27
Michael

Fearing his worst instincts, especially since Ares was so very good at bringing them out, Michael still tried to take comfort from Gabriela's promise.

Holding her close, he wondered.

What could three ancient Greek gods . . .

Because it was *clear* that this was Hades at work.

. . . be making a bet over which causes them go to this much trouble? And why take Hermes and Hephaestus hostage rather than including them in the bet?

As she clearly didn't have an answer, Gabriela just pulled back to look at him. They could both hear Loviatar stewing in a corner.

I don't know, but maybe we can find out when we meet him, 'cause I don't think Loviatar's going to leave without letting him know EXACTLY how she feels.

Making this obvious, the Finnish goddess was nearly smoking with anger. Looking around, Michael wondered if he was going to have to throw a quick blessing to keep everyone from noticing, but all the humans were far too caught up in what the mirrors had taught them.

"Come," Loviatar ordered, striding over through a curtain and into a backstage area.

They followed because, well, it was Loviatar. Also, the only way to get answers was to have someone to ask them of.

She stood before a final mirror which showed the goddess as a truly fierce Amazon in a full leather catsuit, complete with a very complicated, almost horned chandelier thing on her head.

She looks like a Jack Kirby character, Gabriela noted, as Michael stared at her. *You know, the creator Stan Lee stole all the credit from?*

He continued to stare.

Never mind. Edgar was into comics.

Blinking, he wondered.

Is that why you're still a virgin?

Has NOTHING to do with it, trust me.

Loviatar, of course, was paying them no attention, glaring at her fierce image.

"Show yourself to me, you lecherous cretin," she demanded.

A moment later, the mirror swung inward, and they were greeted by a three-headed dog which jumped up on Loviatar excitedly. Suddenly, her voice was almost sweet.

"Yes, Cerberus, I missed you, too. Now, show us to your master, would you? There's a dear."

The three heads barked, as the one tail wagged frantically, and they followed the beast in toward what could only be called a lair.

Michael did notice Gabriela risk one look in the mirror to see herself much as he had always known her, at least in her more traditional form, beautiful and bewinged. He heard her breath catch and sighed.

Will you never understand how lovely and special you are, my one?

Uh, hello! Raised in a compound by those who made it clear that I was eminently expendable.

Now who's being formal? he smiled.

You're rubbing off on me.

He had to try to move Gabriela on, as she noticed Cain staring at himself, as well. He was shining with magic and life, and Michael smiled, as Thorschild kissed his cheek, her wings—and some lightning—shining all around her.

"Told you," she whispered.

Admittedly, Michael sighed to his own partner, *you're not the only one with self-image problems.*

They followed along in Loviatar's wake, as they had all day, into somewhere which was clearly both fairly far underground and in a different dimension. Michael took Gabriela's hand just in case. Thankfully, she just smiled at him.

It was quite a long walk, but eventually they came within hearing distance of a man giving loud orders, and finally to the man himself.

Hades was of operatic proportions and dressed in a cape of black feathers. He had his short hair dyed stark white and a beard which just screamed "Mephistopheles." Cerberus kept running back and forth between him and Loviatar like an excited puppy, all three heads drooling.

Hades was in mid-shout to a cringing flunky when he spotted the goddess.

"Oh, yay. You're back."

"Miss me?" she smiled.

Michael noticed that there were four, very muscular men in Roman gladiator outfits over in the corner who were watching interestedly.

Folding his arms, Hades glowered down at her.

"Not particularly. I've moved on."

Gesturing toward the four men in the corner, he sneered.

"Muscle men do what you want and don't threaten to eviscerate you afterwards."

These Greek gods really get around, don't they? Gabriela noted.

Well, Zeus was reputed to have "seduced" women in the form of a swan, a white bull, and a shower of gold, among other things, so I suspect they come by their reputation of getting their freak on honestly.

She looked at him. *That was a little less formal.*

You're rubbing off on me, he smiled.

Watching Loviatar pretend to pout was a very surreal experience on its own.

"Oh, come on, lover. Don't tell me you're not in on this little bet."

"I'm *very much* in on this bet. In fact, I'm going to win it."

Cerberus was whimpeering for attention from Loviatar, until she started scratching the middle head behind its ears, still staring at the god of the underworld, who didn't stop to hear her opinions.

"Now, if you think I'm going to ask Ares to let you go when he incarnated you fair and square, you're even crazier now than when you loosed those diseases."

"If I remember correctly, it was you who gave them to me."

"They were keepsakes!" Hades screamed. "Like a bouquet!"

He had quite the voice for screaming and quite the cave-like environment to do it in. Everything echoed.

"Oh now, lover," Loviatar moved in on him, touching his leg, which was about the only decent part she could get to, given that Hades was standing on a small stage. "Don't you remember when we . . ."

Her next reminiscence was detailed and explicit. And very odd. Especially the chicken.

Gabriela stared.

Okay, I know I'm a virgin, but that's not normal, is it?

She looked a little worried.

That, my dear . . . Michael assured her, running his hand warmly over her back. . . . *is not even in the same GALAXY as normal.*

Oh, thank god.

She let out a relieved breath.

I love you, but I'm not ready to try ANY of that.

Neither was Michael, who blushed along with her.

Glad to hear it.

They continued to listen.

And I think the wildebeests will be, too.

The descriptions of sex play by way of Fellini with a dash of *American Psycho* continued to make all of them stare.

Eventually, Loviatar changed the subject, although it was unclear whether that was because Hades appeared rather dewy-eyed with memories.

"And why did you create that bizarre attraction upstairs? It did nothing to flatter me."

"It's not for flattery, you hellhound."

Loviatar smiled as though it were a pet name.

"I'm the god of the underworld, where the dead face the consequences of their lives. Do you know how tedious that becomes? I thought if maybe I could convince a few to be better people and move on to Elysium, I might get a holiday a little more often."

Michael supposed this made as much sense as anything.

Still, Loviatar objected. "It doesn't seem to work on everyone."

It was true. The grandmother who'd stopped them before going in didn't seem to be the least bit concerned, had just seen it as "a bunch of mirrors."

"Depends on the person," Hades shrugged. "Some have some serious karma to work out, which they find out when they see their pasts. Others don't. Some have fears about their future they haven't faced. Others are pretty settled on where they're going. Some need to know where their current path takes them, while for others it's only to more of where they are right now."

He grinned.

"For most, it's pretty terrifying. There's nothing scarier than facing down your own truths."

This was difficult to argue with, but Michael had no idea where it left them.

Loviatar asked, as well. "And what does all this get you?"

"Like I said," Hades shrugged. "More downtime. Also money. You would not *believe* how much perfectly comfortable people are willing to pay to feel an emotion much of the world stews in on a daily basis."

"You're using it to buy your presents for the contest?"

"Eh," the underworld god hedged, "more like using it to bribe the right people. A museum guard here, a curator there, and you can walk away quite peacefully with almost anything you want."

"And when you win this bet?" she wondered.

His smile spread like an oil slick.

"Then the world will see what I *really* want."

Chapter 28
Gabriela

With this disturbing pronouncement, they left the underworld, as Hades made it clear he wasn't telling them anything more. Gabriela saw the three-headed dog, all six of its ears drooping, as it pined and whined after Loviatar, as they returned through the portal.

To her surprise, they didn't end up either back in Niagara Falls or at the theater but instead back in Cain's world.

She was a little alarmed but only showed her thoughts to Michael.

Is this wise? Loviatar can probably be trusted at least not to be on Ares' side.

Although that said nothing of what she might do if someone gave her an axe.

But we still don't know what Isis is up to.

Michael looked at her.

I agree, but I suspect that Cain and Thorschild have thought about this as well. Maybe they've just come to some sort of decision.

Apparently, they had, the pair about to speak when Loviatar cut them off.

"This is a very light, sweet place. I don't approve."

"It's Cain's," Thorschild said.

"It's ours," he contradicted, with a brief smile to her.

The formidable goddess rolled her eyes.

"Children," she groaned. "Always so sentimental."

One eyebrow raised, she refocused.

"And why are there a hundred sea creatures making that racket?"

Gabriela looked over to see all her ocean friends, whistling, sonically signaling or just waving a tentacle or two. Letting Michael's hand go with an apologetic look, she ran over to them for a moment, rubbing a wet, silken head or two.

"Yes, I missed you, too."

The noises they were making got louder.

Um, Isis? Michael reminded her. *She didn't know you were Poseidon's daughter before.*

Her hand stopped in mid-stroke of a dolphin's head.

Well, crap.

Leaving them, she returned to the group, although the secret was already out.

Loviatar's arms were crossed, one eyebrow raised at Gabriela. The stuffed minotaur she had won at the arcade was still on her shoulders.

"You do not have enough interest in the art of bladed weapons to be termed a true woman, but you become less typical upon acquaintance."

Gabriela started to wonder if high-flung speech were a both a godly and angelic trait. Still, what to say to that?

"Um, I think I like you, too?"

Thankfully, Loviatar smiled.

Thorschild and Cain led them into the house, where Tatiana—wearing only a bikini—was using Billy, who was down on all fours, as a pommel horse to practice her vaults on. He seemed oddly happy with the situation. Nearby, Seraphina continued to knit.

Tatiana had just finished a truly remarkable display of twists and turns and landed with both her arms raised, seemed to be waiting for applause. The best she got was Billy's "Ooo, nice one!" and Seraphina's only half-interested, "Your left foot moved."

"Darn, thought I'd stuck it that time," she grumbled.

She seemed about ready to take up her starting position again when she spotted them.

"Oh cool, company!"

Putting on a lacy robe which didn't really hide anything, she smiled.

"I'd rather practice naked, but Seraphina says she sees too much of me this way, as it is."

It was about then that Gabriela noticed there were two newcomers in the corner, an attractive, well-built Asian man with reddish-black hair and light blue eyes sitting in an armchair with a woman with curly brownish-blonde hair and a distinctly Roman nose, who was half-seated on its arm.

Possibly noticing their looks, Tatiana introduced them. "This is the head of my family, Kenji, and his partner, Susannah."

Susannah sized all of them up with an expert eye but said nothing.

Gabriela decided that the woman must mean her vampiric family, as, all together, two of the group were generically white, one possibly Jewish, one African-American, and one at least half-Asian. There were other possibilities, but the vampires seemed the most likely one.

Thorschild looked pleased to see them before turning back to the group.

"I think there are some things we should discuss."

Loviatar leveled that deadly eyebrow at her.

"Although, if you'd like, we can go discuss it as women and leave the men to their own devices."

"Good," Loviatar agreed.

That seems to answer the question of whether Thorschild and Cain are communicating like we are, Gabriela noted. *As I assume neither one would wander off without letting the other know what they learned, otherwise.*

I agree. Although pity me left with two vampires and the son of a demon.

Yes, yes. Poor dear.

She ran her hand down Michael's arm and went to follow the women.

Billy's sex tips are VERY specific, he grumped, and she tried not to draw attention by laughing.

So long as they don't involve chickens and wildebeests and do definitely involve you, I'm game.

There was a silence, as Michael either decided not to answer or got distracted by the men around him, so she followed the group through what seemed like miles of corridors. It made her wonder whether the house itself were rather magical. Still, they eventually ended up in a library.

"Wow," Gabriela stopped, staring.

Thorschild just looked at her, as Susannah nearly ran into her. A second later, Susannah stared, thrumming her fingers against the doorframe.

"Never seen books before?"

"Not this many," Gabriela admitted.

About ten at a time would have been a lot when she was growing up, and most of those were written by one of the "Fathers." These looked to be real books, which had been passed down through generations of readers, full of knowledge and legend. And there were *thousands* of them. There was even a ladder attached to a track at the top to help reach the upper shelves.

A little jealous, as she watched Thorschild look over the books lovingly, Gabriela could hear the affection in her voice. "It's my favorite room in the house."

Gabriela would have thought that would be the bedroom with the lovely waterfall, but Thorschild's love for the books was undeniable.

Susannah was still staring at her, though, her question unanswered.

"Raised in a compound full of militant crazies," Gabriela shrugged. "Some of the stereotypes are true."

A general distrust of most "book learnin'" being one of them.

As Susannah did nothing except raise a Loviatar-esque eyebrow at her, Gabriela didn't really know what else to say.

There were a lot of places to sit, and she got the idea that they had all been well-tried out. Thorschild clearly wasn't lying when she claimed to love this room best.

Propping herself on a big, stuffed, cube-like thing and folding her legs up onto it, Gabriela waited to see who would begin.

Everyone settled down in their preferred ways. Loviatar stretched out on a fainting couch in a rather languid pose, Tatiana stomach-down on the carpet, kicking her feet in the air behind her, Thorschild in a well-stuffed easy chair, and Susannah standing near Tatiana with her elbow on a shelf. Isis helped the very-pregnant Seraphina lower herself into a plain wooden chair and took the one beside her. Then, they waited, looking to Thorschild.

"Um, yeah," she started tentatively, before glancing at Loviatar and Isis. "It was my idea to bring the two of you here. Before you ask, it's Cain's world in . . ."

Loviatar waved her hand.

"Yes, yes, child, we goddesses know what a private world is. This is a very nice one for you peace and love types, although I'm surprised to see the fanged ones here."

Tatiana opened her mouth, apparently about to explain, but Loviatar waved again.

"Let's move on."

Isis nodded as well.

The interruption made Thorschild smile, although Gabriela wasn't entirely certain why. Possibly it was some internal comment from Cain she had missed.

"Good. We've gotten you to come here so we can decide what's to be done about our situation."

Looking to the Finnish goddess, she explained.

"I assume you'd be more than happy to do whatever was required to end your imprisonment."

Holding up her hand before Loviatar could answer, she amended.

"Even something nonviolent, perhaps?"

Loviatar leaned her head back. Her now pony-tailed red hair hung off the end. "If I must. I'd infinitely prefer disemboweling."

As this went without saying, Thorschild looked to Isis.

"As I think some of us may have questions about whose side you're on, perhaps you can explain?"

Smiling the smile of the long-martyred, Isis looked at Gabriela.

"I was the one who alerted those Thorschild and Cain work for. If I hadn't, they probably wouldn't be here."

Did you get that? she asked Michael.

I was told the same thing here, yes.

Sighing, Gabriela decided to just ask. Isis would already know who was plotting against the god of war, so they might as well hope that she was telling them the truth.

"What's your history with Ares?"

Wincing slightly, Gabriela hated to just accuse, but . . .

"You've seemed fairly chummy with him these past few days."

Which, let's face it, is the whole time I've known you.

The thought was for herself, not Michael, but he seemed too distracted by whatever his group was discussing to notice, anyway.

Isis shrugged. "Do you know of a better way to find out information than to listen?"

This was certainly true, but the problem with trusting someone who was good at spying was that they might always be spying on you.

As she herself was no spy, Gabriela was certain her look said this for her.

"What have you discovered?"

The history question, she noticed, had gone unanswered.

Probably picking up on that thought, Isis sighed. "I've known Ares for many centuries, though never happily. There have been occasions when I've endured his presence because I had to, nothing more."

Apparently, she picked up on Gabriela's next intended question, answering.

"As to why I didn't tell Michael who our captor was, I was fairly certain but wanted to wait until he revealed himself. I did tell my suspicions to . . ."

There was a significant pause when she was clearly editing.

". . . those Thorschild and Cain work for."

Gabriela hoped this was true. Among other things, Isis was quite a calming presence. She really didn't want to have reason not to trust her.

This said nothing of what the little child's mummy had told her, too, that she was under Isis' protection, although she only now realized she was still wearing the ankh attached to her wrist. Hopefully, even if the goddess wasn't on their side, the object wasn't having any ill effects on her.

Isis went on. "As to what I've found out by listening to him these past few days, it's been very little except that I find him even more repulsive now than I did before. As to what Uriel's up to . . ."

She shrugged.

Thorschild looked at her curiously. "So you haven't learned much?"

"Why do you think I came to lunch with all of you? Five more minutes listening to Ares brag about his conquests, in order, from Greece to Rome to Egypt and beyond, and I might well have tried to kill him myself."

She looked sadly into a corner.

"And then I might never find out where my beloved Osiris is."

It certainly had the ring of truth, although Gabriela was a bit too wary to just believe.

Thorschild picked up there. "So what we seem to have is a contest played by at least three former Greek gods, Ares, Poseidon, and Hades."

She was leaned forward, tapping her finger on her leg.

"As far as we've been able to detect, there's no real rhyme or reason to the things they collect. There's no spell they seem to lead to."

Tatiana and Susannah both nodded, and Gabriela got the feeling that they were quite involved in figuring this out.

"The objects don't build on each other, either. I mean . . ." She looked at them. ". . . you don't need one to collect another, so they don't seem to be building toward some grand prize they're fighting to get the pieces of first."

It summed up their situation nicely, although Gabriela wasn't sure where to go from here.

"So where . . ." Thorschild asked, leaning back again. ". . . does that leave us? Why collect a good deal of magical artifacts and then just let them sit around?"

"To go to war?" Isis theorized. "Perhaps they're there to provide protection to some human who's willing to do terrible things to win."

That brought up the Hitler angle again, which Michael had explained to Gabriela earlier.

Still, Thorschild shook her head.

"No, that would certainly appeal to Ares but not as much to Hades or Poseidon. They're not good, but they don't have the same personal history of battle."

"Besides . . ." Susannah tossed in. ". . . why would even Ares go so far out of his way for some human? He could give him just the Ark of the Covenant or something and let him go on his merry, murderous way."

This certainly seemed true and left the question open once more.

Tatiana spoke up. "Are these objects in some way connected with the other two gods? Might they be trying to get hold on some of each other's power?"

It was a good theory but . . .

Isis shook her head. "The objects are from all over. Many of them are very shiny, but they don't seem to have much in common besides that."

Remembering, Gabriela winced. "Not all of them are shiny. Some of them are a bit gruesome."

"But unusual?" Susannah wondered.

"Yes, definitely that." Gabriela agreed.

What else would someone call all those body parts of the poor supernatural beings she'd killed?

It was Loviatar's voice which distracted her from all the terrible memories, which she also felt Michael trying to soothe.

"You're all being very silly."

Loviatar was now lounging like some '60s sex goddess.

"They're the sort of baubles you give to woo a potential lover, clearly."

Everyone stared at her and then at each other. Even Seraphina stopped knitting.

It made a terrible amount of sense.

"But who are they all trying to court?" Tatiana asked.

Her head back, Thorschild sighed, silent for half a moment or so when Gabriela assumed she was speaking to her partner.

"It's Aphrodite."

As her head raised, she looked certain.

"They're all competing to try to win Aphrodite's love."

Chapter 29
Michael

Somewhat the same conversation had been happening among the men in the house. When Michael wondered why they couldn't all have had this conversation together—the human fascination with separating by gender a mystery to him—Cain just sighed.

"Thorschild thinks—and I agree—that it will be easier to get both Isis and Loviatar to talk in the company of women. Loviatar because she sees men as good for only one thing, and it isn't battle. With Isis . . . well . . ."

He grew cagey again.

"I think there are reasons why being closer to some of the women might make her want to speak more. Plus, Thorschild believes your distrust of her might sadden her into not speaking."

Michael wanted to defend himself, as it was rather difficult to trust anyone when you were all prisoners—which was one of the many hells of servitude. Still, as he now knew about Isis being the one to alert someone in authority to their situation, which had led to Thorschild and Cain joining them, he couldn't deny that she seemed to be on their side.

The four men discussed the possibilities of what the gods' bet was about, as well, but when Michael—and apparently Cain—picked up on the women's new insight, they shared it with the other men.

"It makes sense." Kenji's gaze was distant. "In the ancient legends, mortals and gods alike were always competing for Aphrodite's favor."

Cain looked at Michael. "Didn't you say that Hephaestus was one of the first ones Ares kidnapped?"

Nodding, Michael pieced it together, as well. "Maybe he was hoping that kidnapping Aphrodite's husband would give him a better insight into her?"

There was a shrug from Cain.

"Makes as much sense as anything from a mad war god, doesn't it?"

Sighing, Michael had to question. "I know the legends, but are Aphrodite and Hephaestus still together? If so, wouldn't kidnapping her husband just irritate her rather than win her favor?"

Billy raised an eyebrow.

"Does Ares strike you as the logical type or the type to rape, loot, pillage, kidnap, and burn and see where he is once the screaming's died down?"

"A fair point," Michael agreed.

"They haven't been together for several centuries, according to Hephaestus," Cain put in. "We didn't know to ask him about it specifically, but we did get from him that Aphrodite wasn't the hostage Ares had taken to hold him, and he didn't even seem to know where she was."

This left them thinking, until Michael remembered something.

"Wait a minute. I know Ares was once involved with her, so maybe he just wants her back, but weren't Poseidon and Hermes, as well?"

He looked up at them.

Billy whistled. "That would mean the first two gods he caught were Aphrodite's exes."

"As far as I remember, Hades wasn't ever involved with her, though," Cain pointed out.

Michael sighed. "It doesn't mean he didn't want to be."

"Mm, yes," Kenji murmured. "At some point, she becomes a good time who hasn't yet been had by all."

Um, Susannah just let out a hoot of laughter, Gabriela noted to him. *I'm guessing she and Kenji might have some silent communication going as well.*

And apparently some in-jokes, he agreed.

Aloud, Michael continued, "Wait a minute. Didn't Ares try to in-carnate Aphrodite about a year ago?"

"Did he?" Cain wondered, crossing his arms.

Pie had hopped off of him a while ago and was now napping on Kenji's lap, although the vampire was trying not to touch the cat. Apparently, he got a bit scratchy when that happened with vampires. Michael suspected that he was just being a catlike annoyance in choosing the vampire to sleep on.

"Thorschild and I have only been with you for about three months, so you tell me."

Michael and Cain listened as Thorschild conveyed some version of this to the women, without revealing that she was also listening in on the men.

The two of them would make good spies, Michael noted.

Gabriela answered. *I think you mean they DO make good spies.*

Fair point.

He heard Isis answering this.

"Ares did try, several times, in fact. It was the one time he became truly angry. No matter what he did, she wouldn't be caught."

Cain conveyed some version of this to the two vampires.

"Well, it makes sense. Ares and Aphrodite were supposed to have been lovers even in ancient times. He probably thought he could use that to get an easy win," Kenji put in.

"Do you think the other gods have tried to summon her, too?" Michael wondered.

"Undoubtedly," Cain nodded.

"Then this is a . . . what? Contest to try to get the sparkliest prize which might tempt her to appear?"

Sparkliest? Gabriela wondered.

Sorry. Aphrodite always was supposed to be a bit of a twink. It seemed appropriate.

He could feel her smile.

"Maybe," Cain went on. "Or maybe he's just stocking up presents while he tries to find some method of convincing her to come when he calls."

"Maybe they all are," someone in Gabriela's group said, possibly Susannah, when Thorschild had pointed out much the same thing.

Suddenly, Michael was angry. Ares had taken hostages and forced some of them into serving him. Likely, Hades had done the same thing, if the uncomfortable young vampire in Niagara Falls were anything to go by. Poseidon had done not only this but had created a truly toxic environment where the murder of extranormal beings was typical. As was child marriage. And raping his followers to force them to bear his children, as well as Lady only knew how many other things.

It has to end.

He only realized he was smoking slightly when his three companions looked at him worriedly.

Trying to calm himself somewhat, he explained. "If we let this continue, the three of them—if it *is* only the three of them—will drag this on for years, allowing the suffering of who knows how many for how long."

Letting out a deep, angry breath, he looked at them all.

"We have to find some way to bring them together to vie for their prize. Once Aphrodite's made up her mind, the rest will hopefully let their hostages go."

Gabriela clearly understood his thoughts and conveyed some version of them to her companions, but asked him the same question Kenji did.

How?

Michael didn't have an answer for this directly, but he did have half of an idea.

"Perhaps we can tell Ares that we saw Hades, and that he thinks he's close to winning? If he believes that . . ."

This idea was conveyed to the women, and Isis agreed to be the messenger. Soon, it seemed they had done as much as they could.

Just as they were getting ready to go back, though, Kenji motioned Michael aside.

"I know I don't know you, so I hate to bring up something so delicate, but . . ."

He paused, and Michael wondered if Susannah were urging him on.

"I'm sure you know that vampires can tell a lot by scent."

Nodding, Michael wondered where this was going.

Kenji stepped even closer, his voice low.

"There may be more danger in leaving your partner a virgin than you realize."

Uncertain which of a million reactions to focus on, Michael stared.

"Let's just say that the concept of 'virgin sacrifice' is one which goes back into the ancient world."

His eyes looked into the angel deeply.

"It may be far safer if Ares doesn't get any ideas."

This was probably true on many levels, but Michael wasn't at all ready to work on the one the vampire was suggesting.

Kenji just gave him a half smile and let him be.

Susannah was telling me pretty much the same thing, Gabriela put in. *Although not in quite such delicate terms.*

Sighing, Michael wondered over the odd life he now led. *The vampire relationship advice was bad enough. I draw the line at more fanged sex advice.*

He heard her mental giggle and cherished it. Still, he couldn't see going through with anything like such a suggestion. Gabriela deserved him wholly, not just for a "nooner," as Ares insisted on calling it. Until they had a chance to truly escape and be on their own—assuming The Lady would allow that—he was going to have to live with Gabriela just being a very tender friend.

Chapter 30
Gabriela

Any memory of the warning they'd both been given was forgotten when Gabriela emerged from the house to see all the sea creatures still clamoring for attention, greeting her with a happy riot of clicks and whale sounds and seal barks and many other sounds. It was a cacophony but one she loved.

While she hated to leave her animal friends again, she did force herself to accompany the group, knowing Ares might grow suspicious if they were too much longer.

It was not a moment too soon.

As they came back through the portal, they heard Ares screaming. Even though they were a long way from the main theater itself, it was difficult to ignore. The walls were nearly vibrating.

All of them running, they arrived to find a visitor. Gabriela nearly hissed.

"Father Deacon."

As she was too distracted to even try, Michael translated for the rest of them softly. "That's Poseidon."

Poseidon, Gabriela decided, did not look like a god from the sea. Now that his compulsions had been dismantled, he looked like any insane militia goober who wanted to remake the world in his own, idiot image.

Weirdly, she did realize that she was a little bit happy to be his daughter, but it was only because of the bond with the sea and its creatures. As to him . . .

"He looks like Eric Roberts," Isis mused, clearly as confused as many of the rest of them.

Loviatar had her arms crossed and was glancing him over assessingly.

"Eric Roberts if he started a death cult," she noted, almost approvingly.

Gabriela did have to admit that kind of summed up the effect of the militia outfit.

I'll give Poseidon one thing, Michael told her privately. *If you're going to choose a type, Eric Roberts probably IS the king of confident smarm.*

Father Deacon was standing in the middle of the theater, staring at the ceiling, looking supremely bored. Ares was screaming directly in his face, his appearance ever more what anyone would expect of the god of war. In fact, he now had a giant, slavering hound on either side of him, both of them looking like they wanted to take out Father Deacon's throat. Uriel, now entirely manly except for delicately-painted long red nails, stood to their side, trying to keep Ares from gutting the god of the sea. The angel was being ignored by both of them.

Now that they were closer, the actual words Ares was screaming were clearer.

"You think you can just come in my house and demand one of my prisoners? You dare?"

Without a word, Gabriela took Michael's hand, suspecting just who Father Deacon—she could *not* stop thinking of him by that name—was demanding.

This was made clearer as he finally looked back at Ares, his entire attitude supremely laid back. "Dude, chillax."

He held up his hand, and Gabriela suspected that the "DudeBro" attitude was entirely for the benefit of annoying the god of war. He was often a bit more yell-y at the compound.

"She's my flesh and blood." He grinned evilly. "We both know that has privileges."

Suddenly, the warnings Kenji and Susannah had been giving them seemed much too real.

Uh, Michael?

"*Virgin sacrifice.*" She felt him shudder. *Unfortunately, I was thinking the same thing.*

"Um, I hate to be indelicate," Thorschild put in. ". . . but Susannah mentioned something. Gabriela, you don't happen to be . . ."

Gabriela sighed. She might as well just take out a billboard.

"A virgin, yes," she murmured, as Fath—. . . Poseidon and Ares' argument raged on. Although really all the raging seemed to be from Ares.

Michael was quite literally steaming again.

It was disturbing to Gabriela that she found that weirdly hot. Going from "Sex? No thanks!" to meeting someone who seemed a total stranger, to having all her lifelong illusions torn away, to learning fully who and what she really was and recognizing Michael's place in her soul, to now sorta wishing the angel would get over his politeness and agree to a little mutual ravishing in a little over a day wasn't for the faint of heart.

"I won't let them," he growled, understandably ignoring her thoughts to focus on far more immediate issues.

Loviatar seemed to finally stop appreciating the show and stared back to Gabriela. "You mean you've never . . ."

"Nope," Gabriela interrupted, not wanting to know what words would come next, given the bizarre sex talk the goddess had had with Hades.

"Even all those times you snuck off alone with the angel?"

Gabriela shook her head, which made Loviatar do some steaming herself.

"Humans!" she cried.

Unfortunately, that got the attention of the arguing gods for half a second or so.

"Oh, hey, sweetie," Poseidon waved at his daughter. "Daddy's coming to get you in just a minute, don't you worry."

ARE there any more worrying words? Gabriela wondered.

Probably depends on who your daddy is, Michael noted. *But in this case, no, there aren't.*

He was standing in front of her now, making it clear he was going to do whatever it took to keep her from harm.

To her surprise, Isis first touched Gabriela's arm and then took a place beside him. The goddess wasn't steaming so much as glowing, but she was immensely beautiful, a magical wind fluttering her long, dark, wavy hair.

"They will not harm you while I live," the goddess promised.

Michael was clearly as confused by this as Gabriela but didn't try to stop her. When Gabriela explained silently what the little mummy girl had told her, he just wondered.

Why?

Noooo idea.

The moment wasn't made any less contentious—or ominous—when a loud explosion took off the double doors at the top of the theater, and Hades marched in, decked in full black feathers and now . . . sequins. The three-headed dog barked in behind him but quickly abandoned him to lope off toward Loviatar, panting happily.

Loviatar greeted him by crooning and rubbing him under one of his muzzles.

"Cerberus!" Hades commanded, but none of the three heads listened. "Damn dog," he muttered.

Then, his entrance somewhat ruined by the defection, he marched down the aisle to confront his fellow contestants. It didn't help his attempts to impress any that Ares' hounds now jumped and pecked at his feathers.

Ignoring them, Hades raged.

"Did you think you could bring her into being without me? The bet is between all three of us, you cretins!"

Poseidon waved him off with a small "pff" noise. Ares turned and started screaming about how they were disrespecting him by entering his theater this way.

The argument went on, but it was clear who was at the center of it.

Gabriela decided to actually say what she was thinking, as it wasn't just for Michael. "So, they're planning to kill me, I assume, to try to bring Aphrodite here?"

Thorschild put her hand on one of Gabriela's shoulders, Cain coming to her other side. Pie leaped over from Thorschild's shoulder, where he had been hissing and spitting at the gods, to perch on Gabriela instead, still spitting.

That sort of answered the question, as little as she liked it. But . . .

"Why? Why would a virgin be an enticement for Aphrodite? I'm not really one of her followers, in any sense."

Thorschild squeezed her shoulder reassuringly.

"If they were keeping to history, you would think a prostitute would be a more beloved follower for her. Mythically, she's supposed to get pretty mad when a woman decides to stay virginal, so . . ."

Clearly not getting it, either, she trailed off.

"No." Isis's voice was more commanding than Gabriela had ever heard it before. "This is a traditional contest between men. They fight by presenting treasure to the woman they all seek to claim. Women are just possessions to them. And what is the possession which such men most seek to claim?"

It didn't really need to be answered. As serious as it all was, as well, Gabriela sighed, saying just to Michael, *I feel like a bone every dog wants.*

That IS what they've set up, yes. He wasn't steaming any less.

All of the gods entirely ignoring the way the group clustered around Gabriela to protect her, they finally appeared to have come to a compromise.

"Then it is agreed," Hades pronounced, possibly because he had the deepest voice for doing so. He had stopped Ares' dogs from attacking his cloak at last, although they both had mouthfuls of black feathers.

"We shall all burn the virgin girl, Gabriela, alive as an offering to Aphrodite, so that she might judge all our tribute to her and choose her favorite."

The crowd around Gabriela moved closer, and she was grateful for them. If she had any powers which weren't strictly mortal, they were mostly related to water, and there wasn't a lot of that in the theater to work with.

"But first . . ." the god of the underworld grinned. ". . . to get Aphrodite's attention . . ."

Hermes came forward with a prisoner, neither of them looking comfortable with their role.

". . . we shall kill Hephaestus."

Chapter 31
Michael

M uch as Michael had thought he'd wanted it earlier that day, seeing the three gods deciding to bring their game to a close didn't
bring him any peace. As he hadn't realized that this would involve the
possible murder of the woman he loved, that wasn't surprising.

Ares moved in on them, the other gods watching with grins.

"Come on, Michael. Be reasonable."

Cerberus nipped at him, but Loviatar held him back, stroking his
side.

"It wasn't like you were doing anything with her, anyway."

Gabriela seemed to pick up on his intent, saying to him, *Can you
truly kill him and the other two?*

Sadly, Michael didn't know the answer.

*I'm not entirely certain they CAN be killed. I don't know how they
think they'll destroy Hephaestus.*

Then is attacking him going to get us anywhere?

What are you saying? Although he worried that he was figuring it
out.

*Wherever this is going, they need to bring Aphrodite here. Without
that, this never ends.*

He was appalled.

And you're willing to die to let that happen?

He knew she understood. Hephaestus might be hard to kill, but Gabriela was mortal. Well, half-mortal. If the immortal parent were the one trying to kill her, he didn't hold out a lot of hope for her survival.

I suspect there's more at work here than we can see, Gabriela went on. *Whatever Cain and Thorschild are here for, I doubt that they plan to let this go on any more than you do.*

Yes, but they're both at least half or partly mortal, as well.

His heart, his whole body really, was quaking with some combination of terror and a near-berserker rage, and he wondered again how the humans survived such feelings.

He was locked in a death glare with Ares, so he couldn't look away, but he could feel that Gabriela managed a quick look to Thorschild, who now stood beside her. The woman nodded at her just barely, once.

Still, given the plans of three different gods, it wasn't terribly encouraging.

"No," Isis stepped firmly in front of her, distracting the god, giving them more time to talk.

I WON'T let you be harmed! He began to wonder whether he should just grab her and take her someplace—anyplace—else.

Clearly, she saw his intention.

If you do that, all these people will still be prisoners. I'm certain your Lady sent you here for some reason. If she's all you believe her to be, it wasn't just to watch them all suffer.

And they would, at Ares' hands. That much was certain.

Put a blessing on me, she urged. *Make me as invulnerable as you can for a little while.*

It had worked with Edgar's knife before, Michael knew. While part of him was ready for holy war, that vision in the mirror in Hades' castle made him pause. If he let his rage free, the thought of where it might lead was terrifying, especially with far too many nearly-mortals around him.

He didn't like it, then, but did as she asked, trusting that those around them had plans he couldn't yet know and ready—if things truly went bad—to do what was needed.

Isis, unaware of this conversation, still stood guard.

"I will not allow it. You will not take her."

That unearthly wind blew her hair even more wildly, and her whole body seemed wreathed in light.

"I am not your slave, Ares."

The god's eyebrow rose. Now, instead of the black leather, he was wearing perfectly-fitted black armor, delicately traced with various signs of protection. When he moved closer, he stalked.

"Is that what you believe, my goddess by conquest?"

Michael saw Isis shudder and suspected that, whatever the origins of that term, it went back to the Romans' conquering of Egypt. A moment later, the god snapped his fingers, and an attractive man who looked a bit like Isis appeared in a cage.

"Osiris," she murmured, clearly torn.

At the moment, the man seemed to be unharmed, other than being caught in a rather oversized birdcage.

Ares raised his fingers again. "One snap, and he'll suffer."

His grin was gleefully cruel.

"Is that what you want?"

While obviously torn, Isis did step aside.

Ares' grin spread wider. "How about if I remind all of you what's really at stake?"

With another snap of his fingers, the entire balcony of the theater was filled with cages. Mostly, the cages were filled with people—or, at least, human-shaped immortals.

Loviatar's eyes were filled with tears as she stared at one cage which held only a double-headed axe, though. "My little pörröinen pupu," she whispered with nearly a sob in her voice. The axe seemed to vibrate in sympathy.

Soon, almost all of Gabriela's defenders had backed off, if warily. All except Michael.

The angel glared at Ares.

Michael... he heard in his head and wasn't certain whether she believed that he was ignoring her earlier pleas or not.

He didn't get time to figure it out, as Ares grabbed Isis and soon had her held firm, a sword with a small sickle-like protrusion pressing just against her throat.

"I can destroy more than just Gabriela here, Michael."

He heard Isis gasp, saw a bit of blood run down her neck, and threw a blessing at her—hoping it would in any way work correctly, as he'd never tried to mix their magics. How Ares had managed to cut her was a mystery. The god's eyes were now a burning red, as though reflecting bright flames, and there were raised blades on the shoulders of his armor.

On the balcony, Osiris called out from his cage, "Isis, no!"

Cain put his hand on the angel's arm, his voice very soft.

"Please, Michael. Have faith."

It took a moment, but Michael gave in, stepping away, smoking even more.

Gabriela... he said, only to her.

I know, Michael.

With a grin, Ares flung Isis to the side, where she put a hand up to her throat. A moment later, the injury healed.

Let's hope everyone here is as immortal as we hope, Gabriela finished.

It wasn't much of a plan—was pretty much "let's see if they kill you before something happens." Still, Michael had never imagined a more noble sacrifice than Gabriela at that moment.

Not fighting, she merely removed the still-arched, spitting cat from her shoulder and handed him over to Thorschild, clearly unwilling to see the beast harmed. Thorschild held the upset creature in her arms, stroking it lovingly and clearly keeping it to her tightly to prevent it from taking on the god of war for Gabriela's sake.

Michael knew exactly how it felt.

Isis too had a hand on his shoulder, and it occurred to him that she was also gentling him. He just hoped that any of them had more of a plan than, "Let's burn Gabriela and then see where this goes."

While he watched, he couldn't help the smoke which rose from him. Having to stand there and watch the angel who was part of his soul walk to her kidnapper without blinking was killing him.

Ares had willed into being two large stakes in the middle of the theater. When he tied Gabriela's hands behind her, the kindling appearing out of nowhere and piling up around her feet, Michael thought she looked like Joan of Arc.

Considering what had happened to that particular servant of The Lady, he wasn't encouraged.

Hephaestus was soon tied to the other stake, Hermes looking at him miserably. There wasn't a pyre around him, though, just that deadly sword with a sickle on its blade which Ares was now coming toward him with.

"Poseidon, you fathered this brat. Do you want to do the honors?"

Hades handed him a flame lit no doubt in the underworld, and Poseidon, grinning, knelt down.

"Sorry about this, sweetie," he said to Gabriela with a wink. "You win some children, lose others."

He touched the flame to the sticks.

"It's all part of the game."

Surprisingly, the flame caught only slowly, and Michael saw from Ares' grin back to him that it was being done just to make this more painful.

Isis and Cain were both holding him back now, as he could look at nothing but Gabriela. Thorschild was still struggling to keep Pie from breaking free and wreaking havoc.

Michael understood. He was no longer certain his blessings would be enough.

Magically, the flames lit up each stick around the outer edge of the pyre before slowly beginning to circle their way up. Gabriela looked both terrified and resigned.

Cain and Isis had to hold him back even more, and Michael wondered just how far he should let this charade go on before he took out everyone he could.

The master of ceremonies in this hideous blood carnival, Ares stepped up, sword in hand, its sickle now to Hephaestus' throat. Hephaestus was a very large, powerful god, but he just looked saddened and defeated. Hermes actively shook, as Ares forced him to hold a golden chalice ready to catch the blood.

As the fire encircling Michael's beloved moved within a half inch of her legs, Ares' voice screamed out. Already the flames were several feet high. "Aphrodite! I offer this virgin demigod as a sacrifice in your honor!"

Having let this go on much too long, Michael was now trying to break free, but something beyond simply Isis and Cain seemed to be holding him back. In an agony of a need to protect, he started crying out, "*Gabriela!*"

Ignoring him, Ares started to dig the blade into Hephaestus' throat, some blood running down.

Hermes screamed.

"And I kill the man you left for me once!" Ares shrieked. He now appeared to be covered in the flames of war. "*Come to me!*"

For a moment, nothing happened, other than Michael's mad, useless struggles. He didn't know what held him back and didn't care, *needed* to get to Gabriela.

Then, to his surprise, Isis screamed out in ancient Egyptian, "Goddess of love! We struck a bargain! Appear before me *now!*"

The flames had reached Gabriela's feet, and Ares' blade dug into Hephaestus' throat, as the god of the forge let out a small gurgling sound.

And then all hell, finally, broke loose.

Chapter 32
Gabriela

For the first time in her life, Gabriela had been praying to The Lady fervently. Mostly, it wasn't for herself. She just feared all too much what Michael might do if she were truly harmed.

It didn't help that it was difficult to focus, as the flames were starting to singe her jeans, and she was afraid her legs were next. The ring he had given her when she had first met him—the one he had used to help break Poseidon's spells—seemed hot on her hands, and she wondered if the flames were going to burn her with it, too.

Just as she saw Michael so close to breaking free, however, just as the heat was starting to merge into pain, there was a flurry of movement off to her right. And then all the ghosts—who she hadn't noticed were missing—and Loviatar's marble lions came roaring in at once.

It took a moment to identify the ghosts as more than a simple, arctic wind which settled around the flames and froze them eerily in place. Several of the lions, too, started jumping up and down on them, which—being that they were marble and a good ton or two a piece—made the whole theater shake.

Ares' hounds had already run away, whimpering, and were now peering timidly around the front seats at the devastation.

Hades was shouting out, "No! Bad lions! Stop that!"

They didn't seem to listen. Several of them already had him on the ground.

A moment later, someone was behind her, untying her hands. While she had expected it to be Michael, she soon saw the face and what seemed to be the very solid form of the attractive male, Asian ghost.

Once she was freed and the flames had been solidly lion-quashed, he looked at her worriedly.

"Are you harmed? I'm sorry we got here so late. It took some time to find where Loviatar had hidden her friends."

She couldn't quite tell what had happened to poor Hephaestus, who had been just as endangered as she was, as she was quickly surrounded on every side by ghosts, who worriedly reached out for her and tried to help her off the pyre. Since they were all fairly insubstantial, it didn't go anywhere, although somehow the now-solid ghost's efforts did. As her knees had gone a bit weak, Gabriela was thankful.

The ghosts murmured a cloud of sympathetic things at her, including:

"The brute!"

"Oh, your pants are ruined. How unseemly!"

"How dare he treat a lady that way!"

Generally, the dead's feelings seemed to be turned very much against the god of war.

Even the Lady in Red was standing beside Poseidon, looking dismissive. "This lady's not for burning," she noted.

Poseidon took a swipe at her, but, since she was a ghost, she didn't even notice.

Once she was off the pyre, Gabriela saw that at least twelve of the marble lions had pounced Ares. Some were trampling, others biting, a few roaring in victory. Had he been mortal, he would have been dead. As it was, he was just extremely inconvenienced.

Loviatar was goading them on. "That's it, my loves! Get the bastard!"

Several of the other lions stood blocking Poseidon from coming any closer, a few still on top of Hades. Cerberus was barking excitedly and jumping up and down like a giant, three-headed chihuahua.

Thankfully, Gabriela noticed Hephaestus sitting in one of the theater chairs, his neck not showing any sign of being slit. Apparently, he had survived, as well.

He was pretty much petting Hermes' head, the messenger god weeping in his lap.

"Ssh, my love," Hephaestus soothed. "He hasn't harmed me."

It was a tender scene which explained several things to Gabriela at once.

Still, she didn't get much time to think them over, as the semi-solid ghost led her to Michael who not only clasped her to him tightly but surrounded them both in a kind of burning flame.

Michael, it's all right. My pants . . . well, Thorschild's pants. Really, I'm going to go through that woman's whole wardrobe . . . are singed, but I'm fine.

He said and thought nothing, but she still felt in him the dark need to destroy everyone who had been even remotely responsible for trying to harm her.

I'm OKAY, Michael, she pressed. *Look inside me and see how little I want you to start behaving like Ares.*

The idea clearly shocked him so badly that he pulled back from her and said out loud, "You think I'm like him?"

Her fingers stroked soothingly over his cheek. "I think that anger goes nowhere good." She kissed him and felt his whole body shudder.

At that moment, she also realized the now-solid ghost was still standing beside her, as though waiting to see whether they were yet safe from Michael's wrath.

She went back to talking between themselves. *I think you should remember that there are many more lives at stake here than mine.*

It took a second, but he finally smiled. *Pull the angel card on me, willya?*

Laughing, she kissed him softly again. *You did say you were fine with me keeping you in line.*

As much as she liked his formality, she found she enjoyed the everyday Michael, too.

One part of this had been brought to an end, then, but it was really only Loviatar's lions which was keeping it from restarting. Well, that and the fact that Ares had to keep rehealing himself from lion stomps.

Hades was staring at Loviatar accusingly. "How could you use these lions against me? I was the one who introduced you to them in Halicarnassus."

"I'm aware, lover," Loviatar smiled. "And I loved getting freaky in a tomb."

Michael and Gabriela looked at each other but said nothing.

"But they were all so sad and broken."

Looking down lovingly at several of the stone creatures, as they nuzzled around her, even displacing a whining Cerberus, she finally placed the stuffed minotaur she had worn on her shoulders all this time into a chair of its own and petted them.

"I always wanted to liberate them, even more when they were imprisoned in that museum, and make them whole again."

I'm a little surprised she hasn't hacked someone's head off, Gabriela pointed out.

Thankfully, Michael seemed to be calming. *Perhaps seeing her pets do it for her is enough.*

There was still the issue of three rogue gods to deal with, of course, and none of the prisoners in the large birdcages had been set free. And that didn't even go into the ones in the compound or in Hades' world. Nothing had been resolved, then, just a sacrifice or two interrupted.

They heard Isis speak. "This isn't over."

Looking to her, they saw her nod toward the stage.

"Not till the lady you've all been courting has her say."

A formidable-looking woman in a pink business suit and matching heels stood on the stage, smoke rising from her. Her ice blonde hair was up in a perfectly-upswept bun, and her nails matched the pink of her outfit perfectly.

Glaring at each of the gods who had started this bet in turn, she was shaking with fury, her blue eyes burning. Her voice was surprisingly louder than anyone might expect from someone wearing so much pink.

"I was in a meeting!"

Gabriela noticed behind the angry woman another, very human-looking woman with long, wavy brown hair, holding a tablet and staring around wonderingly, seeming like she might faint.

The goddess was clearly fuming, but there were weirdly . . .

Are those rose petals showering from her? Gabriela wondered.

Michael was much calmer, but she wasn't certain if it weren't a little from shock. *I suppose a goddess of love is only allowed to show so much anger.*

No one had seemed to give Aphrodite this note, as she stomped to the front of the stage, rose petals piling up around her. "Just what have you *idiots* done *now*?!"

Chapter 33
Michael

Michael had seen many things in his long, angelic life. A pissed-off goddess of love in a pink business suit wasn't one of them.

Staring as much as everyone else, and still holding Gabriela close to his side in case any of these misbegotten gods got any ideas, he watched Hades entreating her, both his arms raised. The lions had at least let him get up to his knees, which was a good position to plead from. "Oh, great goddess of love . . ."

Michael wondered for a moment whether he'd spoken first in hopes of getting in before his competitors or because he'd been the only one who hadn't been involved with her previously and didn't know her temper.

"I bring thee . . ."

"Oh, can it, kidnapper. You're just as bad as these two."

Kidnapper? Gabriela wondered.

Ever heard of Persephone? Pomegranates? The Greek mythological origin of summer and winter?

She just looked at him, and he didn't even need her to say it this time.

Right. I'll explain later.

They continued watching the show, even if he still held her close in case anyone got any ideas.

Aphrodite leaped off the stage in a truly inhuman way, landing neatly on her very high heels without any obvious effort, and started to march toward the three gods. Loviatar had apparently allowed her stone lions to let Ares stand up but continued to guard him. For once, he looked both uncertain and disheveled.

One step toward the threesome, though, Ares' dogs stopped cowering and started to attack, just as Hades, clearly lost, complained, "Kidnapper? Have I taken someone of yours?"

Aphrodite let out a grunt of irritation and, ignoring Hades for the moment, pointed at the dogs of war.

First, they stopped their attack, then whined, then looked at each other, then . . .

"Oh dear," one of the primmer ghosts—Margo, maybe?—said, turning away.

Ares stood aghast. "Throat Ripper! Scrotum Biter! Stop that!"

Scrotum Biter? Gabriela wondered.

I suppose it's just the other end of the spectrum from "Tweetie Pie."

Clearly annoyed, Ares looked at her, as his dogs continued . . . well, getting to know one another *much* better. "They're both male, you realize."

Aphrodite held up her hands in faux shock, her voice mocking.

"Oh no! A same sex relationship! What an unheard of novelty! The ancient Spartans who worshiped you would be soooo shocked!"

Her pointed stare said more than any history lesson in attitudes toward extremely intimate male bonding could.

She rolled her eyes. "And it's the 21st century already. Get over it! And you . . ."

Refocusing on Hades, her gaze narrowed.

"*How* many centuries did you keep poor Persephone prisoner?"

Her hand rose before he spoke again.

"Yes, I know where she is, and *no, absolutely not*, you are *never* going to find her."

Hades' mouth hung open, as he tried to form words but was clearly too shocked to begin.

Aphrodite held up her hand again, gesturing imperiously. "*Consuela!*"

The shivering woman on the stage seemed to shake off some of her fear at hearing her name, her head rising.

"To me, please!"

The goddess, who in truth was rather plus sized, waited, as the rather timid-looking woman came up to the front of the stage where her employer had leaped off, pondered it, and then looked up piteously.

Gary the ghost, who was now standing next to Michael, although he didn't remember him getting there, whispered, "I'd go help her, but it looks like she might faint if she gets another shock, and some people aren't ready for ghosts."

Michael nodded.

Isis took pity on her, giving her directions through the wings to the stairs.

Aphrodite waited until her assistant was with her again. "Take all this down, Consuela. I want a full transcript."

Somehow the order seemed to put Consuela's mind back in place. "Yes, Ma'am." She soon stood with thumbs ready over the keyboard of her tablet.

"Now. You lot."

Aphrodite glared at them, then looked behind them to the remains of the pyre as well as the stake which had held Hephaestus.

"What moron thing have you been doing *this* time?"

Suddenly, the three bragging gods seemed a whole lot less ready to talk, staring determinedly at their feet.

"How about you, love?" Aphrodite glanced over to Isis. "Can you explain what they're too cowardly to?"

"*Coward?*" Ares roared.

"Do shut up, Ares, dear. There's a good boy." Aphrodite didn't even look at him.

Ares went back to staring at his shoes. They and his armor seemed to have lost their spikiness.

Half-smiling, Isis pointed at each god in turn, starting with Ares. "Kidnapping, theft, looting, coercion. Probably all of that for Hades, too, though I don't know all the details there."

The god of the underworld stared innocently at the ceiling.

Eyes flaring, Isis pointed at Poseidon. "All of that, plus rape and murder."

Reaching out, she put her hand on Gabriela's arm, although she had to reach past Michael to do it.

"This is the daughter of that rape, whom he was more than happy to try to murder, as well."

Letting off an angry glow, she took Gabriela's hand.

"She's also the great-great-great-great-gr—. . ."

The "greats" went on for sometime. Michael sort of lost track.

". . .—great-grandaughter of one of my favorite priestesses and therefore under my care."

Gabriela blinked. "I am?"

"She is?" Michael chorused with her.

News to me, she mused.

Isis smiled at her. "Yes, dear. Though your mother, even if she weren't under compulsions so strong she can't remember her own name, has no idea." Rolling her eyes slightly, she sighed. "It's the trouble with this country. Everyone's from so many different places, they have absolutely no idea of their pasts."

Michael wasn't certain whether this was a problem or not but was aware that there were whole business plans which depended on this fact. It wasn't obvious just looking at Gabriela, either, but there had obviously been a few generations in Ireland to cover up some of this heritage.

Their attention was redrawn to Aphrodite, who was quite literally smoking by this point. Stepping up to Poseidon, she gave him a slap so furious that he fell over slightly and had to catch himself against a theater chair. Even the amorous dogs stopped . . . getting to know one another better, sat down, and stared.

"I thought Ares was a bastard," Aphrodite growled. "But you have really gone some, mister."

"But Aphrodite," Ares tried to reason with her. "Back in the day . . ."

"Back in the day, there were slaves and masters in every aspect of life, from the gods to the peasants. Back in the day, there was a democracy that only a very small percentage of half the population got to vote in."

She growled a little.

"Back in the day *sucked*."

"I didn't even mention the private army Poseidon created under compulsions so strong they can't think a single personal thought," Isis continued.

Aphrodite let out something like a scream and slapped each of the gods in turn. They didn't stop her but all looked appalled, Hades especially.

"What did *I* do?" he wondered.

"You were part of this bet, weren't you? Of course it was a bet!" She didn't let him answer. "It's *always* a bet with you lot."

Not letting anyone tell her any more, Aphrodite moved in on the men.

"It's all pretty damn clear. You've been stealing things to try to impress me. Whether you want me or what I can do for you, who knows and who cares? Well, except for Hades."

She swept her hand at him dismissively.

"I know he did this to try to get Persephone back, but that ain't happening."

The growl was low in her throat.

"The 'bride by kidnap and conquest' days are *over*, boys. Wake up and smell the Me Too Movement."

It was a bit of a mixed metaphor, left all the gods staring at each other out of the corner of their eyes, but they said nothing. Behind Aphrodite, Consuela two-thumb typed furiously.

Curious, Michael leaned in to Isis. "How do you know each other?"

"Roman conquest. One of her favorite priestesses . . ." She waved it off. "Anyway, I did her a favor she promised to return one day."

Either Aphrodite didn't hear this or didn't care.

"Now, here's what you're going to do. You're going to let all your prisoners go, including those I see in the cages up there. For any who need some help, you'll provide them with any money or transport they require, without any strings attached. As to all the things you stole, you—no one else—will put them back where they were, as they were. Or, if they were stolen from a thief, you'll return them to their rightful owners."

Aphrodite's smile was wrathful.

"Figuring out the paper trail alone is gonna be *hell*."

The gods were not taking this well.

"Aphrodite, please," Ares pleaded for them, although he didn't get too close, since the stone lions were sitting around watching him curiously and blocking his path to the goddess. "We used to have something."

Aphrodite rolled her eyes. "Yep. It was called lust and daddy issues. I've moved on, boys. Instead of being the patron goddess of prostitutes, now I'm the CEO in charge of a charity which does its best to rescue them from that life and get them counseling, education, and jobs. Instead of the flirty goddess who never met a penis she didn't like, I've realized that most of you were pretty terrible lovers. Selfish . . ."

She pointed to Ares.

". . . and boring."

The finger went to Poseidon.

"I have no *idea* how I put up with you for so long."

"She didn't mention Hephaestus," Hades whispered out of the corner of his mouth, although Michael wasn't certain whether he were goading the other gods or just curious.

Aphrodite smiled over at her former husband.

"Aw, Phaestus, baby. I'm glad to see they didn't hurt you."

She smiled sweetly at Hermes, too.

"And I'm glad to see that you and Hermie finally got together."

"The pink diamonds suit you," Hephaestus smiled.

Obviously nostalgic, Aphrodite looked misty-eyed.

"No one else could ever make jewelry for me like you do. Anyway . . ."

Looking back to the gods who had tried to summon her, she glowered.

"Just in case you didn't get it, 'cause you're all kinda dense, duh! I never slept with Hephaestus. He was gay."

Shrugging, she looked bored.

"I was just his beard."

It does explain why she ran off with every other god in town, Gabriela put in. *Well, sorta. In a bad taste kind of way.*

Something about this made the scales fall from Michael's eyes. *Gabriela . . . Edgar . . .*

Yep. Gayer than a Diana Ross-impersonating drag queen singing Judy Garland at a party for Elton John's birthday, she confirmed. *He and Gerald have been in love for YEARS.*

Michael thought about this, and especially about the man trying to slit his beloved Gabriela's throat.

That still doesn't forgive him.

Eh, Gabriela shrugged. *Let's see what he's like once the compulsions are off. There're some things I did I can't really be forgiven for, as well.*

He wanted to argue against this, but watching Aphrodite put the gods in their place was rather hypnotic.

"It's time all of you went back to wasting your time in some way which doesn't involve hurting others."

She looked Poseidon over.

"When was the last time you were even *in* the sea?"

Poseidon grimaced. "Do you have any idea how dirty the oceans are nowadays? I'd rather swim in sewage."

Aphrodite appeared to be pondering arranging just that.

"Besides, the deserts and mountains are just the places oceans have been thousands of years ago. I like them better now."

The goddess of love glared at him. "So you decided to turn your power over the sea into a power over water. And since humans are around 50 percent water . . ."

Poseidon's grin was absolutely evil. "It makes them *very* easy to control."

"Okay, I think I'm going to need reenforcements for this one . . ." Aphrodite's eyes narrowed.

Suddenly, the idea came to Michael. "Where's Uriel?"

Everyone around him stared, letting him know that they too had entirely lost track of the angel, once the fire and swords had started.

"Here I am!" the angel announced.

He was now fully male, except for red nails and lipstick and his long silver hair back in a flirty, cheerleader-style ponytail. He was also wearing nothing but a silver thong.

"I brought a guest!"

A shadow started to come into view behind him.

Michael gasped. "The Lady." His eyes were wide. "She's finally here."

Chapter 34
Gabriela

Gabriela braced herself for this immense meeting—or reunion . . . or whatever.

How does one act when meeting god? she wondered, but Michael was too agog to answer.

Uriel walked down the aisle in high—if slightly camp—dignity, and Gabriela saw the shadow moving closer. She had no idea what to expect. Would she be rather pretty and feminine like Aphrodite? Or stately and beautiful like Isis? Or maybe wrathful like Loviatar?

Eyes wide, she waited.

A moment later, a grumpy little old lady wandered down the aisle. She was slightly dumpy, honestly, but clearly sharp, kind of like a grand-mother who spent all her time keeping the idiot men of her family in line.

"I heard that, Gabriel!" the old lady pointed at the ceiling, referring to Gabriela by her old name. "I'll thank you *not* to think of me as 'dumpy.'"

Gabriela swallowed. *Oops.*

"Yes, my lady," she said, bowing.

It never did to piss off a supreme being, although her thoughts did go on without her. *Okay, maybe a little old JEWISH grandmother.*

The Lady didn't seem to object to that.

Behind her filed in several dozen other people or beings or whatev-er they might be. All bets were off, these days.

The one Gabriela noticed most was a tall, formidable honey blonde woman in a light gray pantsuit and heels. She somehow commanded the rest of the group, including the auburn-colored wolf and the tall, attractive, black-haired man who walked beside her. Her hand was on the wolf in a manner which looked more like love than control.

The Lady waved a hand, and all the cages in the balcony opened. One more wave, and dozens of surprised people appeared in some of the theater chairs on the right near the stage, including the young British vampire they'd met in Niagara Falls, still in Nosferatu costume and makeup.

With one more wave, all of the people Gabriela had grown up with in the compound filled a section on the opposite side near the back. Many of them still had guns.

Oh crap, she thought.

But with another wave, the guns turned into flowers. That really pissed a lot of them off.

All the ones who'd just appeared looked confused, and the ones from the compound looked murderous. Gabriela saw the blonde woman gesture, and her wolf and man took off in separate directions, along with several other new arrivals, to try to quell any uprisings.

This was a little easier with the beings Hades had apparently trapped. As far as the compound folk went . . .

Lady . . . Gabriela warned, since the woman could apparently hear her thoughts.

The Lady turned just as Poseidon was raising his hand.

"No, I don't think so."

Reaching out toward the sparkles—or clair-lumes or whatever—that the sea god had put forth, The Lady drew them to her somehow and then pulled and kept pulling.

Its effects were rather terrifying.

Not just Poseidon but everyone from the compound started screaming. The more The Lady pulled what seemed to be miles of thick, oil-like ropes of . . . well, Gabriela assumed it was magic . . . out of them, the more they jerked and screamed.

Should we help her or them or somebody? Gabriela asked. The Lady looked much too fragile to be fighting such obvious power, although she seemed more annoyed than strained.

We may have to eventually to get rid of all those lume-noirs, but let her finish first.

Lume-noirs? Gabriela blinked. Her life wasn't becoming any more normal.

Sort of dark magic.

There was a pause, before Michael continued.

If we stay on earth after this, I may need to give you basic magic lessons.

Lessons would be good. She wasn't any less confused.

Finally, the magic or curse or lume-noirs or whatever lay in a giant heap of evil at The Lady's feet.

"Ugh. It's hard to tell anymore whose is whose."

She shook her head, looking back to Poseidon who was now sitting on the ground and looking utterly spent and sad. The russet wolf growled warningly at him and the other gods, the stone lions having made room for him.

"When you set out to do something evil, you don't do it halfway, do you, ocean boy?"

"It was just a bet," he argued weakly.

"Just a bet? Just a *bet?!*"

The Lady was clearly furious, the room darkening as though a storm were passing through.

Uh oh, Michael said in her head.

What? Gabriela wondered.

Ever heard of Noah and the Ark?

Gabriela nodded.

It's a good reminder of why you DON'T make The Lady angry.

This could have gone very badly, but the blonde woman came up very close, putting her hand on her shoulder.

"Lady," she murmured softly. "We still have people to help."

Gabriela decided she must be a goddess. No human could have done that and lived.

"Eh?" The Lady looked at her, and a moment later, the darkness went away. "Okay, fine. But we need to see this through."

There were about a hundred things happening at once now, making it a little hard to follow.

Ares' prisoners had been released, some being helped down the stairs from the balcony to the ones who'd lost them, some flying or making their way down on their own. For a moment, Gabriela thought she saw the spokesman mummy from the museum—*Was it Callahan?*—helping someone who was presumably Osiris down to Isis, but, with every step, the god became more sturdy, so the mummy turned back to help others.

Once he was down to the theater level, Isis ran to him like a giddy schoolgirl, and he caught her in his arms, twirling her around and around.

The attractive dark-haired man brought the two-headed axe Loviatar had been staring at, trying very hard to keep it from hacking at anybody, including himself.

Loviatar took it in her arms, as it vibrated, apparently happily, and rubbed her face against its hilt. "My little pörröinen pupu. I missed you."

Michael blinked. *Did she just call her axe "little fluffy bunny"?*

I'm not the one who can speak Finnish, angel. Gabriela smiled at him, although she did ponder the merits of him casting another spell or blessing or whatever so she could understand, like he had at the museum.

Reunions happened all over.

Hastrman, who still looked eerily like an animated scarecrow, grabbed up a half-giggling, half-crying little girl who was like a mini scarecrow herself and twirled her around like Osiris had with Isis. A moment later, they were joined by a woman with dyed-black hair who was clearly very deep into goth. Everything she wore was either black and lacy or bat shaped. Hastrman's reunion with her was more passionate but not less excited.

While all this happened, Gabriela's old compound buddies were not as happy. Some were crying. Some were laughing hysterically. A few had fainted, and one or two had clearly gone mad.

Among the latter was Father Friar. Edgar was at his side, trying to get the man to look at him, but he seemed to have become catatonic. Gerald had a hand on Edgar's shoulder tenderly.

To her surprise, Edgar called out to her. "Gabriela, please. I don't know what to do for him."

Uncertain herself, she still went to him. When Michael caught her arm, she just smiled and took his hand, bringing him with her.

"Do you remember everything?" she wondered.

Edgar's eyes were not the mean little points they had been most of the time she'd known him. It had only been when he was talking about comics that he'd seemed fairly human, so she'd definitely encouraged his fixation.

Now, he looked sad and scared and confused. Watching the various events around him, he sighed. "They're not dangerous, are they? They're just living their lives, like us."

"*Have* we been living, Edgar?"

Looking back to first her, then Michael, he nodded.

"I get your point."

Glancing at his father sadly, he sighed.

"He's not ever going to wake up from this, is he?"

"Do you want him to? Do you think he can ever accept a world where you're not torturing someone?"

She looked over to Gerald with a small smile.

"Or one where you're deeply in love with your best friend?"

The pair of them blushed, especially as the rest of the compound turned to stare at them. But only one or two moved away. Most weren't as unaccepting as Father Friar. And the rest had problems of their own.

One of these was Gabriela's mother.

Isis and Osiris had stopped reuniting and were now hand-in-hand in front of her. Although clearly still confused, her eyes wide, she got down on her knees.

"Lady," she whispered, as something from a distant past triggered inside her already fractured mind.

Isis' hand ran tenderly over the woman's face. "It's all right, Isabelle. We're going to see that you're comfortable now."

Sadly, Gabriela could see that something in her mother was just . . . broken.

The Lady caught Gabriela's eye, gesturing down at the oily pile of evil magic at her feet. Even the rainbows which shone off it in the lights were not anything holy.

"Most of these came out of her. Poseidon had her so deeply controlled I don't know that she'll ever manage to be normal."

Michael put his arm around Gabriela. *I'm sorry, my love.*

Saddened but accepting, she put her head on his shoulder.

Don't be. I never really knew her anyway.

Although even she knew that this didn't make it any better.

To her surprise, Edgar looked at Gerald once, who nodded. Then, hand in hand, he moved past his father and came to her.

"If you'd like, we can look after her," he told Isis and Gabriela.

"Along with your father?" she wondered, looking past him.

"No," Edgar sighed, holding Gerald's hand tightly. "He needs something I can't give him."

Gabriela just blinked, but Michael filled in the rest. "Forgiveness."

Edgar nodded. "He beat my mother before I was born. He beat me after I was born. If he comes back to himself, he'll just hurt the first person he sees."

Looking them all over, his eyes were begging.

"I'll need help putting him somewhere he won't harm anyone, but there's nothing I can do for him besides that."

Isis seemed to be considering this offer. Finally, she took Edgar's face in her hand and stared deeply into his eyes. When she nodded a "Fine," it seemed to be resigned. "But I will come and check that you are treating her well."

It was somehow only then that Gabriela noticed his hand was still bandaged, which made sense since that scene at the compound had only been a couple of days ago—which was kind of hard to believe, considering all she'd been through.

"Are you going to be okay?"

Seeming to pick up her meaning, he smiled at her, waving it a bit.

"It's the least I deserve for that and a million other things."

He was about to move closer to her, but Michael's look clearly told him not to.

Sighing, he went on. "I'm sorry, Gabriela. For all of it."

Glancing back at the man he loved, he smiled.

"I'm sorry to both of you."

Don't you dare say you're sorry, as well, Michael warned her. *You've done NOTHING to apologize for.*

Five murders, Michael. I ended five innocent lives for NOTHING.

Sighing, he nodded toward the black oil-looking stuff.

No, THAT killed five innocents. That and Poseidon's tricks.

Gabriela wanted to say that, if that was true for her, it was also true for Edgar. The man seemed so at peace now, holding Gerald's hand. There really wasn't a trace of the knife-cleaning obsessive she'd been forcibly married off to.

Still, as Michael nodded at Edgar in partial acceptance before turning her away, she saw his point. She believed that the man would tend the woman who had given birth to her and even suspected that he would do it out of kindness, but he had also tried to kill her. She still didn't know if she would have done the same in reverse, but she didn't want to find out.

The Lady broke up wherever her thoughts were going, yelling out, "Uriel!"

The angel appeared, still naked but for his wings and a silver thong. Gabriela had to admit that he looked really good like that, and the nail polish and lipstick weren't detracting from it.

"My lady," he nodded.

"Take care of Poseidon's evil, will you?" She gestured at the pile of goo.

"Of course, my Lady." Moving his hand in a circle over the pile, he began to envelope it in a ball of rainbow light.

Gabriela and Michael moved over to her, as the formidable blonde goddess who'd entered with her returned as well to speak to her. "Between Marco, Evan, and Carrie, I think I've got everything I need for the report. But we've still got a few questions of what to do with people that need answering."

The Lady sighed. "Aren't there always?"

Forgotten but comfortable just being close to Michael, who had his arm around her, Gabriela noted, *Those are three names I don't know.*

Well, we never did learn Thorschild and Cain's real names. Could be them. Could be someone else.

Gabriela supposed he was right. Thorschild and Cain were now chatting with one of the people who'd come in with the blonde goddess. She looked human, a petite woman with red hair, but when she reached up to scratch her nose, her hand turned into a pointed branch for a second and then turned back.

Gabriela didn't even ask, watching The Lady turn away, till Uriel got her attention.

"Um, Lady?"

The older woman turned back.

"You haven't really said anything about . . ." Uriel gestured down to his new look.

The Lady shrugged. "Meh."

She slapped him playfully on the chest, and he grinned.

"You be you." Turning away, she had one hand in the air. "*Whomever* that turns out to be."

Uriel grinned at the approval and nodded at Gabriela and Michael.

"Bye, guys. See ya next mission, okay?"

Then he picked up his ball of goo and was gone.

I guess he WAS always on a mission, Gabriela noted.

Michael shrugged. *Angels often are.*

This didn't make the question of whether she and Michael would be allowed to stay together any easier, and he clearly felt it as well.

Standing where the three gods' fates were now being debated, they continued to watch. Ares was still looking bruised from his run-in with the stone lions. Hades seemed to have more a bruised ego than anything else. Poseidon looked . . .

Diminished, Michael explained. *It will take him at least a couple of hundred years to rebuild the power he had before.*

Any way we can do the same to Ares? she wondered.

Not while there are still wars and hate to feed him, no. As Poseidon said, the oceans are increasingly poisoned, so he can't draw strength from them alone, and, as he's done nothing to protect them, none of the sea creatures are likely to be on his side.

Sighing, she listened to The Lady.

"You three have acted like dangerous morons for the last time."

Looking up to Aphrodite, she raised an eyebrow.

"I'm guessing you don't want any of them."

"Ick, no. But I do want them to clean up their mess."

Behind her, Consuela continued to type.

"Then . . ."

Wherever it was going, she was interrupted by Loviatar. "Wait!"

She had at least twenty of the stone lions trailing behind her, one of them carrying her beloved "fluffy bunny" in his mouth. Cerberus nuzzled at her side and tried not to let his feet get stepped on.

"I have no interest in the others but an idea for Hades."

She smiled evilly.

"Let me have him. I'll make sure he does his part of the clean up."

"You realize he did all this just to try to find the woman he kidnapped millennia ago and reimprison her," The Lady pointed out.

"Of course. It's the fact that he's a scoundrel that I like."

Her grin grew.

"And it will make punishing him all the more interesting."

The Lady gave another "meh!" face. "Seems as good a fate for him as any. He's yours."

As nobody spoke up to defend him, Hades sagged, knowing defeat when he saw it.

"C'mon, lover," she chucked him under the chin. "If you're very good, I might bring back the wildebeests."

They were about to turn away, Hades now looking speculative, when Loviatar returned to Gabriela momentarily.

"You are too good a girl, but I approve of you, nonetheless. Here."

She held out the stuffed minotaur, presenting it to her.

"As a keepsake. If you need lessons in bladed weapons, look me up."

Her grin grew.

"And if you ever have need of someone to help in battle, *please* give me a call."

"Will do," Gabriela smiled. She held the stuffed animal closely.

Only when the goddess had left with her new plaything and her many animal companions did Gabriela's eyes widen. Reaching in her pocket, she found the small, black cat she'd won at the arcade, too. Thankfully, it hadn't been damaged by the fire. Still, as everyone including the new blonde goddess was staring at her, she stuck it back in her pocket.

She could tell Michael was trying not to laugh. *ARE you planning on calling her?*

If I'm ever looking for someone to help me cut an army in two? Absolutely!

He looked at her.

But, yes, I hope that won't happen.

The blonde goddess looked a little amused, pointing at the two remaining recalcitrant gods, and refocused on The Lady. "What about these two?"

There was no answer, as they were interrupted by the arrival of a man with blue skin. Well, maybe a man. There was a beard, anyway—as well as a large belly and breasts.

"Dita!" he shouted to Aphrodite. "Are you okay? I got a call that you disappeared."

Gabriela just blinked.

No, you haven't gone mad, my dear, Michael told her. *Gods, like humans, come in all forms. Especially in ancient Egypt.*

She supposed this was true when Isis and Osiris came up, still hand-in-hand, leaving Edgar and Gerald to try to help Gabriela's mother up and get her going.

"Hapi!" Isis smiled. "I haven't seen you in a century or two. How's the Nile doing? Where have you been?"

"Meh, it's still there. And I've been here and there. You know." Hapi shrugged. "One minute, starting an ecological group to look after rivers. The next, trying to stop some dam which will all but kill another ancient waterway. The usual."

Pulling himself back from his old, godly companions, he looked at the two men near Aphrodite and frowned.

"These two idiots again? How hard is it to learn that no means no, fellas?"

"Don't worry. They didn't get anywhere with me." Aphrodite waved the thought away. "Still . . ."

She looked around at the remaining group of sad supernaturals Hades had drawn together.

"I've got some newly undead I need to deal with."

Pointing at the remaining compound people, she sighed.

"And I don't even want to *talk* about what Poseidon's been up to." She shook her head. "We're going to need to hire a *lot* more counselors."

"That can be arranged," he smiled.

"Taken up with a love goddess, huh?" Osiris wondered.

"Eh, you know how it is." Hapi shrugged. "We flirted back during the Roman conquest, but she was still . . ." He looked at her apologetically.

"Ech! Don't even!" Aphrodite held up her hand. "I was all 'ooo, Ares, what a big army you've got!'"

Her voice had gone all squeaky with that, and she rolled her eyes.

"Like I said, daddy issues suuuuuuck."

"How many U's in 'suck'?" Consuela wondered, still typing.

"Six," the goddess answered, ignoring Ares' grin. "I just need to get done with a few things here, and I'll come back home."

Clearly trusting that she could handle it, Hapi nodded and went off to talk with Isis and Osiris.

"Anyway, back to the issue of these two," the blonde goddess started again. The red wolf sat by her feet, looking up at her intelligently and supportively.

"Sgt. Jaye . . ."

She was interrupted by Thorschild and Cain this time, Thorschild smiling at her.

"If there's nothing else you need us for . . ."

The goddess is a sergeant in something? Gabriela wondered. *Are there armies of gods?*

The Lady laughed, Gabriela having forgotten that she'd know her thoughts.

"Sgt. Jaye is a member of Supernatural Oversight." Her hand circled. "They handle problems like this."

"They're who we were working for," Thorschild confessed. "And I'm Carrie, by the way. That's Evan."

She shrugged.

"Those other names were getting old."

Gabriela just stared, as she wasn't really sure where to start.

Thors—. . . Carrie didn't let her get far anyway, giving her a card.

"That's my number, if you ever want to call. If you two need somewhere to stay, or you just want to visit your ocean friends again, feel free to give me a ring. We've got lots of room."

"Definitely," Ca—. . . Evan finished, smiling.

Sgt. Jaye—whom she still didn't know what she was goddess of except confidence—nodded to them.

"You've been a great help. But you better get Pyewacket home before he goes mad from lack of scratching certain gods' eyes out."

Pyewacket? Gabriela wondered.

Better than Tweetie Pie, Michael opined.

"Agreed. Marco's gonna hang around for a while just to be sure all the ghosts get to where they should be going, but he's nearby if you have any questions or need us," Evan smiled.

Then, nodding to them, Pye still growling at the gods, they left.

"Sorry to delay things further, but who's Marco?" Gabriela wondered.

The Lady looked at her. "See that tall one at the end of the stage?"

Following The Lady's directions, Gabriela saw the attractive, now fairly solid not-quite-a-ghost who had saved her from the flames.

"He's why all the ghosts followed you. They started chatting with him at the various theaters they'd been haunting and realized he could help them move on. Well . . ." She shrugged. "Mostly. Some just followed to have something to do."

On the stage, Marco was organizing the ranks of ghosts and helping them see the light to move into it. Gary, the terminally-confused ghost, as well as Margo and Eve, waved to them before heading off to their rewards.

Gabriela sighed. "I wanted to thank them for saving me."

"They know, dear. They know." The Lady patted her on the arm sympathetically.

"So . . ." There was a pause, as Michael clearly worked for the right name. ". . . Evan and Carrie have a ghost who lives with them too?"

Must be an interesting addition to the vampires, Carrie thought to him.

He nodded.

"Actually," Sgt. Jaye answered. "Marco was killed trying to save Evan from a demon when . . ."

She held up a hand.

"You know what? Never mind. Long story. Loooooooong story."

"How man—?" Consuela started. She still hadn't looked up from her tablet.

"Seven O's," Aphrodite answered automatically.

"Sorry, just one more thing. Supernatural Oversight hires goddesses?" Gabriela looked into Sgt. Jaye. "And, sorry, are you the goddess of wolves?"

The wolf near her feet gave Sgt. Jaye a look which clearly said, "Humans!"

"Actually, Henry's my partner, and he's a werewolf. But it's his . . ."

". . . time of the month," the dark-haired man she'd come in with finished.

The wolf Henry gave him a look which said volumes.

"Till the moon changes, we're stuck with Mr. Fuzzy Tail here." The dark-haired man gave the wolf a grin which said not only that he knew the wolf wouldn't bite him but also that he was actually kind of fond of him.

"Erick is a comedian who's bucking to get demoted," Sgt. Jaye said, rolling her eyes.

Erick apparently either wanted the demotion or enjoyed her annoyance.

"Sgt. Jaye here is the daughter of an incubus. He calls himself Solitary Brightness if that gives you any idea."

"Oy, him." The Lady rubbed her head. "He was *always* a randy one."

Even Michael winced. "He *was* a bit of a problem. Sorry," he shrugged to Sgt. Jaye.

But the detective just rolled her eyes. "*Tell* me about it."

"Anyway, to the real issue here . . ."

The Lady looked down at the two gods at her feet, drumming her fingers against her arm.

"I think I might know a way. The moon is lovely this time of year. Completely deserted. It's a good place to work on clearing up what they've done."

She grinned a grin which let Gabriela know that she did *not* want to know what a wrathful Lady looked like.

"Ever heard of a *No Exit* situation, boys?"

She pointed at them, and they started to float at her command. Ares struggled a bit, but The Lady was not listening.

"I'll leave a copy of Sartre with you so you can familiarize yourselves with the concept of irony."

She started to move away, leaving Michael to stare back at his partner.

"Um, my Lady?" he stopped her, and she looked curious. "Do you have another mission for us?"

"You just did it! What more do you want?"

Michael said nothing, he and Gabriela still waiting, barely breathing.

Coming back, she looked Michael in the eye.

"Did Ares incarnating you make you lose your memory, too? With the birth thing . . ."

She gestured at Gabriela.

". . . ehhhh, it's a small design flaw, the memory loss. But I didn't think with you . . ."

Gabriela could feel Michael's confusion. "But, I don't remember you giving me a mission to be here."

Her shrug was eloquent. "I left you the ring, didn't I? It kept both you and then Gabriela safe?"

Her look clearly said, *What more did you want?*

Gabriela could kind of hear the cogs turning in Michael's mind and filled them in. *It was the ring which kept you from coming to take me off the pyre, wasn't it?*

Something did, he agreed.

Given what Gabriela was starting to learn of The Lady, this made as much sense as anything. Clearly, certain things needed to happen, and she had left the object as a way to keep those events on course.

Michael gave in, moving on. "Um, okay. But what do you want us to do now?"

The shrug returned. "Love each other, of course. What else do I ever ask for?"

"Ummmm . . ." Gabriela started.

"How man—?" Consuela asked.

"Four M's," Aphrodite answered, watching interestedly.

The Lady just stared at them. "Which part of 'be happy' can't you understand?"

Michael and Gabriela just stared at each other.

"Look," The Lady sighed, Ares and Poseidon still floating and squirming behind her. "I let Gabriel be incarnated knowing I was going to let you go after him. You two have been dancing around each other for millennia now!" she nearly yelled, before they could speak. "I got tired of watching. I figured however Gabriel got born, you two could still have fun."

Both a little stunned, they said nothing.

"Go!" she gestured. "Have a baby. Or two. Or none! What do I care? You can both be men, women, whatever!"

She was still gesturing, as she walked up the aisle with her disgruntled gods in tow.

"Or do Uriel's thing and switch off! Just take a century or two and go have some fun. Always work, work, work with you two. No sense of joy. I ask you, what did I make angels for if none of them understands . . ."

The grumbling continued until she was well into the lobby and they couldn't hear her anymore.

It was an idea which made both of them smile.

Um, if it's all right with you . . . Gabriela started.

Don't worry. I'll keep the dangly bits, he assured her. *I like your form, too.*

Epilogue

About a year after the gaming gods had been dealt with, Gabriela was in Evan's world, speeding through the water on the back of her best dolphin friend with Carrie riding another dolphin beside her. Michael and Evan sat on the beach, smiling at them.

Carrie had an infectious kind of giggle when she was really happy which just made Gabriela want to hug her. When Evan was nearby to hear it, the look of love he would give would nearly change the entire atmosphere to sparkling pink lights. Occasionally, if they were around Aphrodite, it actually did.

"I still feel a little bad for riding a dolphin I don't know the name of," Carrie shouted over the winds which flew past them, warm and embracing.

"Sorry, it's too hard to translate," Gabriela shouted back.

While she could perfectly understand the dolphins' clicks and whistles, she couldn't imitate them at all.

Carrie's dolphin started talking, making Gabriela laugh.

"She does say you can call her, 'Dolphin Who Swims With the Gods', though."

"What's the name of the one you're riding?" Carrie wondered.

After a few long whistles, Gabriela translated. "She Who Shall Not Be Named."

They both laughed.

"I think she's been listening to Tatiana again."

While the dolphins and other sea creatures tended to get nervous if the vampires came in the water—their teeth being too much like sharks, according to the animals—they liked the vampiress enough that they'd cluster around to hear her talk. While Tatiana couldn't understand what they said in response, she enjoyed talking to them, and the dolphins would let her pet them, as well. Both the women had come out to find her talking to them at many a sunset. Since Billy knew she enjoyed it, he never interfered.

"Soooo . . ." Carrie started.

"Four O's," Gabriela broke in, making her laugh.

Aphrodite's ever-present secretary was a very nice woman, but her habits had become a bit of an in-joke. Also, she guessed what Carrie was working up the courage to ask.

". . . did you and Michael finally . . ." She trailed off delicately.

"If you're asking whether I'd make a virgin sacrifice anymore, the answer is no."

It was actually why they hadn't seen Carrie and Evan in six months, having been fairly caught up in each other.

"You really don't need to answer this," Carrie warned. "'Cause it's none of my damn business but . . ."

"Why'd we wait so long?" She sighed. "*Believe me.* I asked Michael that on a nightly basis."

Carrie just looked at her, obviously willing to leave it there but still curious, and Gabriela had to admit that the real answer was more complex.

"He said he wouldn't be convinced that he wasn't taking advantage of me, unless I truly knew him, and I couldn't know him fully after just three days, however eventful they were."

Gabriela petted She Who Shall Not Be Named and thought about it. It was actually kind of nice to have a friend to complain to, in hindsight.

"I tried to point out that he was quite literally in my thoughts, so I wasn't hiding anything, even if I couldn't remember our time together as angels, but he was adamant. Still . . ."

She smiled.

"... he took me around the world, told me about adventures we'd had in various places, and let me experience lots of things I have no memory of seeing before."

Carrie listened silently.

"We went to visit Isis and Osiris in Egypt, as well as Aphrodite and Hapi in New York."

Or an apartment which started in Manhattan, anyway, and then went into an alternate dimension.

"Did you know that Aphrodite has adopted Ares' dogs, although she now calls them Stud Muffin and Perky Tail?"

Carrie laughed. "Sounds about right."

"We even stopped in on Loviatar," Gabriela went on. "... who's now somewhere near the Arctic circle in Finland." Staring off into the memory, she smiled. "The Northern Lights there are unbelievably beautiful."

Clearly, there was something about the way she sighed which tipped her friend off.

"Was it the Northern Lights which did it?"

Gabriela laughed. "Yeah."

Flashing an embarrassed look to Carrie, she tried not to blush, changing the subject a little.

"Loviatar offered to let us stay, but she's keeping Hades in a really complicated dungeon thing in an old castle, and it's a little too weird for both of us, no matter how much Hades seems to like it. Plus, her stone lions have colonized every inch of the grounds, so you have to be really careful walking around."

Carrie seemed ready to let it go at that but did ask one more thing.

"Are you happy?"

"Yeah," Gabriela sighed, replete. "I sort of feel like I've gotten my soul back."

And Michael did, too, she knew.

Carrie smiled at her. "Yeah, I know what you mean. Oh, look, more dolphins!"

Gabriela barked out a laugh. "Okay, Carrie, ready for dolphin games?"

Carrie didn't look sure.

"Be nice to her, okay, everyone? Remember that Carrie is not a child of the sea."

Back on the beach, Michael and Evan watched the women, as the dolphins played with them.

One dolphin used its nose to push Gabriela straight up into the air, where she flew up and did several somersaults before diving back into the sea. Then, with a "Whoo-hoo!" Carrie was pushed up into the air sideways in a mummy-like pose before spinning around several times and splashing back in, still on her side. She was giggling the entire time.

Neither woman was insubstantial, so there was a bit of jiggling going on in several outlying regions, which their bathing suits did nothing to hide. Michael and Evan adored it.

Not only would anyone who tried fat shaming on his island have found themselves back in the real world with a thump, but Evan—it was clear—truly loved everything about Carrie and had no desire to make her change. Michael felt the same about his own beloved.

Both men were smiling.

"I appreciate you letting us visit." Michael stared out at Gabriela with love. "She really enjoys being with Carrie. And Tatiana and . . ."

". . . the fanged crew of the Jolly Roger?" Evan smiled. "They like having her around, too."

Seeming entirely at ease, Evan watched the women for a moment more.

"Carrie didn't get the chance to have friends when she was younger," he said sadly. "I cannot imagine ever denying her anything."

Michael looked at him, saw all the desperate love in Evan for his partner that Michael felt for his own. It was one of the reasons they understood each other so well.

"She loves you," Michael reminded him.

"I know," Evan smiled back to him, but it wasn't overconfidence. It was pure, and absolute, gratitude.

Michael knew entirely how he felt.

They were silent for a while longer, just watching the women play.

Finally, Evan broke into their thoughts.

"So, given that it's been six months since we saw you . . ." He let the statement hang much as Carrie had.

"Yes," Michael agreed simply. He knew the man wasn't asking for details, and not only would he not have given them, but he couldn't. It was sweet and arousing and made him feel both unworthy and unspeakably grateful all at the same time. There would have been no way to put it into words.

Evan just smiled. "I know."

And Michael thought, given the man and Carrie's relationship, that he probably did.

"So what are you going to do now?" Evan wondered. "You're always welcome to stay with us."

In some ways, Michael was tempted. Evan and Carrie were starting to create a family—not of their own biological children, or even of anyone else's children, but of people like them. The supernatural misfit, the lost, the abandoned were all starting to collect in Evan's world.

At first, they'd be scared or defensive. Then, between the visits of the odd, garrulous vampires and the love for everyone and everything Carrie just streamed out of herself like a lighthouse, as well as Evan's adoring devotion to her, they found their place. After a while, they'd be taught self-defense by Marco or go on a mission brought by Sgt. Jaye and Henry to go help others like them. It was somehow a perfect and happy little world.

"We've been discussing that," Michael answered finally. "We're thinking of offering our services to Aphrodite."

Evan looked at him curiously.

"She's helping the mundanes who need her, but she's been looking for someone who can help her track down more of the abused gods and demigods, like Persephone, someone who's capable of rescuing them from their mythological captors and helping them live a new life."

Evan's obvious and honest happiness in knowing that others were being helped out of their bad situations made it even more clear why Carrie treasured him. Even Michael could see that.

"That sounds like a wonderful thing to do." Evan smiled at him. "Let me know if you need our, or Supernatural Oversight's, help."

"I will," Michael assured him. The S.O. were pretty much made for keeping the extranormal in line.

There had been a lovely tree behind them this whole time, with multiple small branches all carrying what looked to be small red berries, although they didn't look very edible. In this case, Michael would never have thought of trying to eat them, anyway.

The reason for this became clear, as the tree started to reshape, eventually taking on the form of a young woman with red hair.

"Okay, I've had a lot of sun today. I'm full. I think I'll head inside and see what Tatiana's up to."

Rowan the tree nymph had been a bit of a surprise to Michael when he'd first met her, but she was apparently an old friend of Evan and Carrie's. Even her name was slightly doubt, as they often called her "Siobhan." Michael had decided they would explain if they wanted to and left it at that.

Evan raised a hand to wave her off.

"Do you think she was listening?" Michael wondered.

"Absolutely," Evan smiled. "Trees are very good at that."

Despite himself, Michael laughed. It wasn't as though he'd been saying anything secret, anyway—although he could now count on the vampires knowing his and Gabriela's plans. Given the whole scent thing, he suspected they already knew any possible sex secrets they might try to keep.

The two women they loved came into the shore at last, and Carrie said goodbye to the dolphin reluctantly.

"Why'd you stop?" Evan wondered. "You seemed to be having fun."

"I was," Carrie agreed. ". . . but you seemed to be signaling. Besides . . ." She looked at her hands. "I'm getting pruny."

Gabriela laughed, wringing out her wet, red braid over She Who Shall Not Be Named, as the dolphin clicked happily.

"What?" she asked when they looked at her. "She likes it. Who am I to say no?"

The dolphin let out a complicated series of whistles, rose up on her fin and danced backward for a moment or two, and then did a backflip. Gabriela just grinned.

"Complicated goodbye," Evan noted, one arm now around a wet Carrie.

Gabriela laughed. "She was just telling me that she can feel the baby moving."

Everyone stared.

"Don't ask me," she shrugged. "According to the dolphins, being pregnant is when you should be the most active. I don't judge."

Evan and Carrie smiled at one another and then headed indoors, leaving Gabriela to walk into Michael's open arms.

"I'm all wet," she noted.

"You're so happy you're glowing. Who am I to object to a little water?"

Kissing her head, he sighed, closing his eyes. *Have I told you how much I love you?*

Well, it was maybe four hours ago, so, no, you've been terribly silent on the subject.

He laughed. *I love you.*

And I you, my heart.

Utterly at peace, Gabriela held him closer. They had agreed to stay with Carrie and Evan for a couple of weeks, which, generally, she adored. Still . . .

Um, Michael?

His hands were running warmly over her back, his lips soft on her neck. *Mm?*

Just how soundproof is our bedroom here?

She felt his smile against her skin.

I'll take care of it, my love.

A moment later, they kissed and both understood what it was like to have a world all their own.

It continued until they heard Tatiana's voice from the house. "Guys! Twister!"

They pulled back, smiling at each other.

Either Rowan or Tatiana always wins, he noted. It was very hard to beat both a dryad and an undead ex-gymnast.

But it's so much fun to see how they'll win this time, she smiled.

Then, with some new sea lion friends barking happily from the side of the island, they went inside to enjoy the luxury of each other and their friends.

Want to Dive Further into the *More in Heaven and Earth* Universe?
If you'd like to see more of Carrie and Evan's story (and many more odd vampire encounters), then try out the quirkily-humorous new adult urban fantasy, *Cursed in White*, and see how they decided to start working for Supernatural Oversight:
https://storyoriginapp.com/universalbooklinks/
e87acb90-55a4-11ea-96d7-8b1d557e3d27

To learn more about Sgt. Marilyn Jaye, Henry, and Erick, try the quirkily-humorous paranormal mystery, *Unearthly Remains.* Join the immortal Marilyn, as she struggles with two murders and her unprecedented attraction to newly-turned werewolf, Henry: https://storyoriginapp.com/universalbooklinks/ae69fb58-66a1-11e9-9b5b-b3150184f041

or you can pick up its short story prequel, "Things to Do at the British Museum When You're Dead," to discover what it's like for her human partner, Erick, when he's just starting out with Supernatural Oversight. You'll also meet Callahan and find out more about the mummies and their champion: https://storyoriginapp.com/universalbooklinks/9b54fbf6-8fc5-11e9-8110-2fee6bca5160

If you'd like to read a quirkily-humorous, new adult urban fantasy, try *Protecting the Dead.* Come learn about the adventures of Lydia as she struggles to understand the supernatural world and the paranormal creatures who inhabit the Roanoke Apartments in her first job while also dealing with several angels and The Lady: https://storyoriginapp.com/universalbooklinks/3caa27a2-66a3-11e9-8eff-bf586265c024

If you'd like something with a few more chills, try the new adult magical gothic fantasy, *Moonlight, Magnolias, and Magic.* Join Annabella as she learns all about witches and some terrifying family secrets and tries to avoid becoming her ancestral home's next sacrifice: https://storyoriginapp.com/universalbooklinks/7b82271c-ba55-11e9-8f5b-9f4e4f93fd97

If you'd like to lose yourself in a community full of witches, sorcerers, centaurs, odd cats, and reluctant time travellers, then try *A Wild Conversion* and see what happens as Emma and Frederick have to unravel a conspiracy which goes back several generations: https://storyoriginapp.com/universalbooklinks/d9d33bfa-d811-11ea-9ef7-63f05ee3f6c7

Or, if you'd like to take a look at the whole *More in Heaven and Earth* series and learn all the corners of this paranormal universe, then you can find the series page here: https://storyoriginapp.com/universalbooklinks/ee1fd0f4-c70a-11ea-9bd7-7fb4b81d8cb1

To join Katherine Gilbert's More in Heaven and Earth Newsletter and get behind-the-scenes info and updates on new releases, sign up at: http://eepurl.com/dCcccL

To find out more about her books, check out her webpage at: http://www.katherinegilbertauthor.com

For all other inquiries and questions, you can either contact her at katherine.gilbert@katherinegilbertauthor.com or message her through her Facebook page: https://www.facebook.com/Katherine-Gilbert-Author-102573417043950/

About the Author

A lifelong believer in love, general silliness, angels, and universal plans, and a fervent fan of all things paranormal, Katherine Gilbert grew up in the '80s around Reagan fans who thought she was nuts. She teaches at a South Carolina community college and publishes what she writes in hopes that there are others with the same spirit out there who need a smile on their faces, too.

Made in the USA
Monee, IL
26 January 2021

58716362R00152